MONEY GAMES II

Paid For In Gold

Kimberly Barnes

Urban House Publishing

P.O. Box 1826

Montclair, N.J.

07042

Email: urbanhousepublishing@yahoo.com

Telephone: (973) 744- 5067

Fax: (973) 744- 5067

See us at Face book: Urban House Publishing

More Books by Urban House publishing coming to print soon!!!

Cover Designer: K. BARNES

Image: Sergy Galushko / Dreamstime.com

ACKNOWLEDGMENTS

I would like to thank Rasool Jacobs for believing in me and helping me embark on this endeavor. Without his encouragement and business mind, this could not have become a reality. I would also like to thank my family, especially my husband Celester for allowing me the time to work on this manuscript. To my three children, effectionally known as Rue, Nini, and J.B, You are my inspiration. A very special thank you to my granddaughter, Khalia, for helping me with the computer formats AGAIN! To my parents William and Mary, I would be nothing without you! RIP, Mother. I LOVE YOU ALL!

DEDICATION

Writing this novel would not have been possible without the advice and insight of my old friends from Trenton. George, you gave me some excellent details about the military, their "toys," and awesome suggestions when editing the first draft of the manuscript.

R. Jacobs, (yes, the well-read Urban Author), thank you for helping me smooth out some of my overly confusing dialogue and providing me with a sounding board for the plot.

I must give special thanks to my good friend and editor, Patrick. You were definitely an inspiration and helped me move the story with all of your great advice. There really are no words to show my appreciation to you. To Billy, my legal advisor, thank you for all of your hard work.

Without the four of you, this work would never have been worth reading.

Any mistakes, omissions, or errors dealing with the military, weapons, tactics, high finance, or economics are purely my own. I did take some liberties with locations, some famous politicians, and other public individuals, but no harm was intended. This is a novel and the characters, along with the events described in this story, are purely fiction

PROLOGUE

In Part two of this Trilogy, Susan DiGiovanni has come into a fortune worth billions as well as ownership of a massive gold mine. Unfortunately, it cost her the love of her life as well as making her the target of a cabal trying to take control of the world. Roland Troth is the man Susan has to take down so she can excerpt her revenge.

Troth, a member of a secret society, has reached out for help from a man even richer and more powerful than himself, Maxwell York. York is interested in one thing, establishing neofeudalistic society with him and his associates controlling the world. To Clean up Troth's mess he hires Daniel Sampson, an ex- Special Forces operative. In a strange twist, Sampson falls in love with Susan and convinces her to team up with him to take down the entire cabal of elitists.

When the most powerful of men in the world's secret societies start to fall, a power-play to fill the voiddraws entire nations into the fray and puts the United States in a state of panic.

Susan and Sampson, the indirect cause of international collapse, looks for a way to escape and survive to fight another day.

Chapter One

Maxwell York was walking around his Cape Cod estate. Strolling through the south garden adjacent to the seawall, to him, was like walking in Eden. The rose bushes were in bloom and the beds of perennials were coming in nicely. Japanese maple and ginkgo trees elegantly lined the cobblestone walkway that was laid out in looping arches around the grounds.

The estate was secluded and secure. Surrounded by high walls and the 20-room mansion to his back, there was no one to bother him and he felt completely at ease.

Standing on the seawall, staring out to the vast Atlantic Ocean to the east, Maxwell found himself reminiscing about his heritage, the long line of ancestors connecting him to the land he was standing on and to the island thousands of miles in the distance. On his mother's side, he could trace his lineage back to the Mayflower and then further back to Royal blood. On his father's side, the Blue Blood ran deeper but then merged with the line of the Rothschilds prior to America's war for independence.

If anyone had the right to the land he was standing on, it was him. It was his family who financed the Virginia Colonies. One of his relatives had been a major investor in the Dutch East India Company, jump-starting trade with the colonies. It was his family who assisted William Penn in developing a commonwealth out of nothing but an empty frontier. If it hadn't been for the York family, he wistfully thought to himself, the Americas would still be under the control of savages.

Maxwell was exceedingly proud of his heritage. Seeing how the United States had devolved into a hodgepodge of races and cultures, where everyone demanded equality at the expense of the upper class, made him cringe. It was not the way things were supposed to be, and York longed for the day he and his kind could reclaim all the rights, powers and privileges they had ceded to the minorities, the poor, the homosexuals . . . everyone who wanted what he possessed.

It was coming, he knew. The day was coming when the class distinctions would matter again and the world would be a much better place. In his earlier life, when he arranged or financed arms deals, he did not care how many lives would be lost through the use of the military hardware he merchandised. The people who were killed were peons, nothing but parasites using up his resources.

There was a time when the saying, "The world needs ditch-diggers too," was correct. The serfs, slaves, and lower castes had their place and their purpose. Maxwell York knew that day had passed. With the rise of technology, robotics, and absolutely no need for unskilled labor, there were simply far too many people. It was something he thought of often while standing on the seawall looking at the ocean and imagining the three-masted ships sailing in to settle the New World. Back then, his forefathers believed the resources were endless.

The fundamental question of Economics is the proposition that there are limited resources and unlimited demand for those resources. The way he saw it, everyone else was chasing what rightfully belonged to him—things they neither earned nor had a right to. To solve the fundamental economic question and resolve the constant conflict between supply and demand, York always reached the same conclusion, they had to eliminate the demand.

But how many? How many people would have to "disappear" so the ones who remained could forever live a life of comfort and ease? How many should remain? Who should remain? If the entire world had to support only a handful of people, what skills, what trades, what philosophies should be carried forward. What were the true necessities of life that would ensure survival, good health, and comfort?

York often pondered the numbers, the way to determine who was worthy of saving, and then dream about how wonderful the world would be if they could eliminate everyone else. The entire Earth would be his garden, his Eden. That was the way things should be, that was the way he wanted to mold the world.

"Mr. York, sir?"

Andrew Stevens, York's personal assistant, stood a respectful three feet behind his superior and mentor. Dressed in the finest blue, pinstriped Armani suit with matching paisley handkerchief and tie, Stevens looked like he belonged in a Paris boardroom not standing on a coastal seawall in Massachusetts.

"Yes, Andrew?" York did not bother to turn around.

"Your visitor is here."

"Yes of course. Please, show him out."

Andrew, extremely well-groomed and polished, nodded and walked down the path toward the main house. Having his thought process interrupted did not bother Maxwell as much as receiving a visitor. It had been a long time since he exposed himself to an outsider. Even though the man coming to see him, Roland Troth, was a junior partner doing very important work, dealing with him face to face was an anomaly.

Being out of the public eye, unknown to the masses and the media, was paramount to York. If he and the other senior partners were to accomplish their goals, staying in the background was a necessity. That entailed trusting others, such as Roland Troth, to managing the unseemly details. It was only because of the magnitude of the trouble Troth caused that Maxwell York agreed to see him. There was simply too much at stake to allow some junior partner

8

to bring them all down. He had to be dealt with, one way or another.

Roland Troth was only one of many hedge fund managers York and his compatriots used to expand their wealth, influence, and control. But, Troth had gotten himself caught up in some difficulties. Political intervention had been required to free him from some ridiculous scandal dealing with confidential memos from federal agencies. That was a minor affair compared to the flash-crash mistakenly initiated by Troth's traders. How that came about, no one seemed to know. Persuading the SEC and NYSE to halt trading and reverse all the erroneous trades had not been as much of a problem as placating the media and the masses. It was way too soon for people to get even angrier and more suspicious of the financial markets. The partners still needed the markets to work for them.

York felt the difficulties developed because Troth was too greedy and moved too quickly. Because he had not stopped to consider all of the relevant factors and implications of his actions, the events had mushroomed and became a threat to York and the senior partners.

It was stunning to Maxwell York and the others when they learned Troth had unwisely used a gang of rogue former military thugs and then lost control of them. Because of their trail of bodies and blood, they had the entire nation in a panic for weeks and almost caused an international incident. The bombing of the building in Williamsport, Pennsylvania and the attempt to purloin the cache of gold had not been properly planned, executed, or sanctioned. Those events, in and of themselves, were not necessarily bad and could be used for their benefit. But, there was a right way to do things and a wrong way. Troth had gone about things the wrong way.

If bringing in so much scrutiny and drawing so much attention wasn't bad enough, the one-time "superstar" trader and analyst had been financially clobbered, almost completely wiped-out. To York, it was the most disappointing of Troth's failures. The losses had set them back significantly, but it was not devastating. Roland Troth had managed to lose tens-of-billions of dollars and was outsmarted by a bunch of ciphers from some small town in Pennsylvania. Although the losses were huge, they still only represented a percentage of the assets under the control of Maxwell York and the other senior partners. It was just money—with time it would come back to them.

York did wonder, however, if Troth was worth saving. Before the latest misadventures, Troth had proven himself to be loyal, dedicated, and exceptionally brilliant when it came to manipulating the markets. He had been successful and could be once again. York needed to know if Troth had simply been a victim of circumstances or if he was losing his edge.

It was way too late in the game to trade and train a new horse. If Troth was able to be salvaged, York was willing to give him another chance. But, if Troth was losing his sense of perspective, no longer worthy of being a member of the elite group who would prevail in the coming changes, he would have to be eliminated.

York heard the men approaching. He turned and examined the countenance of his visitor. Roland looked like he had aged many, many years since the last time York had seen him—although that had been on television when Troth was leaving the courtroom a free man. It had been many years since the two men saw each other in person.

Troth's face was pale and gaunt. The skin around his neck sagged like he had recently lost a lot of weight. Before the recent ordeals, people always said Roland looked terrific for his age, somewhere between 75 and 80-years old.

The white tuft of gray hair blew in the wind and, although it was a warm fall day, Troth appeared to be cold and was bundling himself in his jacket.

As they neared, Roland's eyes were big and plaintive; looking for any hint of the reception he was going to get, seeking mercy. He knew better than to reach out to shake hands, a gesture of "equals." Maxwell York was not his equal. Troth, along with Andrew, his escort, stopped a yard short of where York stood waiting.

Andrew bowed slightly, "May I present Mr. Roland Troth."

York acknowledged Andrew and nodded to Troth, "Roland." There was an awkward silence.

Then, Andrew asked, "Shall I have Stewart bring you something? Coffee, maybe?"

"That won't be necessary, Andrew, Mr. Troth will not be staying long."

With no further discussion, Andrew left and headed back to the mansion, leaving the two older men on the seawall. It was morning, the bright sun slowly rising on the horizon and hardly a cloud in the sky. Yet, the negative gloom accompanying Roland Troth was like a wet blanket on a cold day.

York gestured for Troth to come closer, to join him standing on the precipice of the wall leading down a rocky cliff to the ocean below. The carved-stone balustrade was the only thing shielding them both from a fifty-foot drop and certain death.

"So, you insisted on seeing me and here you are. What exactly do you have to say for yourself, Roland?"

*****

Driving around Williamsport was something Susan would probably never get used to. Hardly any traffic, drivers who were polite, and the ability to go from point A

11

to point B without seeing thirty cops along the way, was so different from where she learned to drive. North Jersey: Route 17, Route 4, and Interstate 80—where she cut her teeth behind the wheel—was better training for defensive driving than any NASCAR circuit. Living in a small town without the automotive madness did have its advantages.

The cherry-red Shelby Cobra she was driving, fully restored and pristine, as if it had just come out of the factory, growled as she stepped on the gas and accelerated through the steep switch-backs heading up the mountain. The gorgeous fieldstone and glass house she was staying at was at the top of the mountain and came into view once she made the last turn, racing up the final rise.

The car and the house belonged to a friend, a dear friend who had died earlier that summer, Mario Mezzara. Mario was one of nineteen people who were killed when the building they were in exploded in some commando-like attack. The assault and destruction of the office building in Williamsport had been covered internationally for weeks as a terrorist attack. But, Susan, and almost everyone else in the small town, knew better.

Driving Mario's car and living in his house had been Tommy's idea. Tommy was Mario's partner, and also the partner of another man Susan had lost, her true love, Donald Clearmont. While still recovering from knee replacement surgery, having had his knee shot out, Tommy thought it would be a good idea to have Susan stay close, so it would be easier to get together and make plans. Tommy's house was the next estate down the lane. Only a few acres separated the only two houses at the very top of the mountain.

The garage door opened automatically and Susan pulled the Shelby into the three car garage. She cut off the engine, but did not immediately get out of the car. It was something that was happening to her more and more frequently, an eerie sense that she was losing her grip on reality. She sat in the car, breathing deeply, trying to clear her head.

The anxiety and panic attacks had been coming and going for months, ever since her life had changed so dramatically.

What she thought was an idyllic life—married, a nice house in a quiet Bergen County neighborhood, stability—it was all gone. The once typical "Jersey-girl" had lost that old life and had changed. All she retained from that former life, the most important people in the world to her, were her children, Chris and Lisa. However, they were not with her.

Chris and Lisa remained safely hidden away in Costa Rica, being cared for by two trusted friends, Carlos and Helena. Susan did not feel it was safe to bring them back to the states, at least not yet. Until they were sure Roland Troth could do them no harm, she would have to keep the kids half-a-world away from her.

Coming back to Pennsylvania was something Susan knew she had to do—it was all part of the twists and turns Fate had thrown at her.

After the love of her life, Donny, had died and left her in control of several trusts: the Seven Rams Gold Trust and the Clearmont Geology and Mining Trust. She became an instant billionaire, and responsible for the well-being of hundreds, maybe even thousands of people. Many other participants in the Clearmont Geology and Mining Trust had perished in the bombing, increasing considerably her responsibility, and the wealth she controlled.

When Mario was killed, his participation in the trusts and his personal wealth had to be distributed. It was in probate, but would most likely fall to her, Carlos and Tommy, the three remaining members of the Seven Rams Trust.

Susan knew, after the attacks, the killings, and the destruction, they had a huge responsibility to try and make the people in the tiny suburb of Williamsport whole. They also had to expand the gold operations at the foundry in Pittsfield, Pennsylvania, and take the mines in Canada and Peru public. There was so much to do and Susan knew she was in way over her head.

Besides the stresses of helping to run the trusts, both she and Tommy agreed they had to do something to help out the region. The massive amount of money and property they acquired beating Roland Troth at his own game was being put to use trying to rebuild the economies of western Pennsylvania, segments of Ohio, and large swaths of West Virginia. Trying to economically repair what Troth had destroyed was a huge responsibility and something Susan never imagined herself doing. Using the funds they were able to wrest from Troth's control for anything else would have been wrong. Troth's money games had hurt so many people, giving something back to the ones who had lost the most was just the right thing to do.

Beyond all of the money issues and dealing with trusts, the main change, the thing that really weighed on Susan's mind more than anything, was the fact she had killed a man.

Yes, the man was a creep, and he had confessed to killing Donny, but the image of pointing a gun at his head and pulling the trigger—watching his head explode—was something she was having trouble getting out of her thoughts. Even though the man was working for Troth and had plans to hurt more people, to Susan, killing someone made her feel different. Either she would have to learn to live with herself and convince herself she did the right thing, or she was going to go insane.

Finally able to breathe and silence the noise in her head, Susan got out of the car and headed into the house. She immediately went to the kitchen and got a cold bottle of water. Over the summer, she had gained weight and was making an effort to cut down on her caloric intake.

Although the weight had gone to all the right places, swelling her breasts and rounding out her bottom, she didn't like the way it felt. At 39-years-old, she prided herself on being curvy, but retaining the form of a much younger woman. She ran her fingers through her hair, which she allowed to grow out again, no longer feeling the need to disguise her appearance. When the phone rang, she already knew who it was.

"Hi, Tommy."

"Hey, Susie-Q! You comin' over?" Tommy's voice was deep, yet chipper, and always up-beat.

"Are you done with your physical therapy yet?"

"Yeah, my wife won't let me slide, not even for a minute."

"Good!"

Tommy's voice changed to one of feigned hurt, "Oh, so now you're gonna get on me, too, huh?"

Susan smiled, knowing Tommy's work-ethic was beyond compare. He had shocked the doctors with his recovery time and adjustment to having a replacement knee. Both Susan and Darla, Tommy's wife, knew that by chiding Tommy, he would work that much harder and get stronger even faster. He was the type of man who took teasing as a challenge. It would not be long before the big man, all six-feet, five-inches of him, would be out jogging 5-miles every morning, and lifting weights very few humans would even think about touching.

Susan asked, "So, what's on our plate today?"

"How about buying a few thousand acres near Canton, Ohio, and building a plant that makes engines to run on natural gas?"

"You found a site?"

"Yup!"

"Do you have a designer in mind? A plant manager lined up? Did you decide what technology to use, what kind of engine?"

15

Tommy laughed. "That's why I'm calling you! Now get that tiny behind of yours over here and let's get to work." Tommy was the one with the big ideas and big plans to transform the entire Mid-Atlantic into a natural gas economy.

Together, Tommy and Susan had already established three retraining centers, gearing up to help the 40-something-year-old, unemployed, semi-skilled laborers. The residents of the rust belt had to move away from the habits and practices of the industrial age and into the technology age. Retraining the workforce to specialize in new trades, such as precision machining using CAD or CAM, would give the men and woman the skills needed to be employable. Also, as Tommy and Susan had planned, the workers would be able to work for them developing a whole new economy for the area.

Investing in the training centers was something Tommy was proud of, and financing the evolution of the economy starting from scratch was exhilarating. His enthusiasm was contagious.

It was Susan's turn to laugh. "Let me shower first and then you'll see my fat ass, Tommy."

"Susan? One more thing . . ."

"Yeah, what's that?"

"I think I figured out how to get to Troth."

"I'll be right over."

Chapter Two

Sitting behind the wheel of the Rolls Royce, donning the standard black jacket and even the tacky driver's cap, the driver could not stop picking at his beard and scratching his chin with a gloved hand. He was so unaccustomed to having facial hair, the months-old, wiry whiskers continued to make him itch. Major Daniel Sampson, USMC (Retired), was not trying to disguise his facial features from his boss, Roland Troth. Instead, he grew out the beard and stayed under cover to protect himself from Military Intelligence, the FBI, or any other government agency who may be watching Roland Troth. For Sampson, being seen alive would not be a good thing.

*****

Several months earlier, after he witnessed his partners, his comrades-in-arms, taken out by two Hellfire missiles launched by a couple of A-10 Warthogs, he took off and went into deep cover. Armed only with a Springfield Armory 9mm and the Sykes Fairbairn commando dagger strapped to his calf, Sampson hiked his way over mountains and some rough terrain into the Allegheny State Forest where he secluded himself at the edge of a steep cliff.

Living off elk meat and drinking out of a stream, he lived in the wild for about two weeks until he moved on. During his routine recon hikes, he saw no evidence of search parties or trackers. Also but for standard civilian aircraft, there had been no fly-overs. Either they did not know he existed or they didn't care. Feeling it was finally safe to move, Sampson made his way north, on foot, until he reached the New York State border and Route 17.

Even though it would have been easy to hijack a car and drive, Sampson did not want to draw any attention by leaving bodies around or generating missing-persons reports. He didn't even want to be in a stolen car. Hiking all the way across the Empire State, drawing as little attention to himself as possible, was the prudent move and, for him, not a difficult thing to do. Moving only at night and sleeping during the day, and staying out of communication with some of his closest associates, was also simple, since he trusted no one.

Near the end of his withdrawal, his weeks of seclusion, Sampson took one small detour. He hiked into the town of Port Jervis, the tiny town on the border of New York, New Jersey and Pennsylvania. Since it was still summer, people were hanging laundry out to dry. He was able to clandestinely snatch up some clean clothes and, after washing up in a local stream, change. Going into town may or may not have been a risk, since Sampson had no idea if he was being hunted, so he was extremely careful and laid low. It was a risk he was willing to take in order to gather some much needed intelligence.

After a quick stop at a busy diner, he went to the local library and got on a computer. He did not waste time looking through a multitude of media publications or Googling for information. Sampson used what he had retained from his days in the military when he served under the direction of the most elite special forces operators. Instead of hunting for and seeking tidbits of slanted public information, he went directly to the main source.

Using the passwords his now dead boss J.T. Snyder, had given to him, Sampson logged onto the super secret MIN-OPS network. The Military Intelligence Network was created to provide the brass in the Pentagon and the Joint Commission Task Force's Rapid Response Unit with the raw data from every element of United States intelligence agencies. Incorporated with the system were databases and the ability to sort out the information in a way that drew connecting lines between seemingly random people or events. The technology was the latest in artificial intelligence and had access to everything everyone knew. The system was developed so the mistakes and lack of communication that allowed 9/11 to happen would never happen again.

Checking the MIN-OPS network, Sampson discovered he was not invisible. His name had been connected to the attacks in Williamsport and the squads the military had taken out in the vans. Oddly, none of it was connected to Roland Troth, although Troth and some of his associates' names were peppered all over the documentation and reports.

To Sampson, what he read told him that Troth had somehow used his status to weasel his way out of the cluster-fuck they were in and do it without turning on them. The people who did turn on him, Jose and Smiley, were locked up in a hospital ward in Gitmo. Lucky for Sampson, they had no idea if he was dead or alive or what had happened to him. Also lucky for Sampson, because of the smoke when the two vans blew up in front of him, the military had been unable to lock in on him and get his image when he took off from the tractor trailer that was behind the destroyed vans.

As far as all of the agencies, commissions and military were concerned, Sampson was dead. The vans and the men inside had been all but vaporized and there was no way to tell who was who. Knowing exactly what the people who may be pursing him knew gave Sampson a big measure of relief. But, he could never reappear as he was, and Daniel Sampson would have to forever remain "dead."

From Port Jervis, Sampson had trekked to Greenwich, Connecticut, making child's play of Roland Troth's security detail and alarm systems. Waking Troth up in his plush bedroom by gently poking him in the nose

19

with a dagger was a night Sampson would not soon forget. Roland had screamed and almost jumped out of his own skin.

Even though it had been James "Toby" Snyder who mostly dealt with Troth and his underlings, Sampson had also met with Troth and C.B. Ross, taking on special assignments and one-man jobs others in the three squads— now all dead—did not have to be privy to. Through those interactions,including the hit on Troth's right-hand-man C.B. Ross, Sampson and Troth had formed a much closer relationship.

Showing up in Roland's bedroom and poking his nose with a dagger was Sampson's way of showing affection. If he had wanted to kill Troth, it could have and would have been done. That was something Troth understood almost immediately, and it convinced him that Sampson was still on his side.

Although still disturbed and shaken over the lost money, all the land he had been forced to sell at a huge discount, and the problems his security detail had caused, Roland Troth felt better having someone on his side, even though Sampson was a psychopathic killer.

Over the next few days, the two men were quick to combine resources and compare notes. Sampson was able to assure Troth that the Feds were probably going to leave him alone, although from what Sampson had read on the MIN-OPS network someone, somewhere was going to eventually ask questions and investigate. Sampson also provided assurances that Troth would be safe—he promised to make sure no one got near him or did him any harm.

During their debriefing, Roland was able to convey to Sampson everything that happened to him, how he was arrested, locked up and humiliated in jail. Then, he told him all about the man he was so anxious to have a meeting with, a man named Maxwell York.

Troth explained how he had called and asked—no, demanded—to meet with the one man who had the power to make everything right. Not hearing back from Andrew Stevens, who was supposed to set up the meeting with York, had made Roland paranoid that the senior partners were going to come after him, maybe even punish or kill him for everything that happened.

To Sampson, that was an enlightening discussion. Up until that point, he had never heard of Maxwell York, or had the slightest clue people existed who could buy and sell the likes of Roland Troth. The revelations continued, and Troth related everything he knew about York, the senior partners, and their plans—which wasn't very much.

To Sampson, what he learned from Troth changed everything and was stunning in its magnitude—if Troth was to be believed. There was a time in his life when Sampson used to laugh when others spoke of the Illuminati, or other cabals of powerful men aiming to take over the world. It was a common joke to blame everything on the "New World Order," and compare the state of affairs to the novel, "1984." But, seeing the absolute fear in Troths eyes when he spoke of Maxwell York, and hearing Troth's voice quiver when he related the spheres of influence of the senior partners, made the hair on Sampson's neck bristle. If they scared the hell out of Roland Troth, Sampson thought, it must be one mighty powerful group.

Because his still powerful network of contacts still existed, and because Troth had really started to trust and believe in Sampson, Troth decided to help Sampson with something that had become a necessity if they were going to succeed. A very well known plastic surgeon from Brazil, along with an anesthesiologist and two nurses were flown to Connecticut and escorted to Troth's estate. All of the necessary medical equipment and supplies were shipped in from another source in Europe. The medical team spent two grueling days changing major aspects of Sampson's appearance.

The surgeries, as gruesome as they were all took place in the privacy of a finished basement. There was no way for anyone to know what was going on in Troth's estate.

With a new nose, tightened cheeks, less oval eyes, and a lower brow-line, Sampson looked five years younger and of a different race. Except for his strong chin, he looked almost Asiatic. The worst and most challenging procedure came the next day. One of the doctor's specialties, and the reason Troth had specifically hired him, was altering fingerprints.

Using the well-preserved skin from the hands of a cadaver, the doctor successfully peeled off Sampson's flesh from the wrist down and transplanted all new palm and finger prints. Hours upon hours were spent as the doctor meticulously tried to weave together the delicate nerve fibers.

After the surgery, the doctor told Sampson that the sensitivity in his hands and fingertips would never be the same, and the healing process would be painful, but eventually he would adjust. The doctor was not wrong— the pain was intense and Sampson was afraid he'd never be able to have the same sensations in his fingertips. But, day by day things improved. The gloves he was forced to wear were meant to improve circulation and protect from cuts and infection, but to Sampson, it made it more difficult to tell how well he was healing. There was nothing more he could do but wait and hope the sense of touch would improve. Besides changing his DNA, which was impossible, everything needed to change his identity had been accomplished and Sampson was satisfied.

It was only a few weeks later that Troth got the call from Andrew. Maxwell York had agreed to meet with Troth. With the time that had passed, and with Daniel

Sampson on his side, Roland Troth had managed to regain some of his old spunk and a touch of his once legendary ambition. With Sampson as his consultant—like having the Devil whispering in his ear—together they planned for the day of the meet and how to handle whatever may come. They both had ideas and ambitions, but first Troth had to survive that meeting.

*****

Sitting in the Rolls, Sampson checked his watch and then felt under his jacket for the 9mm semiautomatic. He wished he could feel the smooth steel of the slide or the ridges of the grip, but there was almost nothing. His fingertips were still pretty much numb. Looking toward the front door of the Cape Cod mansion, he saw the door open and watched Roland Troth walking out. Troth meandered down the walkway toward the waiting car.

As if it was something he had done his entire life, Sampson opened the driver's door and stepped out of the Rolls Royce. Efficiently, and with proper deference, he opened the back door for Troth and shut it after the old man got in. Sampson hustled around, got back in the car and slowly drove it up to the large, iron gates blocking their exit. As soon as the gates opened enough for the big car to get through, Sampson drove away.

"How'd it go, Roland?"

"Well, to be honest, better than I expected."

Sampson was all business. "How many guards did you see? How many on his staff?"

Roland started to unbutton his jacket. He reached in and pulled out a device no bigger than an IPod-Mini with a wire attached to it. Reaching back into his jacket, he unhooked a small black plastic bubble with a lens on the front. He leaned forward and dropped the device and the camera on the front seat next to Sampson.

"Look at it yourself." Troth said dryly. "The man is almost alone."

Sampson looked into the rear-view mirror, trying to read Roland's expression. It was blank. "You know, Roland, when you didn't come out right away, I almost went in after you."

"That would have been a mistake."

This time when Sampson looked back Troth was smiling. "Yeah, why's that?"

"Because Maxwell York just gave me my life back." Roland's voice was, for the first time since he and Sampson had reconnected, strong and displayed self-assurance.

"Does that mean we're not going to kill him?" Sampson was obviously feeling let down, disappointed that the sands were shifting under his feet again.

Troth hesitated, thinking of his response. Finally, he answered, "I don't know. I haven't decided yet."

Chapter Three

Major General Adam Smythe had left the command center of the Joint Commission Task Force's Rapid Response Team the day before. The trip to Cuba and stay at "Gismo," the naval base at Guantanamo Bay, had become a necessity once word reached him that one of the two remaining home-gown terrorists was ready to break.

Lieutenant Ortega-Suarez had turned out to be one tough nut to crack. Getting him to talk, they had resorted to some extraordinary measures. It had taken months of tactics: water-boarding, stress positions, and electric shocks to reach this point and the general wanted to see and hear for himself what a former military man had to say for himself. The hard work they put in over the summer was about to pay dividends.

Major General Smythe and his support staff were reviewing the briefing files in front of them. Smythe was sweating more than he could ever remember. The Cuban heat and humidity had caused wet circles of sweat to form under his arms and along the collar of his immaculately pressed khaki shirt. The air system in the secured Intelligence Office did not help.

The fact that Ortega-Suarez, along with the rest of the hit squad they had taken out, were all ex-military was a poorly kept secret to the politicians and the public at large—hence a major embarrassment to Smythe and his superiors. What had been kept pretty much under wraps was the fact that Jose Ortega-Suarez and Joseph Francis had survived and were being held in Gitmo for interrogation ever since the attacks.

Laptop computers with special encryption cards plugged into the USB ports sat on the desks in front of the officers. The one in front of Smythe was logged onto the super secret MIN-OPS Military Intelligence Network so that Smythe's team could get background information as needed or enter any findings they may gather. Looking over the data concerning the forensic investigation of the vans, it was a problem for them that the scenes were such a mess. Not only were they unsure if everyone involved was killed on that Pennsylvania highway, they also didn't know who had provided the home-grown terrorist group with funding, advanced weaponry, and top-secret military hardware recovered from both scenes.

General Smythe pressed a button on an intercom. "Major Burkley, bring the subject in and secure him."

"Yes, sir."

Smythe paused for a second until he saw a green light on the wall turn off and a red light turn on. Displayed on several LCD screens on the wall, five Marines were carrying a naked, cuffed man into an almost empty white room. The prisoner was bald and had bruises over the back of his legs. His calves and ankles were covered with gory scars and remnants of sutures. Both ankles and feet looked crooked and disfigured.

The general knew the man's ankles had been shot by some large, black man who Ortega-Suarez and Joseph Francis had unsuccessfully tried to kidnap. Even after several surgeries at the military hospital, neither man was able to walk.

The Marines, wearing leather gloves and helmets with masks, set the prisoner down on the rubber covered steel chair and secured him in place with leather straps. As soon as the squad left, an officer with an Army uniform walked into view along with a smaller man, obviously a civilian. The civilian donned an expensive looking tan suit with shoes to match. The tips of his curly brown hair looked damp with sweat.

The general pressed eight digits on a security panel and waited for the air-locked door to hiss open. He then walked down the hall to the interrogation room, the door being held open by one of the five Marines who were on escort duty.   Smythe strode in and nodded to Major Burkley, who returned a half-hearted salute.

"General Smythe, I'd like you to meet Dr. Simon Liebman of Mossad."

Smythe extended his hand and shook with the leading pharmaceutical researcher from the Israeli version of the secret police.   The man's hand was soft and the shake delicate.

"Doctor.   I sure hope everything will work as reported."

With only a slight accent, Dr. Liebman responded, "Yes, General.   I think you will find that this particular compound will get you the answers you need.   It has taken years of research, and I am sure you will be pleased with the results."

No one even looked at or spoke to Jose, who sat passively strapped to the chair.   Without any prompting, Burkley wheeled a stainless steel cart over to the middle of the room directly in front of Jose.   Dr. Liebman took a hypodermic needle and a vial from the top of the cart and started to extract a precise amount of a brownish liquid.

Dr. Liebman looked at Smythe and indicated for him to come closer.   "General, this serum is something we have worked on for decades.   I assure you that the subject will tell you whatever you want to know."

"How does it work?"

"There are two mechanisms," he replied as he reached down and grabbed a packaged alcohol swab off of the cart.   There were a series of other items on the top shelf including prepared ampules of self-injectable morphine. "The direct effect of the main compound is the sensitization of the pain receptors in the subject's brain.   If something hurts him, he will feel ten times the sensation.   The second compound is what you may consider a type of truth serum—but instead of being a hypnotic from the barbital family, it's more closely related to phencyclidine and acts

27

on the same pathways as alcohol. But, this compound is much more effective than alcohol and it does not cause the drowsiness, slurred speech, and the like."

Everything that was being said was meant for Jose's ears. Part of the process was to make sure he believed the shot he was about to get would overwhelm his will to keep secrets. Even as he sat there with absolutely no affectation, unable to react, he knew what was coming. The psychic numbing from prior trauma had required even-increasing levels of pain and degradation. His mind no longer knew exactly how to respond to the fear and anxiety. Yet, hearing he was about to relive the same agony he had gone through before with Liebman made his skin break out in a cold sweat.

*****

The top pages of the file Smythe was reading highlighted the information Ortega-Suarez had provided and a chart outlining his association with an entire group of former American warriors. Jose Ortega-Suarez had given up the names of the men who had demolished the building in Williamsport, and the names of his partners in the vans that were destroyed outside of Pittsfield. He had provided the name of their group's leader, J.T. Snyder. But, Smythe knew there had to be more intel to be extracted.

The men Jose had given up were all one-time special forces commandos of one type or another. They had gone off the reservation and committed some horrendous acts. Smythe looked up the classified personnel files of those men—each and every one of them had been drummed-out of the service for antisocial or criminal behavior. The general noted how they had a common employment in the private sector with a very well-known military contractor, AMPERS, Inc., a company that had come under fire and gone out of business.

Smythe's eyes focused on two names in particular: Captain James Tobias Snyder, U.S.A., (Ret.); and Major Daniel Sampson, U.S.M.C., (Ret.). From prior personal experience, he already knew who Snyder was and that he was the founder and CEO of AMPERS; the one who organized and recruited ex-commandos as employees. After reports of abuse of Iraqi citizens surfaced the company folded. He was familiar with the company and knew of its reputation. It was no surprise then that the once high-flying military contracting company fell on its own sword. Fortunately, Snyder was one of the confirmed dead because the man was one ruthless son-of-a-bitch.

More disturbing to Smythe was the fact that Major Daniel Sampson, U.S.M.C., (Ret.), had not been a confirmed kill. He may or may not have been blown up by the Hellfire missiles that took out the vans outside of Pittsfield, but there was no DNA evidence to support the conclusion that he was dead. Intimately familiar with that man's highly classified military records, Sampson was someone who the General feared. The thought of him still alive and on the prowl sent shivers down the old man's spine.

After he finished reading the summaries, Smythe was sure there were pieces missing and he had to be sure Jose Ortega-Suarez had given up every last bit of information he possessed.

*****

Two Marines shoved their way through the door, dragging and pulling a naked, seemingly unconscious woman through by her arms. As soon as Jose saw her, his eyes became as big as saucers. He started to thrust and shake like a wild animal, trying to break loose from the leather straps holding him to the chair. As he pulled and

29

tugged with all of his might, he could not help but to grunt as spittle and gasps of breath issued from his mouth.

Once he recognized his attempt to get free from the chair was futile, Jose started shouting, "Jen, no! Oh my God, Jen! You . . . you can't do this to her!"

Major Burkley turned to General Smythe and told him in a conspiratorial tone, "It's his wife . . . it's her turn."

When the Marines let go of the woman, she laid on her side quietly. It was obvious she had been sedated, but she was still partially awake. The woman was completely naked and her skin looked filthy. Her mousy brown hair had been tied back tight into a ponytail so that Jose could see her clearly. Jen's face was turned up and she had a plaintive look in her dark brown eyes. White, powdery streaks formed lines of salt from the tears that had dried on her cheeks. It gave her a very sad, desperate look.

Burkley slipped on latex gloves and grabbed two electronic leads. The leads were attached to a device on the second shelf of the cart wired to several large lithium ion batteries on the bottom shelf. He squirted conductive gel onto the leads and turned. Squatting down next to Jen, he reached between her legs and pushed them apart. Although the General could not see what the Major was doing, he knew the leads were being attached to the woman's labia.

The doctor swabbed Jen's shoulder as he explained, "In addition to the drug, we are also using electric stimuli because Mr. Ortega-Suarez has used this method himself and he knows exactly how effective it is." Doctor Liebman bent down and injected a compound into Jen's shoulder. "It will be almost instantaneous."

Jose Ortega-Suarez started to scream.

Focusing her eyes the best she could, all she could think of was the love she felt for him and how much she wished she could touch him. Her vision cleared when she felt the man poke the needle into her shoulder. The concrete floor in the barracks was cool compared to the

30

steamy Cuban air.   For reasons she did not fully understand, Jennifer could not move her arms or legs, but she could feel them. Her eyes could move and she felt new tears running down her cheeks, but she wasn't exactly sure why she was crying. She could hear Jose's voice; he was screaming but she couldn't put his words together. There was nothing she could do to help him because she couldn't move. Oddly, that did not seem to upset her.

Where was she? How did she get there? Who were these people standing around looking at her? Why didn't she have any clothes on? It must be a dream, she thought.

Seeing Jose strapped to a chair and the look of horror on his face confused her, but her addled brain was unable make sense of it all. She wanted to speak to him and ask him what was wrong, but she couldn't get her tongue or lips to move.   Suddenly, what Jose was screaming started to come together in her brain, but what he was saying made absolutely no sense at all . . . why would Jose be telling them to stop, to give her the antidote and he'd tell them everything? That wasn't like him at all.

She was more convinced than ever that it had to be a dream because she actually started to feel pleasure in her special places—even while watching Jose go into a panic. It was a strange sensation and Jen not only stopped crying but felt like she was getting closer to having an orgasm. Her head was spinning and without even realizing she had regained the capacity to make noise and even move, Jennifer started to moan.

"Oh my God!   Stop it, stop hurting her!" Jose screamed. "I told you, I'll tell you everything just give her the antidote!"

Major Burkley looked at the doctor and nodded. Then, he faced Jose, who was straining at the straps holding him to the chair. He had a grimace of pain on his face and huge throbbing veins popped and throbbed at his temples.

"Okay, Jose. The doctor is going to stop your wife's suffering and make her well. But first, you have to promise to tell the truth and, I swear to you, if you're lying to us, you're going to see your wife tortured and then die right in front of your eyes." Burkley paused for effect and then continued, "We have most of it put together, Jose, so we're going to know if you're lying—you understand that don't you?"

Jose nodded. He knew Burkley was telling the truth because in the prior sessions, they knew of things he had not told them. Even though Jose had absolutely no conscience when it came to strangers, and he had tortured people with impunity, there was one person he really, truly loved—the only one who believed in him and stood by his side no matter what. Jose just couldn't stand to see or hear his Jennifer being tortured. Looking into Burley's eyes, he said, "I swear to you—I'll tell you the truth!"

Doctor Liebman bent over and injected a dose of saline solution into Jen's shoulder. The previous shot had not been the truth compound he had described earlier, but a powerful derivative of MDMA, better known as "Ecstasy." Liebman knew the drug would reverse the earlier induced paralysis and give the woman a very nice psychological experience—and so the injection of saline solution would not only allow her to continue her trip, but it was given to her to appease the true subject, Jose.

"She'll be fine." Doctor Liebman said as he stood and turned.

Major Burkley reached down and gently pulled the electronic leads from Jennifer's labia. As if right on cue, she just then started to smile and sighed contentedly—which caused Jose to sit back, relax and breathe deeply himself. Major Burkley opened the door and went out in the hallway, indicating to the Marines waiting outside to come in.

"Take her to the clinic and have the doctors check her out. Then, follow Protocol A-6 and put her into the guest quarters—make sure a female is with her at all times." Burkley stepped aside to give the squad easier access.

"Aye, aye, sir," a sergeant responded. The group of Marines gently picked her up and carried her out the door.

"General Smythe?" Burkley indicated to Jose and nodded his head toward Jose.

The General walked toward Jose and stood directly in front of him. Jose had to tilt his head back to look him in the eye. "Tell me, who was your source of military hardware? Where did you get your weapons?"

Jose breathlessly murmured the answer. "AMPERS."

"They're out of business—either try again or we'll bring your wife back in here."

"Wait! Wait! Let me explain. After our company lost the contract in Iraq, we had everything we were given by the military and CIA—all of our equipment—shipped back here. When we got back and the company fell apart, some rich dude in Connecticut hired us and we stored our stuff at his building."

Smythe turned to Burkley. "Major, you and the doctor are going to have to leave."

Burkley's face twisted up in an expression mixed with confusion and outrage. "What, what do you mean I have to leave? I have Top Secret security clearance—this is my investigation . . ."

"You don't have security clearance for this, Major. Now get out, and that's an order!"

Tight lipped and with a face as red as a beet, Major Burkley snapped to attention and saluted his superior. He turned on his heel and walked to the door. Doctor Liebman followed closely behind and walked out of the room with the Major. The door closed behind them and the electronic lock clicked.

Smythe marched over to the wall directly across from Jose. There was an opening and a camera used to record all interrogations. Underneath it was a small control panel for recording. He made sure the device was turned off and walked over to the cart. He reached down and picked up three injectable morphine ampules. Sidestepping the cart, he moved towards Jose. The General looked at his face and saw that Jose knew exactly what was coming. He was not only resigned to it, but seemed happy about it.

Taking a vial in one hand, Smythe pulled the protective sheath back, exposing a series of needles in a circle. Palming the other ampules, he reached out and touched Jose's neck, looking for a pulse—his jugular vein.

"So, what was the name of this rich guy in Connecticut, hmmm?"

"Roland Troth."

"That's what I thought."

Smythe poked Jose's jugular with the morphine dispenser and pushed, injecting the first dose. Then, seeing the spots of blood rise up where the needles had punctured the skin, he pushed two more doses directly into the circulatory system. The drug quickly overwhelmed Jose's brain. Almost immediately, his head nodded down. Less than a minute later he stopped breathing and was dead.

General Smythe walked to the door and pushed the button of the intercom. A second later, a voice responded from the Control Center. "This is Control. Go ahead please."

"This is Major General Adam Smythe, clearance number 4-NINER-4, NINER-BRAVO-SIERRA-TANGO-ALPHA."

"4-NINER-4-NINER-BRAVO-SIERRA-TANGO-ALPHA. Roger that. Go ahead, Brass Hat, clearance is confirmed."

"We have a Protocol A-6 in progress in the clinic. That order is rescinded and is now a D-2. I'm also issuing a Protocol D-2 on detainee Joseph Francis in holding cell 112. Interrogation Room 101 has a Protocol D-1."

The voice asked, "That's your ninety, correct, sir?"

"Correct, but I won't be here. Immediately schedule a top priority flight to Andrews Air force Base and have an armed escort take Major Burkley and Doctor Liebman to the plane ASAP."

The man repeated the exact orders back to General Smythe for confirmation. Those orders would be routed through the Base Commander for documentation and then completed as covertly as possible. Satisfied everything on his end was under control, the General keyed open the door and left Jose's dead body in the interrogation room for disposal.

*****

Walking out of the building on his way to the tarmac, Smythe extracted a cigar tube out of his back pocket and pulled an ersatz Cuban cigar out with his nicotine-stained teeth. He bit off the tip of the cigar and spit it out. As he paced purposefully towards the awaiting plane, he lit the cigar up and tried to focus on enjoying his only vice—but he was unable to enjoy it.

Ruefully, he thought to himself that killing Jose was the dirtiest task he ever had to perform—but it was his duty. Handling Major Burkley and the Doctor would be a little more complicated—but not nearly as messy. Once he filed his report and blamed them for killing the prisoners, they would disappear—the doctor back to Israel, and the Major to some post on the other side of the world.

The smelly cigar smoke burned Smythe's throat and left a bad taste in his mouth. As terrible as he felt about killing a man in cold blood, and ordering two others covertly disposed of, it had to be done. At least that was what Senator O'Connell said. With the upcoming congressional hearings on the terrorist attacks, and the Armed Service Committee squeezing every branch for budget cuts, no one could ever discover the details about the American terrorists responsible for the destruction earlier that summer using hardware sold by American defense contractors.

The senator knew, and had explained to General Smythe in no uncertain terms that there could be no interruption of funding and absolutely no more congressional oversight of spending on national defense issues. He had received the exact same messages from FBI, NSA, CIA, and Homeland Security liaisons. The pressure they put on him had been enough to make his head pop. Without coming out and saying it, the people compelling him to act let it be known he had to handle the extermination. They had been able to obscure the truth about the group who executed the attacks. But, if someone produced testimonials from the detainees about what really happened it would be severely detrimental to the national security apparatus.

General Smythe felt that the fact the men were brought to Gitmo in the first place—and not killed on the spot—had been a huge mistake. They should have taken them out just like they did Osama bin-Laden . . . dead men tell no tales.

Although not understanding exactly why, the General was told to find out if either Ortega-Suarez or Francis had given up the name Roland Troth to anyone else. Then, they would also have to be neutralized. The ugly task of silencing men held inside of a highly secure military base had fallen to Smythe. He was the only one who could gain access and the standing to pull it off. No one would dare to question his veracity or his version of what happened.

They had to continue with the farce and stick to the cover story they had created at any cost. It was, Senator O'Connell said, all about protecting American liberties and freedoms.

In return for risking everything, and continuing to cover up the truth, General Smythe had accepted the $500,000 payment and the promise of a lucrative consulting job as soon as he retired—if he was not appointed to some Cabinet position. For all of that, he would figure out a way to quash his conscience and get over killing a man. What really mattered was that he had done what was necessary to keep his department funded and his country safe.

Chapter Four

Darla Jones was a very active woman and it showed. As chiseled as her husband Tommy was, she was trim and fantastically smooth all over. Her chocolate skin did not have one blemish or crease that wasn't supposed to be there and her high cheek bones had the natural glow of good health. Her taut muscles and the long, slender limbs of her 5-foot, 10-inch, frame were that of a distance runner. At the age of forty-two, Darla could have easily passed for thirty.

Walking down the marble-tiled floor barefoot wearing tights and a pink body suit with a flowery camisole draped loosely over her shoulders, Darla reached the heavy, oak double doors in the front foyer and opened them. "Hey, Baby. Good to see ya!" She greeted Susan with a kiss on the cheek and a quick hug.

"Hey, Darla. How are you?

"Oh, I'm just fine, just fine. Come on in."

Susan walked through the foyer into the large open space beyond an interior set of doors and a short hallway. The grand room was cavernous, with a modern architecture that eliminated walls between rooms. The kitchen simply blended into a dining area which sat across from a formal sitting area that was directly attached to a family room with a wet bar recessed into the north wall. The carpeting was plush, specially made to be durable and it was embellished with some intricate, traditional African pattern. In all of the right places, the floor was traversed with Italian marble tiles. The tiles also covered the kitchen area and led out of the huge room to other hallways. Folk art and majestic paintings dominated the walls of the otherwise tastefully decorated room.

The most striking feature of the grand room was the south wall, which was made of huge plates of glass, providing an unobstructed view to the city in the valley below.

"Is Tommy decent?"

"Girl, is that man ever decent?" Darla stepped to the kitchen and opened the fridge, pulling out a pitcher filled with carrot juice. Pouring two glasses she handed one to her visitor. It was a ritual they always followed.

Sipping at the juice, Susan didn't say anything. She knew Darla would not let her go until she had something nutritious in her stomach. Even though just a few years older, Darla had come to think of Susan as a little sister and immediately noticed how Susan wasn't taking good care of herself. Darla had plans to change that as her nurturing, sometimes domineering, nature took over.

"Did you eat today?" Darla asked.

"No." Susan answered flatly.

The answer made Darla shake her head and reach into the cabinet behind her for a protein bar. "Susan, eat this, okay? Protein in the morning gets your metabolism going . . . and by the time you finish, Thomas should be out of the shower and dressed."

"What would I do without you, Darla?"

"I don't know . . . probably starve yourself, thinking that's gonna help you lose weight and keep it off."

"I know, I know, but . . ."

Darla interrupted her, "When are you gonna start running with me in the morning, hmmm?"

Without the women noticing, Tommy walked into the grand room from the right hallway leading from the master bedroom.

"Whatcha mean, run with you?" Tommy demanded.

When he wanted, his voice was almost as big and booming as he was. His powerful bass startled both of the women and made them jump, which in turn made Tommy laugh in delight.

"Damn you, Tommy! You scared me!" Darla complained.

Putting on a mock-angry voice paired with a comical hurt expression, he asked, "Well, which one of you two gonna answer me? How come I'm not included in your morning runs?"

Water and sweat beaded on the top of Tommy's big, bald head and on his exceptionally muscular chest. The early morning sun shining through the windows made the drops glisten against his dark skin. He was dressed in baggy, white boxer shorts and had a pair of tongs covering his feet. A damp, white, terry-cloth towel hung limply in his left hand.

Susan looked at his right leg. The scar running from his shin to his thigh directly over the kneecap had healed well. But, there was no hiding the fact that Tommy's knee and leg had been through some serious trauma. The muscles in his right thigh were just a bit less defined than the left—the result of atrophy. After being shot in the knee by one of Troth's men it amazed her he was walking without a cane. And, there he was, anxious to start running.

"Tommy, why don't you go and get your wet-ass dressed? We've got company, ya know." Darla snapped, donning a sour face that showed her disgust at his laxity.

"Aww, shit, Darla, ain't nothing she hasn't seen before!"

Putting on the thickest southern accent she could muster and waving an pointed, thin index finger in the air, Darla responded, "She ain't seen your johnson before—now go get dressed!"

"How ya doing Tommy?" Susan interrupted, trying to defuse the debate and ignoring the fact that he was standing right in front of her while all he had on were drawers.

"I'm good, Susie-Q, got a great workout in today."
Tommy took the towel and wiped the sweat off of his head,
face, and chest. Then, he continued, "I'm starting to feel
like my old self again." He took the huge beach towel and
wrapped it around his waist, knowing that would please his
wife. "I do think we should all start running together, it
would do us some good, you know relieve stress."

Seeing Tommy cover himself, Darla's face lost the
negative affectation and she went back to being the
extremely gorgeous woman she was. "What stress do I
have except you?" Darla joked walking up to Tommy and
arching up to kiss him on the cheek. "I'll be in the yoga
studio. You two are welcome to join me . . ."

"I wish I could, Darla," Susan answered, pouting.
"But, I gotta steal your husband for a few hours and work
out some of these details."

"Work, work, work . . . what am I gonna do with
the two of you? Haven't you learned anything?" With her
final words, Darla turned and gracefully walked toward the
hallway leading down to the other rooms in the house.

As she walked away, Tommy couldn't help himself.
Susan was touched by his affection. He acted as if it was
the first time he ever saw such a beautiful form. Darla was
Tommy's only addiction, and although they had an open
marriage, there was no question he loved her as much as
she loved him. They, for sure, would grow old and die
together.

Both Susan and Tommy knew they wouldn't see
Darla again for hours. Once she retreated into the solarium,
what she called the "yoga studio," she may as well be on
another planet.

"So," Susan asked, "what's this about getting at that
motherfucker Troth?"

"Shhh! Keep your voice down, Susan! What the
hell's wrong with you?"

"What? What did I say?"

41

"Darla thinks all this shit is over. She doesn't know all that much about Roland Troth and doesn't believe he's the one behind killing Mario and Donny and everyone else . . ."

"How could she not know? Everyone knows!" Susan's voice was incredulous.

"'Cuz she doesn't live in the past and if the government says 'it's over,' in her mind, it's over and done and she moves on."

"Yeah, I know the philosophy . . ."

"So, let's keep our discussions about getting at Troth and taking his old-ass out on the down-low. How does that sound?"

"Yeah, okay, but who's left to go after that piece of shit besides you and me? And, if you can't help me . . ."

"I never said I was out," Tommy interrupted. "It's just that I don't want her to know what I'm—I mean—what we're up to."

"Fine. But still, what happens when we have to leave and go find Troth? What are you gonna tell Darla? What if it gets ugly again, don't you want her ready to protect herself?"

Tommy didn't respond but had a sort-of twisted expression on his face as he thought. Finally, he answered, "Okay, Susan, you win. Sooner or later she's gonna know and she won't be happy—so I may as well take the heat now and get her ready just in case Troth does get stupid." Tommy paused again, thinking. "I don't know, maybe we can convince her to go to Costa Rica for a few months."

The villa in Costa Rica, where Susan's children were staying, still felt like a safe haven to them. There had been no indication that Troth's men knew anything about it.

"That's a good idea," Susan mused.

"At least there she'll be out of the line of fire."

"So, it's settled? You'll tell her tonight that you and I are going after Troth and we're going to take him out."

"Susan, I'm not gonna say all that, but I'll tell her enough."

"Do you think she'll go—or even believe you?"

"Oh, she'll believe me . . . but whether she goes or straps on a few shooters . . . that's for her to decide."

"You know, Tommy, that's why I always liked you."

"Why? What do you mean?"

"You letting us woman make decisions for ourselves like big girls." Susan smiled.

"Oh, kiss my ass! Come on, we got some business to discuss."

*****

Tommy and Susan moved to his home office, a small room between the great room and the master bedroom that once served as a bedroom for one of Tommy's sons, Eric. Having graduated from college with honors and then getting drafted by the Seattle Seahawks, Eric was well on his way to a bright future. The day Eric was drafted and signed a multimillion dollar NFL contract, Tommy boxed up all of his younger son's belongings and put it in storage. A week later, with the help of some of Donny Clearmont's former computer-geek interns, the room was transformed into a digital office with all of the latest gear and fastest internet connections.

Darla hated that particular room because of what Tommy had done with it—so she steered clear of the computers and huge plasma monitors hanging on the walls. It made that particular room the only place not influenced by her classy taste and elegant decor. The electronically cramped space could only be described as "macho."

Tommy sat back in a large black leather captain's chair. His feet were up on the mahogany desk and an unlit cigar was gripped tightly between his teeth. Susan was sitting off to the side, leaning back and sinking deep into the soft, black leather of a puffy love seat. Directly across from her was an enormous television hooked up to several game consoles she did not recognize. She noted that there was nothing in that room connecting him to his former profession as a lawyer. It wasn't the first time Susan was in his office, but she always seemed to be distracted whenever they talked in that particular room.   "Boys and their toys," she mumbled, looking around at the Bang and Oulfson speakers and other insanely expensive gear.

"What's that?" Tommy asked, partially grinning.

"Nothing . . . I was just thinking, you have no idea how all of this stuff reminds me of Donny. He had a room almost exactly like this in his house in Jersey."

"No kidding?" Tommy looked around the room, as if taking in details for the first time. "That makes sense since the same kids who did this place learned from him." He reached across the desk and tapped several keys on the computer's keyboard. "Hey, Susan, I want you to check this out."

The television across from her came to life. After Tommy clicked on a command, the TV displayed an internet site. It was a copy of a recorded broadcast. A well-known journalist and a professor from Harvard filled the screen. Tommy manipulated the device to fast-forward to the segment he wanted Susan to hear.

The reporter and the professor were in the middle of an interview, discussing the movements that continued to generate anxiety for governments around the globe. Both Tommy and Susan had their eyes on the screen and paid close attention as the professor articulated how the members of the European Union were next the group that would be in trouble with the defaults of the sovereign bonds issued by Portugal, Italy, Greece, and Spain. Susan sat and listened patiently.

"Finally," Tommy sighed, "this is the part I wanted you to see."

"Professor Hayes," the reporter asked, "What does this mean for the United States? How is the devaluation of the dollar tied to the Occupy Wall Street movement?"

"John, the vast majority of the people in this country either no longer have the ability to afford their basic necessities or are barely making it from week to week. There are fourteen million homes under foreclosure, and that number is rising. The prices for food and transportation have increased dramatically, and forty million Americans have no access to healthcare—everything is just going to get worse.

"Those in charge feel that the only way out of this stagnant period is to pump more money into the system—and that's a function of the Federal Reserve. I tend to disagree. If they continue down this same path, there will be hyper-inflation, and it won't be long before it'll take a pound of dollar bills to buy a loaf of bread. When you see that happen, you're really going to see a movement in this country."

"So, what you're talking about, Professor, is basically a huge devaluation of the dollar right here at home, maybe even a revolution—if I'm hearing you correctly."

"Yes, John, that's exactly what I'm saying."

The reporter asked, "So what do we do? How do we protect ourselves?"

Professor Hayes did not hesitate, "Buy gold and horde it, it's going to be the only means of survival once the dollar collapses and this nation falls apart . . ."

Tommy pecked at the keyboard and the television went blank. "I guess Donny was right, huh?" he asked, ruefully, thinking of his now-deceased partner.

"Yeah. Actually, he told me it was something his father predicted decades ago, after Nixon took the U.S. off the gold standard."

"He told me that, too, and so did my father. The thing is, Donny was really the only one of us who listened and paid attention to what the government was doing. I guess we better increase production at our mines in Peru and Canada, huh?"

Susan didn't respond immediately. The trust's mining operation had to be handled, but it wasn't the reason why she rushed over. Even though she was not exactly anxious to talk about it, hearing Tommy's take on Troth and how to get retribution was all she really cared about. The fact that Tommy may have thought of a way to get to Troth was all she could focus on because she still believed none of them would truly be safe—not even her children—until Roland Troth was either brought to justice or killed.

"I don't mean to ignore what you're saying, and I know what happens at the mines is important, Tommy, but, please, tell me, what's your idea—how do we get to Troth?"

Tommy reached onto his desk and grabbed a thumb-drive off of the desk's blotter. "This is the recording Carlos gave you of Paul Joseph's interview right up to the point of the attack. Have you seen it?"

Carlos, one of the original Seven Rams, was still in hiding in Costa Rica. Carlos was as active in helping to run the affairs of the trust as he dared to be. Even from Central America, he tried to keep up on the developments in the states and help as much as he could by taking care of the mining operation in Peru. Technology made their clandestine communications possible, but he still had to be careful.

Susan looked away and answered softly, "No. I couldn't bring myself to watch it."

46

When the men employed by Troth had attacked the trust's office building in Williamsport, a man named Josephs who worked for Troth had come to warn them and explain what Troth was up to. But, before the interview ended, everyone in the room was killed and the entire building destroyed. Besides Susan, Tommy, Carlos, and Michelle—the only ones remaining who really knew all the details—no one else knew what Josephs had told them. No one else knew the damning evidence against Troth even existed.

Fully aware of how that session with Paul Josephs ended, with Mario dead and the all-too-clear scene of a young woman getting her head blown off, Susan had a serious aversion to watching it. At the same time, none of them knew what to do with the copy of Paul Joseph's confession implicating Troth. The government put the kibosh on any real investigation into the bombing in Williamsport and Troth's involvement. Because all of the law enforcement agencies were acting strange—like they were somehow compromised—neither Susan nor Tommy had any idea who they could trust. The proof that their fears were not some sort of paranoid delusion was the fact that even though Roland Troth was initially arrested, he had eluded punishment and remained unscathed. Everything related to the bombings and attacks in Pennsylvania had been tagged as a national security issue. Just by having a digital copy of some of the events from that tragic day put them all at risk of criminal penalties. Tommy, a former United States Attorney, knew they were in dangerous territory.

"Before the attack started," said Tommy, "Andy was doing a great job and Josephs pretty much laid out everything Troth had been doing for the past few years. The way I see it, though, it could be argued that Joseph's statement was just him trying to save himself. I mean, his statement is pretty self-serving and even though some of it was against his own interest, it's not clear if a court would allow it as evidence."

"Why's that?" Susan asked.

"The constitution's confrontation clause. The evidence would be deemed testimonial, but because it's a recording and there's no way to cross-examine Josephs it would violate Troth's rights for a jury to see it." Tommy explained.

"That's just another good reason for Troth to kill us. We were witnesses and maybe he'll silence us too so we can't testify against him, right?" Her words were dripping with sarcasm.

Tommy stood silently. He had no answer for her, but they both knew that was one of the main reasons they had not come forward.

Angrily, Susan asked, "Okay, so what the hell was the point of making that recording of Josephs if we can't use it?"

"Susan, it's not like Mario knew Josephs would be assassinated, and it still might be admissible. But, the important thing is it'll give my people some ammunition— a direction to go and lots of leads to follow up on." Grabbing the tiny drive and waving it, Tommy added, "There's a heck of a lot to work with on this thing. We just have to be sure who we're giving it to is wearing a white hat, if you know what I mean."

"Wait a minute, back up a second. You just said, 'my people.' I thought we couldn't trust anyone . . ."

"Yeah, I did think that, but let me tell you, Troth isn't connected in the way we thought he was connected."

"What do you mean?"

Tommy stood, putting the cigar in an empty ashtray and walking around the desk dominating that side of the room. He had managed to get dressed and was decked out in a pink Polo shirt and white, three-quarter length baggy shorts. On his massive feet, he still wore the same leather slippers that looked to be twenty-years-old.

"Everything we know or we think we know about conspiracies and government cover-ups, we get from television or the movies, right?"

"Yeah," Susan answered, and then added, "or maybe a good book."

"Okay, right, now, throw everything you think you know out the window because it's all bullshit. Troth and his cronies are connected, yes. They know powerful people, yes. They have politicians in their pocket, absolutely . . . but they are not some omniscient, all-knowing, all-seeing, all-powerful entities."

"Tommy?" Susan interrupted. "Can you please stop being a fucking lawyer for a second and talk to me, I'm not the goddamn jury and this isn't your closing argument."

The comment made Tommy chuckle. "Okay, okay, check it out, I still have a lot of friends in the Justice Department, and a few old colleagues of mine have been keeping me up to date on the investigation into everything that went down."

"I thought you said they closed those investigations off—you know, everything falling under that national security tag."

"Yeah, sort of, but the government is like a thousand-armed octopus and one arm never knows what the other arms are doing. Like when the SEC came and served me with a Wells Notice, or the IRS inquired about our trusts with those stupid subpoenas, well, they all have their own investigators, right? They all started to dig and guess what? Shit keeps on leading back to Troth. These investigators made inquiries with Homeland Security and the FBI and they've been getting pushed back to some top dog at the Justice Department—and the man there has been getting his toes stepped on by Military Intelligence, JAG, or some other military outfit."

"And all roads lead to nowhere, right?" Susan asked, sure that the answer was a definite.

"Nope! I don't blame you for thinking that, 'cuz you don't know how the government really works. I've been in the belly of that beast, so I do know. You'd think a national security tag would be the end of it, but the last thing you want to do when you're working in government is step on another agency's toes. It's like saying 'Go ahead and whip out your Johnson, whoever's is bigger wins'."

"Yeah, I get that part," Susan commented. "One guy takes authority away from another and there goes their power and influence."

Tommy smiled, "Exactly. But, more importantly, there goes the funding. With no funding these departments are powerless—and a case like this: military hardware, terrorism, commodities, and a crashing stock market—that would let Justice add a few more billion dollars to their budget and hire another ten thousand employees. What my friends are telling me is that there's a war going on right now inside of the Justice Department between people who want to keep Troth out of what happened this summer and others who want to tear him a new asshole. The bosses, they just want the entire situation to go away like it never happened. A terrorist attack under their watch is terrible for their polling numbers."

Susan asked, "What you're trying to tell me is that Troth doesn't control everyone and there are people who know he was responsible?"

"Absolutely. No question about it. He and his people can't hire or bribe everyone and there are way too many holes for Troth to plug. Sooner or later, the dam just might burst. Conspiracies never work like the books or movies because too many people are too ambitious and wanna make a name for themselves."

"But . . . I mean . . . he has to have a lot of connections to get out of the deep shit he was in, right? How the hell did he get out of jail so fast?" Susan asked.

"I don't know and I have no clue what this bullshit intervention by the military is all about, but they do have to be pretty powerful to do what they did," Tommy responded. "I really don't know how far up the line this goes, but what I do know is several U.S. Attorneys were talking about taking some of what happened to grand juries, and when their bosses told them 'No,' they threatened to either go public or walk away from their jobs."

"What happens if one of the U.S. Attorneys takes the attacks or the market manipulations Troth did to a grand jury?"

"All hell will break lose with firings, accusations, charges, counter-charges, and congressional hearings."

Her eyebrows knotted together skeptically.

"I don't know, Susie-Q, I really don't know. But what I do know is that we still have the recording of Paul Josephs spilling his guts about Troth's involvement and I got a handle on a few of the good guys who may be willing to go to the wall to bring him down."

Susan smiled weakly. "You know, that's more than I hoped for because I really didn't want to try and take him down alone."

The phone clipped to Tommy's waistband started to vibrate. Sliding it free, he looked at it—there was no display showing him who was calling. That made him lift a brow because only a select few people knew his number.

Intrigued, he answered it in his deep voice, "Hello? Thomas Jones speaking."

"Mr. Jones? I am calling on behalf of Mr. Roland Troth. He asked me to call you and arrange a meeting."

"Troth wants to set up a meeting with me?" As he said this into the phone, Tommy looked squarely at Susan.

The man on the other end responded, "I believe there is some unfinished business . . ."

Chapter Five

Roland's helicopter landed in Greenwich twenty-minutes earlier and he was driven in a Lincoln Town Car from the heliport to his estate. As soon as he entered his manor, he was informed by his staff that a visitor was waiting for him in the study. Troth, however, had other matters to attend to before he took the meeting. He did not care how long the man in the study had been waiting, nor did it matter that the appointment was set for an hour earlier. Sometimes, these things could not be helped and the man awaiting his return would not dare question the delay.

Gerald Jacobs, a vice president at Troth Hard Assets and Resource Fund, approached him in the foyer. Jacobs was one of the many employees of Troth's hedge fund who was arrested and later released with all of the charges against him dropped. A few months before, Troth had chosen him to be his second in charge—since the prior two individuals who held that position had been murdered.

At one time, Jacob's black hair with gray streaks gave him a dignified appearance. However, over the past few months, working so closely with Troth and knowing the fate of his predecessors, had turned his hair almost completely gray.

"Welcome back, Mr. Troth." As he spoke, Jacobs did an uncomfortable bow of his thin body and a terse nod of deference with his narrow head.

"Thank you, Jerry. Did you make the call?"

"Yes, I did, sir. I have the details of the arrangements logged into your calendar." Going from a high-flying trader in derivatives, an executive, to being what was basically an over-paid, severely overqualified receptionist was humbling, but Jacobs was not the type to rock the boat.

Troth nodded with approval. "Good. Very good. Now, let's see if I can get some leverage before we start negotiations with Mr. Jones."

Troth strode haughtily down the opulently decorated hallway with his head up and shoulders back— his ego having been restored through York's absolution. As soon as he crossed over the threshold and entered the study, a wiry, tall, impeccably dressed black man rose to his feet.

Stanton Frazier was dressed in a black suit with a thin black tie. His shoes were not new, but they had obviously been buffed for the occasion. Using an index finger, the Assistant Director of the FBI nervously pushed the stylish tortoise shell glasses up his nose. He stepped forward and offered a hand, "Mr. Troth, sir."

One of several men with the title of Assistant Director at the FBI, Frazier had graduated from City University of New York and then Rutgers's Law School while he worked as a detective in New York City. Instead of taking the bar exam, he had applied to the FBI. That was many years ago, a career ago, actually. He had retired as a field agent. The political appointment as a Assistant Director did not come as a surprise to him, even though no one in the world of politics knew who he was. Decades of secretly working for Roland Troth's now deceased underling, C.B. Ross, had assured the appointment that allowed Frazier to continue collecting payments for being part of Troth's network. The job, the title, the money, it was all a reward for his loyal service of feeding Troth information no one else had access to.

The way his appointment worked, Stanton Frazier was given a lot of autonomy and formally only answered to three people: the Director of the FBI, the Attorney General, and the President. Even though he personally was not personally connected in any way to merit such a valuable appointment. Instead, it was a favor granted by someone

54

very high up in the administration in return for enormous campaign contributions. It was just the way things worked—and those were specific details he didn't need to know.

Troth did not take Stanton Frazier's hand. Instead, he gave the Assistant Director a terse nod and gestured toward the sofa, "Please, Stanton, have a seat." Both Troth and Frazier sat down with Troth in a chair beside his visitor. "The reason I asked you here is to request a favor."

Frazier raised his eyebrows. Not only was it highly unusual to be beckoned to the residence of his benefactor, something that would usually be forbidden, but to be asked a favor instead of being ordered to do something set off alarm bells in his head.

"What is it, Mr. Troth? You know I'm willing to help in any way I can," he grudgingly acquiesced.

"You've had your men investigating Thomas Jones and Susan DiGiovanni, correct?"

"Yes, sir, and we've provided you with all the information we could find."

Roland leaned forward in his seat, fixing his gaze on Frazier. "But why haven't you arrested him?"

"Because there's nothing to arrest him for—he's a former U.S. Attorney and he's clean as clean can be."

"Listen and listen closely, nobody—and I mean nobody—is that clean. I don't care what you do or how you do it, you have to turn up the pressure on Mr. Jones and do it in a way that will both drain his resources and distract him. And, Mr. Frazier, I can't have it coming back to haunt me—do we understand each other?"

Stanton rubbed his temples trying to relieve some of the stress he felt building in his brain. Feeding Troth information was one thing, but taking the lead on a bogus arrest was much more serious. He thought his days of actively sticking his neck out had ended earlier that year. Helping Roland Troth the previous summer should have sufficed, but it seemed like his service would never come to an end.

Frazier's formal assignment revolved around antiterrorism, specifically home-grown "lone wolves" who were active threats. But, Frazier had managed to get his nose into many different areas and provide lots of helpful tips to Troth and his hedge fund traders. For the past few years, he had been able to do exactly what he was placed in that position to do—yet stay out of the spotlight. Unfortunately, his ability to be all but invisible evaporated when the building in Williamsport was blown up and a State Trooper was killed. Home grown terrorism, his primary responsibility, could no longer be ignored.

Leading the initial investigation had fallen to him and it had been his unofficial responsibility to try and protect Troth's interests before handing over the investigation to some top-secret, special unit of the military. Stanton Frazier had earned a nice bonus from Roland Troth. For his part, Troth paid what one would expect to have a very powerful insider covering for him inside the FBI.

The summer was hell for everyone involved in the case and the cover-up. Trying to protect Troth, Frazier knew, was going to lead to problems, especially if the special military investigators connected the dots—which he knew they would. But, Frazier had no choice, he had to do what he was told. The money Troth had given him was already spent and the dirty deeds that could land him in jail forever were already done. Now, Troth was asking him to arrest a man on trumped-up charges. Not just any man, though—Thomas Jones, who was already being watched by numerous government agencies. It was a dirty task that could potentially put Frazier's ass in prison—and he was much too old for that.

"I'll do the best I can, Mr. Troth," Frazier finally relented.

"No. You'll do better than that and you'll also make sure Ms. DiGiovanni is taken out of the picture. I want them both charged. I want them both arrested. And, I want them both locked up so they know what it's like."

*****

The quick trip out of Old Greenwich along the curving, narrow lanes displayed to Stanton Frazier what real wealth meant. His home in Arlington, Virginia, was a McMansion and had cost him a bundle to have built. But, the estates he passed as he meandered toward I-95 were the real deal. These were gated properties, some of them even looked like castles, with roving patrols and immigrant gardeners raking leaves off of five-acre lots.

Frazier did not begrudge those people their wealth. Instead, he felt fortunate he and his family had been able to share in the dream—even if on a smaller scale—thanks to his benefactor, Roland Troth.

Frazier patted his pockets with his free hand looking for his cell phone, forgetting he had left it and all other electric devices at home. Traveling to Greenwich had been a risk and he had taken every precaution. Because he knew exactly how the government worked, with their tracking capacity, even bringing along a cell phone was out of the question. He couldn't fly, he couldn't use credit cards, and he was driving his brother-in-law's car. That way, there was no trail and he could deny even being in Connecticut. Heading home, Stanton wondered, once again, what he had gotten himself into.

It had been many, many years worth of payments funneled through one of Troth's subsidiaries that allowed him and his family to live a lifestyle most people dreamed of—but what he had been asked to do in return for that money this time just felt wrong. Earlier in his career, the most he was ever asked to do was pass on tips about investigations and keep Troth's people informed about companies or executives who were under investigation. Troth's funds make a financial killing knowing who was going to be indicted and what firms would be fined before anyone else—and Frazier had participated in those profits.

Years of working for Troth, and as a FBI Special Agent, passed before anyone asked him to actually get his hands dirty and alter evidence . . . but even that was no big deal. In the 1990's, the entire FBI crime lab was corrupt and incompetent, with technicians and so-called "forensic experts" finding or dismissing evidence to suit whatever prosecutors wanted. It wasn't until 1999 that the institutional fraud was discovered and the FBI crime lab cleaned up. But, by then, he had moved on—except for the fact that Roland Troth had him by the balls and wouldn't let go.

As a one-time idealist who thought of himself as a dedicated public servant, having a part in altering evidence had at first made him hate himself. But, his daughter did want to go to Georgetown and he did need the money—so he expunged the fact that his duty, honor, and sense of justice all had price tags attached to them from his consciousness and did what he had to do.

The reward for his ability to alter the course of a few major cases while assigned as an adjunct to the crime lab, and continually keep feeding Troth's firm information, was lots and lots of money— not to mention the appointment to Assistant Director after he retired as a Special Agent. Now in his late fifties, Stanton Frazier felt secure in his position and was fine with continuing to help Troth—at least he did feel secure until all hell broke loose.

The things he had done to protect Troth and shield his firm were very serious and had required him to become part of a massive cover-up. Frazier himself was at risk of being discovered, he knew, and there was no going back to make things better. In his mind, he was already all-in and felt he had no other choice but to continue to do Troth's bidding. As soon as he got back to D.C., he would figure out what to do about Thomas Jones and Susan DiGiovanni.

Chapter Six

Sampson drove the Rolls back to an associate's compound in Hyannis. Grabbing his leather carry-all, and the mini-camera sitting in the passenger seat, he put the keys up under the front visor and exited the car. With an expressionless face and the purposeful stride of a former military man, he started to cut across the cape and hike toward the beach on the Atlantic Ocean. Wearing black cotton trousers, a white knit shirt, and black shoes with rubber soles, the only thing that made him stand out were the flesh-colored gloves he wore to protect the recently transplanted skin.

It was a seven mile hike before he reached the beach and then several more miles south along the rocky beaches until he reached his destination. He knew to look for the rock outcroppings and cliffs south of the national preserve on the northeastern shore. That was where Maxwell York's mansion sat facing the Atlantic Ocean. From the earlier helicopter ride, Sampson knew he could scale the fifty-foot cliff up to York's backyard without gear. There were many crevices and cracks leading up to the seawall. The hardest part would be the man-made concrete and stone segment of the facade, part of some bygone fort and the foundation for York's walled-off compound. He was a little concerned about his grip and the lack of sensation in his fingers, but the deficiency couldn't be helped. He knew it was something he could overcome.

After the earlier recon, he knew trying to get through the front gates or over the twenty-foot high walls protected by electronic trip wires and cameras would have been silly. It was amusing to Sampson that York's security apparatus believed the cliff and seawall provided protection. That was a huge weakness he, or even a first-year member of any JSOC unit, would exploit.

Reaching back into the leather bag, Sampson pulled out a device that closely resembled an Apple IPhone. The similarity in form and function was intentional so as not to draw attention to the true nature of the clandestine service's gear. Beyond the usual applications, a start-up firm working for DARPA had programmed in many neat little tricks that were especially helpful to spies and the military.

Swiping to and tapping the icon for an application, the multipurpose communications device wirelessly connected to the recording device in his bag and uploaded the digital recording. Sampson put two custom-molded earplugs into his ears, pressed another icon on the device to play, and started listening to everything Roland Troth had said and heard and seeing everything Troth had seen during the private meeting he had with Maxwell York.

*****

Sampson walked onto the beach and turned in the direction of York's estate. Listening and watching the recording for the third time, he paid very close attention to even the smallest detail of what Troth secretly captured during the meeting. The camera and microphone had worked well and everything—from Troth being led through the house to him walking out the back door to meet York— was crystal clear.

Because of the setting on the mini-camera, and the way Troth had stood during the meeting with York, all that Daniel Sampson could see on the screen when the two older men were talking was a tight image of York's face and the upper part of his torso.

As displayed on the screen, Maxwell York's hair ruffled in the wind like wings, the gray locks being held in sections by some sort of gel. He had deep creases in his pale cheeks and forehead, but they did not take away from his attractive, rugged face. He had a strong, prominent chin with a dimple in the center. A few gray whiskers grew out just a little from the hard to reach cleft. The ice blue eyes, at times, made him look cold and callous, but at others made him look wise.

Guessing that Maxwell York was in his late eighties, maybe early nineties, Sampson made a mental note to check out the government archives of the OSS, CIA, and FBI dating as far back as World War II. He pressed the earplugs tighter against his ears so the ambient noise of the waves crashing into the shore and seagulls flying above were completely blocked out. He kept walking at a rapid pace, knowing exactly how far he had to go before preparing for the climb.

York's voice was, at times, thin with age but his authoritative tone was evident as he addressed Troth. "Roland, you've had no need to know the rest of what we've planned until now, and I tend to believe because you didn't know, that was the reason why you acted so rashly. I mean, my God, man, what were you thinking?"

Troth's voice came through clearly, but he could not be seen on the recording as Sampson held the device closer to his eyes. York's distinguished face stayed prominently centered on the screen. At the same time, Sampson could tell Troth was extremely nervous by the shaky tone of his voice.

Troth responded, "You have to believe me, Maxwell . . . I . . . my firm, we had nothing to with the market crash or what those men did in Pennsylvania . . . I was on our trading floor and saw it myself, we were locked out of our system, we were helpless to stop . . ."

"Quiet, Roland." York interrupted calmly, yet sternly. "Now, listen to me; you seem to be lacking faith in our movement or else you wouldn't have gotten so greedy—you wouldn't have panicked. Isn't it true that the value of the dollar has gone down like you were told it would?"

"Yes." Troth replied meekly.

"Isn't it also true that the price of gold has surged up to where we projected? All of this was planned, what, thirty, forty-years ago?"

Instead of responding, Troth nodded meekly.

"Didn't the wars come and go just like we said they would, just like we told you they would—and don't we control most of the world's oil resources?"

"Yes, Maxwell, and I made prodigious profits for you along the way, didn't I?"

"Yes, you did, Roland, you were very successful and very loyal. You did what we asked of you, but how could you have failed when you had every change in the geopolitical weather spoon-fed to you by us and your expert networks? A trained monkey could have made a profit."

Sampson studied the cold blue eyes of York as he spoke. In those eyes, he recognized a man who had realized true power. Sampson thought the stare must have sent chills down Troth's spine as his superior put him in his place. York knew the real secret of Troth's success. It must have been humiliating to Troth, the master manipulator, to have his purported genius in trading put into the proper perspective.

Getting no response to his last comment, York continued, "So, you were well aware that these changes were coming. You were made aware of the political diversions and actions we would take to further our cause, correct?"

"Yes, Maxwell."

York turned and faced the seawall. Speaking to Troth without looking at him, he asked, "Then why didn't you contact Andrew when you needed more capital? Why not use our resources at the Fed?"

"I did call, Maxwell!" Troth protested.

"But you called too late—after the damage was done. Roland, if you want to do this right, you have to trust us. The partners are not happy. Roland, do you trust us?"

"Yes," he responded earnestly.

"Will you do anything you're asked to do?"

"Whatever you want, Maxwell."

"Good." York turned back to face Troth. "Now, I want to tell you a little about the rest of the plan because I need your trust."

"What is the rest, Maxwell? Over the years, I've had only scant details from others about the changes to come . . . and I've been a major part in the consolidation of wealth, helping to find and finance the technologies to replace manual labor, but the endgame? No one's told me even though I am a partner, aren't I?"

Sampson was impressed by the way Troth regained some of his nerve and got directly to the point. By ingratiating himself and letting onto what he did and did not know.

Maxwell responded, "Yes, you're a partner, a junior partner, but a partner none-the-less—and that's why we're talking right now and you're not dead."

As he walked, Sampson surveyed the area to make sure he was not being watched or followed. He knew a lot of what York was saying about the world and the faltering economic situation was true. The world was going to hell economically and politically; everything Troth had told him before the meeting was being confirmed by York. He had a hard time believing the shocking scope of what they were doing. But, it was true. York and others aligned with him were behind most of the world's conflagrations and they were planning more, including altering the world's population. The next part of the conversation made Sampson rewind and listen several times. He wanted to pay especially close attention to what was being said so that when he did what he planned it would be easier to gather more information.

Troth burst out a series of rapid-fire questions, "So why the rush? Why was Andrew pressing me so hard to acquire tangible assets so quickly? I mean, if all of this is not to take place immediately, why was I told to act now?"

"Because, Roland, part of it is happening now—and not long from now disruptions are going to take place that will change the world. The rest of it, the final phases; well, just like you, I'm going to die a natural death long before any of that matters. Still, I want everything in place and ready for the last phases of Project Stasis before I'm gone. We're very close to achieving that. Yes, my chosen successor, and my future children—clones of me, actually—will then be able to administer everything just as we had planned."

Sampson, hearing that particular statement again, had to force himself to set the implications aside so he could focus on the next part of the reconnaissance.

York continued, "Before I die, before the partners all die, I don't want to leave anything to chance. As a matter of fact, the long-term, final phase of Project Stasis has already started so we are way beyond the point of no return."

Troth interrupted anxiously, "Will my health be jeopardized?"

York glared distastefully at Roland and answered, "Don't worry it won't impact you, Roland. It's a relatively recent development that all of the genetic technologies have come together to accomplish what we want." York smiled for the first time in some sort of private amusement. He then continued, "Unfortunately, we can't go anywhere just yet. It's our responsibility to finish building the necessary infrastructure."

"Using the markets and laws in place right now, we'll emerge on top. We will be the ones with the means to provide for the world, and people will beg the likes of us to help them, to take charge. When that happens, then we can rest. After that, many years from now, the final phase will take hold and that will free our successors to do whatever they wish. Until then, we still have a lot of work to do."

"But Maxwell . . ."

"No!" York put some depth into his voice. "No more questions. Don't worry about the property you lost. It will all be made available to you again the next time more mortgage backed securities are on the market. Bid for those bonds, you will win—it will just be more expensive this time. When you get back to Greenwich, you'll find another $20 billion dollars has been transferred into the accounts of your hedge funds. I'm trusting in you, Roland, not to make the same mistakes twice. The other partners and I can't control everyone and everything—so if you get yourself into trouble again, we may not be able to rescue you."

"What exactly do you want me to do, Maxwell?"

"Exactly what you were doing—but do it on the up and up. Don't try to manipulate the markets you can't control, and stay away from those exotic derivatives. Finish getting those natural gas pipelines in place. The New York Fed will be auctioning off more mortgage backed securities soon. Figure out which properties we need and buy the underlying bonds; complete the pipelines and the transfer station and that's it. We'll have others take care of the rest. I have partners dealing with equities all over the world and no longer need you in that game."

A sound came out of Troth's mouth that sounded like the start of a protest that he managed to stifle.

Maxwell let out a resigned sigh and then continued, "Just like me, you're getting too damn old, Roland. When you go into other markets I asked you to avoid, we end up trading against each other! Don't you understand, this has

66

to be coordinated." York calmed himself and went on, "However, since you started the project to corner the market on natural gas, I want you to focus on that exclusively and finish it."

The sensitive microphone picked up Troth catching his breath off screen. Sampson heard it clearly through the earphone.

Maxwell went on, reacting to Roland's surprise, "Yes, Roland, of course I knew exactly what you were doing—and I actually thought it was a brilliant idea—except for the fact that you went beyond your scope of expertise. Then, you overreached and got greedy. When you get greedy, you get burned. You will not make that same mistake, will you? If you need more money or have any trouble with leverage, just get in touch with Andrew and he'll make sure you get all the financing you need. But, for that, you may have to wait a while. Just be patient and have faith in me, in Andrew, in the rest of us. Now go and leave me alone, I don't want to have to see you again—and I won't."

Sampson watched the rest of the recording, taking note of the interior details of York's mansion as Troth was led out the front door. As soon as the Rolls Royce came into view outside of the mansion's entryway, Sampson stopped the digital recording and erased it.

The beach started to change and become a much narrower swatch of sand. Sampson looked up and saw he was at a slight inlet of a cove that led to some of the highest ground on the Atlantic shore of Cape Cod. Walking south, the rock wall started to rise on his right and climbed gently in front of an ancient fort. As soon as Sampson reached the bottom of the cliff, where the waves tumbled against the rocks at high tide, he knew up above that point was Maxwell York's unsecured back yard. He would have to wait until sundown to make the climb, but that would give him time to think and several hours to get some much needed sack time.

What Sampson heard on the recording of Troth and York talking sounded more like the plot of a sci-fi novel than reality. But, in the day and age of drones—along with all kinds of military research and development—creating a world where most manual labor was done by computer and robotics did not sound that far fetched. He smiled to himself, thinking a world not unlike the one portrayed in "The Terminator" was not too far off. The technology was available and capable, if that was what York wanted to do.

Another thought that came to him was how Hitler and Maxwell York seemed to have a lot in common. However, the way York spoke, Project Stasis seemed to be a lot more subtle. He was talking about future decades away with a lot more work to do. It did not sound as if there would be some sort of mass extinction, at least not for a while. Sampson's main consideration, though, was figuring out how to make what he knew work to his greatest advantage. As he walked up and over boulders layed out from the shore into the ocean forming a breakwater, Sampson went over the scant details in his head one more time. He still didn't know everything Project Stasis entailed, but he knew where those old men wanted it to lead.

Leaning against a boulder and closing his eyes, Daniel Sampson fell asleep.

*****

The first assemblage included two of the sons of Mier Rothschild; James from Paris and Nathan from London. The only other participant documented by name was the Duke of Wellington. The year was 1815 and the panel, what some claim to have been upwards of twenty men, had been busy planning the final defeat of Napoleon

Bonaparte at Waterloo. The names of the other people in attendance were lost to history.

The scions of Mier Rothschild and their confederates did the only thing possible to insure victory at Waterloo—they hired and paid for the British army to fight Napoleon. But, they didn't just pass off what was the legal tender of the time. Instead, the men were paid to fight for the British in gold.

Using the nascent bond market, Nathan raised money to buy the gold and relied on his network of brothers to get the best price, no matter where the market for the best price was located. Arbitrage allowed Nathan to rack up large profits on the gold purchases while, at the same time, he also collected large fees from the British government for managing the sale of bonds. Nathan's trading activities soon made him the king of bonds and it made him and his brothers very, very rich.

With the soldiers satisfied by their wages—and less likely to decamp—the Duke of Wellington was able to win at Waterloo. It was the first of many wars financed by the Rothschild brothers. However, the Rothschilds were not the only ones who recognized the value in such pursuits. From that original gathering, the twenty or so members who figured out how to beat Napoleon went on to either finance or wage perpetual wars all over the world. And, the heirs of those men became exceedingly affluent in the process.

Maxwell York was a direct descendant from not only one but two of the genetic lineages present at the original conclave. Along with York, there were thousands upon thousands of heirs, but York was one of the last of his generation. Gone were the oldest, most respected members of the neo-aristocracy who, for many decades, worked towards returning the world to where it had once been. York was the most closely connected to the original members—the wealthy men who had engendered hope of a better future for the elite few. With the passing of his compatriots both at home and abroad, he knew that literally thousands of state secrets had died with them. The list included the truth about Pearl Harbor, the Rosenburgs, the Gulf of Tonkin, and the assassination of John F. Kennedy. York, or people York worked with, had their hands in almost everything and worked hard to keep the military industrial complex churning.

But, at age 83, York was not well. His longevity was a surprise to his doctors and his closest advisors. Having been active in the military industrial complex after World War II, and working on weapons programs that led to the deployment of fusion-based ICBMs, they knew at some point York would get cancer, and he contracted thyroid cancer years before. However, the best doctors and the latest treatments were able to extend his life.

Maxwell was proud to have done all he did—but felt a tinge of sadness knowing few of his contemporaries were left. He was the only one who knew the entire story and what they accomplished. Along the way, the neo-aristocracy successfully engineered social discord, armed the world, and enslaved the masses under a mountain of debt. It had been a very productive association.

York knew he didn't have long. But, he was comforted by the knowledge that several vials of his cryogenically frozen sperm would survive him. After testing, it was determined his sperm was fit for reproduction and unaffected by any virus, bacteria, or genetic abnormality. Once the science was perfected, which was getting closer by the day, the DNA from his sperm cells would be implanted into ova with genetic material removed. The cells would be teased back to life and coaxed to divide. Once the cells developed into embryos, the healthiest of the group would be implanted into exceptionally healthy surrogate mothers. Nine months later, several new—but different—Maxwell Yorks would come into the world. And, according to his will and the trust left behind for his genetically identical offspring, they would get the best of everything and want for nothing.

It was because of the frozen sperm and the trusts York had trained his subordinates to only think of working within the framework of a society based on laws. If it were up him, the world would have no need for lawyers, judges, or politicians. And, maybe in an enlightened age to come, they could dispense with the convoluted, unjust constructs of man-made law. But, until that time, they had to rely on the rule of law to ensure the future for the generation of Yorks to follow him.

York felt confident that the men and women coming up—the ones who would benefit the most from the rebirth of feudalism-would do whatever they had to restore the rule of law. They were tutored and taught to think and believe as he had and those directly under him had prospered— with him as a benefactor. All they had to do is follow the path he had laid out for them.

The day was getting on and Maxwell York was tired. He was feeling every single day of his age and wanted to go lay down for a nap. Turning away from the seawall and walking back through the massive, elegant gardens of his Cape Cod estate, he shuffled past the security guards watching him, walking into the sliding glass doors and disappeared inside the mansion.

Chapter Seven

In the weeks after the end of the Little League World Series Williamsport seemed to be getting back to some semblance of normalcy—at least as far as the peoples' routines went. Most of the residents of the small city and several connected suburbs had tried to move on and forget about the attack that rocked the valley and killed so many of their friends and neighbors. But, too many of them had been traumatized, too many lives had been painfully impacted to just let it go. Even as summer came to an end, and the high school football teams started practices for the upcoming season, a haze of sadness, weariness, fear, and confusion still hung over the valley— no matter how brightly the sun was shining.

Susan had gone back to Mario's house where she showered and changed. Minutes later, Tommy pulled up beside the fieldstone and glass house in a black Ford F-100 pickup truck. The glossy paint along with the custom chrome rims and mirror-like bumpers glistened in the sun. Trucks and SUVs were the only types of vehicles he liked to drive. His massive frame simply could not fit into the compartments of expensive sedans. Despite his wealth, and the ability to buy whatever he wanted, the old Ford was his baby and he kept it in mint condition.

She came strutting out of the house, her black pumps clicking against the stone walkway. Susan was wearing what, at first glance, looked like a bright yellow sweat suit. But, the front of the blouse was covered in an intricate pattern of multicolored sequins that sparkled in the sun. The bottom hem of the baggy top hung down to nearly mid-thigh.

"Who you hiding that ass from, baby girl?" Tommy jested as she opened the passenger door and climbed up into the truck.

Tossing her large Gucci bag on the floor, she looked him up and down. Seeing he had on old, worn out jeans and the same Polo shirt he had on earlier, she asked, "You don't like this outfit?"

"I like it, okay," Tommy responded, but then added with a straight face, "I just don't like it on you."

"Shut up, jerk!" They both laughed at their now all-too-common banter. They had become like brother and sister over the past several months and there was nothing—not even silly insults—that was out of bounds between them.

Susan took off her sunglasses and looked behind her. In the usually empty gun rack mounted to the rear window of the cab were two rifles. "What are the guns for, big boy? You planning' on going hunting or something'?"

"Nah, after that call from Troth's man, I just thought it would be a good idea to have 'em handy."

Trying to ease the tension that was right under the surface, Susan quipped, "You know, all you need now is one of them ten-gallon cowboy hats and you and your truck would fit right in with them ol' boys down in Texas."

Tommy turned to her and smiled, "Yeah, imagine that, me wearin' one of them nigga-hatein' hats!"

Susan blushed as he let out a belly-laugh. Hearing a black man use that word made her uncomfortable—even if it was Tommy who said it.

He put the truck into gear and headed down the slope toward the switchbacks that would take them down the mountain. They had agreed to pick up Michelle at the airport—her flight coming in long after Darla's left—and then check out the progress at the construction site. That was where the new building for the Seven Rams Gold Trust and the Clearmont Geology and Mining Trust was being raised.

Despite their attempts at humor, there was still a heavy presence between them and it made the truck's cab

73

seem stifling. The phone call from Troth's associate, some guy named Gerald Jacobs, had immediately sent Susan into a panic. Tommy's reassurances— telling her the caller hadn't said anything other than giving him a time and place where Troth wanted to meet—did nothing to settle her nerves. The whirlwind of activity after the call came made dispensing with the anxiety all but impossible.

Darla had been, by necessity, interrupted in the middle of her yoga routine. Several minutes of explanation and debate later, she decided to go to Costa Rica and stay at the villa. Her other option, arming herself and standing guard in their own home, was not acceptable to her or to Tommy. When Susan was leaving the Jones's house, Darla was running out to a car that would take her to the Williamsport Airport. She was very upset and that was not helpful.

Since then, for both Tommy and Susan, the wheels in their heads kept on turning and hadn't stopped. They were both speculating about what exactly Roland Troth was up to, if they were safe, and what they should do.

"So," Susan said while Tommy guided the truck toward Four Mile Drive, "are we going to talk about this and decide what to do or not?"

"What's there to talk about? Troth wants to meet up with us in Greenwich tomorrow afternoon. It's his place, but we'll make sure someone knows where we're going, and then we'll find out what that motherfucker wants. Any questions?"

"Yeah," Susan responded, disliking his tone. Narrowing her eyes and fixing them on Tommy's face, she all but seethed, "Are you insane, Tommy? I mean this is crazy—we have no idea what that man is going to do, do we?"

"No, we don't—but you know what? I'm tired of running around like a dog with my tail tucked between my legs. The feds are all screwed up—some of 'em are wrapped around his little finger. We really don't know who to trust in the Justice Department and I can't think of what to do but face this asshole and see what he wants. Maybe this is the opportunity we've been waiting for."

Susan was incredulous. She turned in her seat so she was facing him with her back against the door and her left leg bent and up on the seat. "You wanna see what he wants? The man's a killer, Tommy! He had Donny killed, think about what happened to Mario . . .

"I do think about it!" he hollered. "I think about it every single day, Susan! I don't know what you think we should do—run up on Troth and just shoot him?"

Again, there was silence in the truck's cabin. The words hurt her and cut deeply as the image of her shooting another man in the head, and killing him, immediately came to mind. No matter how hard she tried to justify what she had done a pain of guilt—even if she was right to kill that man—always seemed to be right there in her chest. Susan glared at Tommy while he kept his eyes focused straight ahead at the road in front of him.

Finally, he spoke, "I'm sorry I yelled. I didn't mean that."

"You better be, you dick, or I was going to kick your ass."

Tommy turned and looked down at the diminutive woman sitting beside him with her red cheeks, pouty lips and fists tightened up into balls. He smiled a big, glowing-white smile. "Yeah, all right." Pausing, he waited until she smiled back at him and then turned back to look at the road.

"Okay, Susie-Q, if we were going to kill Troth, how would we do it without getting our asses locked up?"

It did not take long for them to cross the bridge over Loyalsock Creek and go in Montoursville. A few minutes later, they were at Williamsport Airport. Michelle was waiting for them outside of the front door. They exchanged war greeting and got back into the truck, heading to the site, Michelle sitting between Susan and Tommy.

"So, what's new? Why are you two so tense?"

"You know how Tommy can be, Michelle, kind of a bull head."

"Me? What about you?"

"Is it about the trust, the building, what?" Michelle probed

"No," Susan answered, "It's a decision he made that I don't agree with."

"If it's about the company, let me help." Michelle was the one with the best business sense and had taken on the most important roles keeping their business ventures running smoothly. She had a doctorate degree in Economics, her professorship at a prestigious college in Costa Rica made her anxious to learn how the real world worked outside of Academia. It was wonderful for her, she believed, to be away from the sterile atmosphere of computer models and theories and really getting her hands dirty. Taking on the task of managing the construction site, making sure the new office building was built perfectly to meet their exact specifications, had given her that opportunity. But working with two petulant, bickering partners could be challenging.

They pulled up to the site where the contractors had made tremendous progress.

"If the site in Pittsfield is moving as fast as this, we'll be in good shape." Tommy stated with appreciation doing the best he could to change the subject. He nodded his head and had a look of pride on his face. The angular, four-story, structure covering the ground where the old building had been was very impressive.

As soon as they stepped out of the truck, Michelle put two fingers in her mouth and whistled in the direction of a trailer. A young man standing near the trailer immediately turned and looked in her direction. She pointed to her helmet and indicated the number two—and then pointed at Tommy and Susan.

"Yeah," she answered, "but Pittsfield is a completely different animal—we're turning that place into Fort Knox. According to Zeke, though, everything there is on schedule and get this, production hasn't dropped off all that much."

No one had to say a word. They just shook their heads in amazement and appreciation. Zeke, the old, cantankerous plant manager in Pittsfield had been given the responsibility of supervising the construction and expansion at the foundry while continuing to manage the main operation, smelting the unprocessed ore coming in from the mines in Canada and Peru.

"How many more people has he hired for transportation and security for the Canadian shipments?" Susan asked, conscious that the people in western Pennsylvania were struggling. The poor economy and lack of job opportunities continue to take its toll.

"About two-hundred full-time. It'll be more when the next group of trainees finally gets their CDL's."

"CDL? What's that?" Susan asked. Of the three, she was the least sophisticated when it came to business matters, but she was learning and never hesitated to ask about what she didn't know.

Tommy answered gruffly, "A CDL is a commercial driver's license. It's required for the men we hired to drive the trucks: tractor trailers, armored vehicles, and the support vans. And, yeah, we're paying them as they train."

"I think this is going to work out great, Tommy."

"What, paying the trainees?" "Yeah that, but I mean the entire restructuring of the trust. I can't think of a better way to get everyone on the same page—I mean, it's a great way to keep everyone working hard and loyal to the company." Susan chimed in.

Michelle confirmed, "The workers all seem to be really thankful for the changes, and Zeke said they're working harder than ever." She was not only managing the construction of both sites, but she was also helping to ramp up the operations for both of the trusts.

As had been agreed upon by Tommy, Susan, Carlos, and Michelle, they were trying to implement a different kind of business model and it was going to be a very expensive experiment if it went wrong. The theory was that if the employees were also owners who took on direct responsibility for the profitability of the firm, not only would the employees be better off and more satisfied, but the business would be more productive and more profitable.

The terms of the initial public offering Michelle had worked out included all employees as partial owners of the operation vested from the start of their employment. As minority shareholders, the employees would actively participate in the management and profits of the business. The tiny percentages of ownership each employee would get from day one would grow as their years of service increased. The plan was being formalized and was part of the Trust's charter to be implemented more broadly after the IPO. The only limitation on what they were calling, "Employee Participation Shares" was that the shares themselves were restricted. They could be passed onto family members, converted to common shares, or sold back to the gold trust; but no one outside of the operation would be able to own those shares. That way, the principals could never lose control.

Not happy that her two partners were being so formal and uptight, Michelle turned to Tommy and asked, "Before we go on, are you going to tell me what's going on between you two or not?"

With the conversation brought back so directly, he no longer had an excuse to delay telling Michelle what they were planning to do.

Touching her shoulder and getting her to turn to him, he said: "Listen, Michelle, we're going on a trip and we need you to hold things down on your own for a while." He had to holler over the beeping warning alarm of a truck backing up.

"Yeah? Where you going'?" she shouted back.

"Greenwich. We're going to see Troth."

Suddenly, the truck's beeping stopped and the level of noise dropped significantly as it pulled out and drove away.

"You're fucking kidding me, right?" She was obviously stupefied and she was still shouting. "Why? What sense does that make?"

"Listen," Susan cut in, "we have to do something and maybe we can talk to him and figure out a way to . . . to, I don't know, be safe."

"I think it's a stupid move, but since when do the two of you pay attention to me?" Michelle turned away, frustrated.

*****

With a large office on K Street, "Old Harold," as everyone called him, had been able to quickly rise to the top of his profession simply because he had no scruples. If a company, PAC, or organization wanted to influence some piece of legislation, he could get them the votes—for a fee of course. Later, hired by someone else, he could just as easily gather support and legislative votes to support the opposite side of the same issue. Harold Lavale was the quintessential hired gun—a lobbyist who knew all of the ins and outs necessary to subvert any possible claims of ethics violations.

The call he received that day did come as a surprise. It had been a long time since one of former benefactors contacted him directly. The last time someone so senior reached out to him was when he was still working for the Justice Department and an associate of Roland Troth had to be discredited. That was a long time ago—but because the target, Charles "Carlos" Rivera-Ortez, ended up being killed in a car crash and Lavale was able to keep the payoff, it was a memorable event in his professional career.

Andrew Stevens was the man who initiated the latest contact. He had dropped the right names and said the right things to let Old Harold know he was an insider and was one to be listened to. Despite getting all of the right signals, wisely, he was still cautious. Despite lax enforcement of influence peddling and campaign finance laws, it was still smart for someone as well known as he was to be very careful who he spoke with and how they communicated when not speaking in a "clean" room. Other lobbyists had learned their lessons the hard way and were busy spending their time counting cinder blocks in the walls of prison cells.

The request for his services by Andrew Stevens, however, had much broader implications than usual and the fee—double his standard $500,000 plus expenses—made Lavale's mouth water, but it also made him extra vigilant.

On the surface, the request was very simple and direct. Stevens wanted Lavale to garner votes from Democrats in support of a Senate bill that was pending before the Intelligence Committee. Unable to be more specific over the phone, the details of the proposed bill had been messengered over. Slouched over in his black leather captain's chair, reading glasses perched on his nose, Old Harold had not even bothered to read the text of the bill Stevens wanted passed. Knowing what MYB, Ltd. did from prior work, he assumed it had to do with military equipment or contracts of some sort. That would also fit in

80

perfectly with the request to lobby for Democratic support—the Republicans would go for defense spending no matter what it was.

More important than the technicalities of the legislation were the particulars about what inducements he had been enjoined to offer the senators in return for their votes. Actually, it was the only thing that mattered because the better the inducements, the easier it would be to get the votes.

What Harold Lavale was pouring over, as if his eyes were lying to him, was what MYB, Ltd. had thrown into the pot to get the bill out of committee. He has seen some sweet deals in his time—but this offer was simply unreal. A big, juicy cut of IPO shares in the hottest internet social networking site was so sweet that he figured he could get any number of senators to dance like circus bears in return for even a small cut.

Knowing he had the right chips to play with, all he had to figure out was who he wanted to join him in the game.

Lavale picked up the phone and pressed a speed-dial button. He knew the call to the private line would bypass the switchboard and would be answered only if the senator was in—so he skipped the formalities. As soon as the woman's voice came on the line, Harold cooed, "Ellen, you sexy little bitch! How 'bout some lunch?"

"With you, Harold? Not on your life!" The woman's response was both severe and coquettish at the same time.

"Well, how about we meet up at the Watergate for some drinks? I'll make it worth your while."

"Okay, Harold, but make it my suite, 8 p.m.?

"I'll be there, Senator Clarkson . . . and you're going to be one happy little lady . . ."

******

81

Ellen Clarkson sat in an all but empty office in the basement of the Capitol Building. The decor was a far cry from her corner office three floors above. The door was closed and it was clear by the way the senator was fanning the documents in her right hand that the air inside the tiny room was stifling. Being in that tiny office next to the loud boiler was the only way to get away from the many eavesdroppers and the prying eyes of staffers on the upper floors. As a powerful senator with many committee appointments, longevity had its privileges, but notoriety also had negative consequences. Everyone knew who Ellen Clarkson was and it seemed everyone wanted to know what she was up to.

As the years of service had accumulated, the stress of the job led to more patches of gray in her undyed hair and deepening wrinkles around her 66-year-old eyes. It had to be the stress, she figured, because other than her hair and the ever more apparent crows-feet, the rest of her looked spectacular—and she knew it.

Leaning on the same desk as the beautiful, smartly dressed Senator Clarkson was her colleague and dear friend, James Neil. They had come into the Senate as freshman in the same year and had endured their first three terms—eighteen years—together. They were both well into their forth term and anxious to finally retire from public service. They knew this was their last hurrah—their last chance to reap the rewards they deserved—before the next election. At the same time, they were as careful as they could be so as not to be caught up in any kind of scandal that could ruin everything.

James, the elder-statesman type, prided himself on being the type of politician who would willingly reach across the aisle and work together with any Republican who had a bill beneficial to the American people. Unfortunately, in the past two terms, very few of the senators on either side of the political divide had put forward legislation beneficial to anyone but themselves or their contributors.

Early in his career, the reality of the D.C. game had bothered him—until he realized most Americans were either disinterested in what the Senate was doing or too stupid to understand. In his last term he had stepped up to the public though and fully intended to fill his own coffers—just like everyone else before him and everyone else would after he was gone.

"So that's it?" Neil asked with skepticism. "We get S-2124-12 out of committee and up for a floor vote and your man will make sure we can buy those shares at the pre-IPO price?"

Pushing a loose lock of hair off of her forehead and tucking it neatly behind her ear, Senator Clarkson responded, "Yes. At this point, that's all we have to do. The Republicans are already on board and if we approve it in committee, the Majority Leader won't think twice about putting it up for a vote. But, you know what, Jimmy, I'm not too sure this is a great idea . . . I mean we're basically giving free reign to the military to police the country." Unlike many other senators, Clarkson and Neil had read what they were supposed to vote on.

"No we're not, Ellen!" James responded, pulling a silk handkerchief from his suit jacket and wiping the accumulating sweat from his brow. "The Posse Comitatus Act prevents the military from engaging in law enforcement. They can't make arrests, do searches, things like that . . . The National Defense Authorization Act won't supersede that! You don't think the Committee's amendment of N.D.A.A. will undo a law that's been in place since 1878, do you?"

"Jimmy, Senator McNamara brought this up at the Armed Services Committee Hearing and talked about how Posse Comitatus has a few exceptions, right?"

"Yeah, like that briefing we got about the Air Force Reservists helping to take out terrorists."

"And the 10th Mountain Division, remember?"

"Right, right, but Ellen, that was a clear exception, national security inter—"

Senator Clarkson held up the palm of her hand to silence him and cut him off mid-sentence, "That's bullshit and you know it! The President ordered that done under the War Powers Act before he knew anything."

"Yeah, but he did have the legal authority to do it— at least as far as the White House Counsel is concerned— and they did stop the terrorists, didn't they?"

Senator Clarkson blew out a heavy sigh. "Listen, James, what bothers me is that subsection of the amendment that transfers command authority of all of those units and all of that equipment to the National Guard. I mean . . . the funding, so what, right? We'd have to fund the division no matter who they were attached to, but the National Guard?"

"I don't see what the big deal is, Ellen? Who cares who orders them around. It'll be a good thing to have special forces around like that—you know, the men who took out Osama Bin Laden. Everyone thinks of them as heroes."

"James, you don't get it, do you?"

"Get what, Ellen, what am I missing?"

"Posse Comitatus doesn't apply to the Coast Guard, the Navy, or National Guard."

"So what?! Haven't you been paying attention? Watching the news? All of these goddamn protesters, those hippies and bums! As far as I'm concerned, they're Anarchists! We need someone around to kick their asses back in line."

"Are you serious, James? Civil disobedience isn't anarchy!"

Gruffly, he responded, "Civil disobedience leads to home grown terrorism, Ellen. The protesters who're carrying signs now are the same ones who'll be building bombs. They have to be dealt with."

"With Special Forces shock troopers? That's like swatting a fly with a sledgehammer, isn't it?"

"Oh, come on, Ellen, you're going way too far with this . . ."

"Am I?"

"Yes . . ." James Neil did have his own concerns, but he kept them to himself and kept his doubts well hidden. Changing the subject he asked, "How many shares of that IPO do you think we'll be able to buy before the open?"

"I don't know, probably 50,000 shares or so—enough for you to buy a house on the Chesapeake after it goes public." Clarkson smiled a very charming but obviously forced smile.

"As long as we sell it all the minute it goes public, huh?" Neil's quip did manage to get a genuine chuckle out of his colleague. "Who's the underwriter?"

"I think its Troth Hard Assets and Resource Fund, like usual."

"I thought they got shut down by the SEC."

"No, they were exonerated. Besides, that was the hedge fund part, we're dealing with the private equity arm."

James asked, "What's the difference?"

"I don't know. I'll find out more when I meet with Harold Lavale tonight."

James Neil did not want to leave anything to chance. "Are you sure all we have to do is get this bill out of committee?"

"I'm sure that's all you have to do. I may have to let Old Harold fuck me, but that's a very small price to pay for a very comfortable retirement . . ."

Chapter Eight

Maxwell York was sitting in the study—seemingly a world away from the high technology, fast-paced, information economy that was taking over the world. Nevertheless, a doorway on the west wall of his study led to another room that was filled with the types of devices and technologies only dreamed of by the most ardent fans of computers and communications.

Inside of the computer room, the walls were covered with large-screen displays with either flashing lines and graphs reflecting the current market conditions or satellite feeds of news channels from around the world. Other monitors displayed data and pictures from military satellites orbiting the globe or databases used by every branch of the federal law enforcement community. In the center of the room were several computer terminals with their own array of monitors. One screen displayed that it was actively logged onto the MIN-OPS network.

The gear assembled on the desks was Maxwell York's corporate nerve center. The equipment developed for the NSA, CIA, or several highly classified military units had the familiar logos of several defense contractors.

Maxwell York was no longer an active participant in his own company, leaving the new age of computer hardware and cyber wars to the people he had hired to run his operation. Many defense contractors, computer hardware makers, software start-ups, and even DARPA came to York's firm to help finance research and development. Different types of new or unproven technologies needed funding and the best way for York's firm to see what was being invented was by offering seed money. Those same companies who came up with great concepts or new military gear were the ones who eventually sold to and installed the systems for the government. By being an early investor, MYB, Ltd., Maxwell York's corporate name, also had access to whatever was being invented, and everything the government used, for its own purposes.

The three men and one woman sitting at the large glass and chrome tables were all dressed neatly in business attire and donned headsets with pea-sized microphones positioned in front of their lips. They were talking on their headsets to other MYB offices in New York, London and Chicago, but in a tone that was quiet and subdued. Out in the adjacent study, York sipped tea and peered down at documents related to other, more traditional, business matters. Andrew Stevens paced relentlessly back and forth in the computer room. His shoulder and foot would come into view from York's position on the leather sofa when Andrew got close to the door. It was comforting for York to see his subordinate nearby and in control of everything.

There was a barely perceptible change in the room's atmosphere. The air pressure shifted or changed directions ever so slightly. It caused the curtains to ruffle, which altered the lighting coming in from outside. The change was just enough of a distraction— different from seeing Andrew's moving shadow—to cause Maxwell York to look up. He took off his bifocals and peered across the room. He noticed that the room's alarm panel was not glowing red to announce it was active, nor green to confirm the system was ready.

"Andrew? Andrew!"

"Yes, Mr. York." Andrew walked through the doorway into the study and stood peering anxiously at his chief.

"Why is the alarm system down?"

Turning his head to do a quick check on the others who were busy monitoring the markets and latest political developments, then walked deeper into York's study. "What? What's wrong Mr. York?"

There was no time to react. A man dressed in all black launched himself from the hallway through the door of the study and jabbed three knuckles into Andrew's throat—immediately followed by an upturned palm thrust into the base of his nose. Andrew fell to the ground gasping for air. Blood gushed out of his nostrils.

With almost inhuman agility, the man all but vaulted through the other door into the computer room. York could not see what was taking place but heard a series of thumps and crashing sounds. He was simply too shocked to move.

In what seemed like seconds, the man in black with his face covered came walking out of the computer room and back into the study. With deliberation, he took several fleet strides toward the sofa where York was sitting and looked around. Seeing the cell phone on the end table, the man picked it up and slid it in his pocket. York noticed the intruder wasn't even breathing hard.

The invader, in a calm, conversational tone, but with a monotonous rhythm said, "I'll be right back-I have to go tie them up." He nodded his head, indicating he meant the people in the computer room. "Don't move, Mr. York. If you do, I'll kill you."

Andrew had stopped coughing as hard but was still struggling to breathe. He tried to get to his knees. York watched the stranger nimbly lunge down to one knee beside Andrew in some sort of deft wrestling move and strike the young man directly in the temple with a bent elbow. Andrew's head slammed against the floor with a loud cracking sound. He was no longer moving at all.

The stranger turned his head and looked directly into York's eyes. Again, in a dry, emotionless monotone, he said, "Don't worry, he's not dead—just unconscious, but he's gonna have a killer headache when he wakes up."

Maxwell York could feel the warmth spreading from his inner thigh to the back of his leg where the wetness started to pool and cool on his silk pajamas and bathrobe. It was the first time since he was a baby that he could remember wetting himself.

"You can take the mask off, Major, I know who you are."

Sampson squinted and shook his head almost imperceptibly, briefly losing his mental equilibrium because of York's correct identification. He sniffed and then sniffed again, making sure the stately old fellow sitting on the sofa could hear him inhale. It was obvious by the way York was sitting and holding his head that he was trying to hide his fear and retain his composure.

"You know who I am, huh? Is that why you pissed your pants?" Sampson asked. "What is it with you old men and your weak bladders?"

"Very good, Daniel—it's okay if I call you Daniel, isn't it? Projecting power by embarrassing me to gain an advantage— letting me know you are in full control of the situation. Very nice." Maxwell uncrossed his legs and stood up. He looked at his adversary, who was standing in front of him but several feet away.

Maxwell took off his paisley silk robe. With absolutely no shame, dropped his pajama bottoms and then calmly retied the robe around his waist. "You don't mind me getting more comfortable do you?" Again acting before deigning to ask permission, York stepped away from the wet sofa and sat down in the recliner next to it.

"Very good, Mr. York, pretending like I'm in charge while you tell me what you are going to do after you do it."

York chuckled. "Power is a funny thing, Daniel, and most people have no idea how to yield it. It was ages ago, but one of my best friends wrote the book on the subtleties of psych-ops."

Sampson walked closer to the chair where York had settled. He stood over the older man while touching his razor-sharp Sykes Fairbairn commando dagger in the sheath strapped to his thigh. Using his other hand, Sampson pulled off the black hood that camouflaged his face. "How do you know who I am?"

"You've obviously underestimated me and have no idea who I am. After the disaster you and the others caused in Pennsylvania, we monitored the situation from here." York indicated the door to the computer room. "The mistake you made was to log onto the MIN-OPS network in Port Jervis. The code you entered triggered a flag. Once you did that, we knew at least one of you survived."

"Does anyone else know?"

"Up to this point, no . . . but they're not sure and they're still looking into if any of you may have survived." York casually crossed his legs, an almost hairless, nearly translucent-fleshed leg stuck out beyond the robe. He continued, "When you went into Roland Troth's residence in Greenwich, we were immediately alerted. Without you knowing, your image was sent to us and it was only a matter of seconds before your identity was known."

There was no need for Sampson to press for anything, York was answering his own volition. The former Marine bent down into a squat, taking on a much less threatening posture. His voice was a little less flat when he asked questioningly, "How? Was it Troth who sent you my picture or someone from the military?"

York Smiled. "No, the military doesn't know. Roland's staff is actually my staff, he just doesn't know it." Changing the topic with absolutely no segue, the old man pressed on, "Your record is pretty outstanding Daniel: enlisting in the Marines when you were but a boy, getting recruited into Force Recon only a year after basic training, and working your way up through the ranks—a maverick. You're one of the most accomplished shooters this country has ever produced."

Seeing absolutely no reaction from Sampson, York went on, "I've read the reports relating to El Salvador, Iraq, and several other—lets just say—black bag assignments. But, the one that really takes the cake was what you did in the jungles of Cambodia in 1972. As I recall, you were so successful in your interdiction, they loosely based a few movies on your exploits—or, I should say, they would have if those files were not classified as top secret. But, may I commend you, Major, on your work for our nation. You made us see what was possible with special forces."

*****

Force Recon, although not nearly the earliest of the elite corps of specially trained, highly capable military men, was at the vanguard of developing the modern day training techniques and tactics used by all of the special forces units. During the Vietnam War, in Cambodia, the men of Force Recon were given one and only one directive: using any means necessary, covertly stop the Vietcong from using Cambodian villages to hide and resupply.

Dropped in behind enemy lines, the Marines in Force Recon participated in assassinations, quick-strike raids, and demolition operations. Sometimes, the men would be left in country to continually harass the enemy or people who were considered hostile. In the early 1970's, Daniel Sampson was one of the most effective operators and he single-handedly subdued large swaths of territory.

What really made Sampson stand out, besides his dead-on accuracy as a sniper and seemingly inhuman physical abilities, was his method of learning about the people's customs, traditions, and religions and using everything he learned to pray on their superstitions. In his sphere of influence, the people who either helped or supported the enemy lived in constant fear—unless or until they came over to his side.

Sampson's personal trademark in Cambodia was skinning people alive and placing the bodies near the villages the Vietcong used, right after the enemy had left. He made sure the desecrated corpses were found with evidence the Communist forces, impelled by evil spirits, had committed the vial acts. The locals would become so enraged that they would go after the Vietcong themselves, Sampson providing them with guidance and support. He was able to convince the villagers to set up remote listening posts to track the enemy, telling them the devices would protect them from the evil spirits.

Near the very end of the war, since Sampson had become so proficient at disrupting the logistics of the Vietcong, the brass planned on using the same methods all along the Ho Chi Mihn Trail. Once he was pulled out of Cambodia, the young Sergeant Sampson was tapped to train others in his methodology. But, before anyone else could deploy, Nixon announced the American withdrawal.

The man who had been so successful pacifying hostile territories was not forgotten by his superior officers. Daniel Sampson was promoted, sent to school, and then dispatched to train others at the School of the Americas. His methodologies were studied and further developed by the military. Other than the skinning people alive, the same techniques Sampson used in Cambodia were refined and not only incorporated by other elite units of the United States military but also adopted by special forces units around the world and the CIA. The controversial School of the Americas was where U.S. personnel trained South American troops in military tactics and interrogation techniques. Many graduates of the School of the Americas went on to become dictators and despots accused of human rights violations and mass murder. Sampson, the young, rising star, surely had left his mark on his students.

In the world of covert operations, Daniel Sampson was a rock star, and his quick advancement up the ranks reflected how valuable he was to the United States military. All of that came to an end when called back to active duty at the start of Operation Iraqi Freedom. JSOC had Sampson dropped in to take out a hostile tribal leader. When things went horribly wrong and his handler, Captain J.T. Snyder, asked for air support, the superior officers demurred and left Sampson to the wolves. After that disaster, everything changed. Sampson managed to get out of a nearly impossible situation alive—but he was no longer loyal to the service he had dedicated his life to. They had abandoned him. He was no longer loyal to the country, it had let him down. A switch was flipped in his mind—but not to ignite the fires of revenge against his superiors. Instead, he retired from the service and dedicated his life to himself. He had come to the conclusion that if he was expendable, so was everyone else.

Sampson's antisocial, sociopathic tendencies came to the forefront—he simply lived for himself and did what pleased him.

*****

Squatting next to Maxwell York in an estate on Cape Cod, holding a bunch of people hostage—ready to kill them all—was not what he wanted to do. It didn't matter one way or another if he had to kill them, but doing so would not get him any closer to what he was after—the money and security to do whatever he wanted, wherever he wanted, whenever he wanted.

The 58-year-old Sampson did not care to reminisce about the past. As someone once said, there was no future in it and surely no money to be made. After spending the past few months with Roland Troth and obtaining a much better understanding about the business world, Sampson was focused on one objective, and that was to monetize his particular skill set.

"Mr. York, I don't care about the Marines, special forces, or the United States. All I care about is one thing."

"And what's that Major?"

"What is Project Stasis?"

Maxwell York was not shocked that Sampson knew Project Stasis existed. Sitting back comfortably into the thick padding of the recliner, York was a little disappointed the former Major—a special forces legend—had been so naive to think he had come in undetected. York knew of Sampson's face-altering surgeries and that he was the driver of the Rolls Royce when Roland Troth came for the meeting. He also knew Sampson walked along the beach heading for the seawall at the back of the estate. Sure, Sampson deserved credit for defeating the alarm system and avoiding, or disabling, the security team on the roof, but York also knew the man had no idea he may never leave that room alive. All he had to do was keep Sampson talking for a few minutes and he would be trapped.

Because of the sudden break in communication the computer room, the Boston office had already dispatched a security team and they were in route via helicopter.

In a calm voice, Maxwell asked, "What exactly do you know about Project Stasis?"

"Not much. That's why I'm here."

"Not because Troth sent you here to kill me?"

"Why would he do that? Deep down, the man's a coward—he's nothing without you and he knows it. You really think he has the balls to put a hit on you?"

The recognition by Sampson of Troth's true nature made York smile. "I believe you're right, Daniel. He doesn't have the nerve. But, it's obvious to me that having you with him has given him at least a little bit of backbone—and that makes him dangerous."

Sampson stood up and walked over to Andrew, who was still lying unconscious on the floor. He bent down and checked his pulse—and then started to slap his cheeks.

Andrew Steven's eyes fluttered and he moaned in pain as consciousness returned.

Turning back to York, Sampson said, "You're gonna need him. Get him to call your dogs off or I'm going to kill you all."

Maxwell grinned at the fact Sampson knew people were coming to kill him. He answered with some amusement in his voice, "You can kill me, Daniel, and it wouldn't change a thing. We all have to die, eventually. What you have to ask yourself is if today is the day you want to die. I'm ready to die, are you?"

Sampson's keen eyes and ears picked up what few others would have been able to see or hear. York's lip had twitched and his eyes had narrowed. When he spoke, York's tone wavered just a little. The signs told Sampson that despite what he said, York was scared to die, but he was not lying about both of them facing the music.

"Okay, Maxwell—its okay if I call you Maxwell, isn't it?—let's get down to business. You know I'm more valuable to you alive than dead, and you know I can control Troth for as long as you need him. Why don't we work together and make the best of the situation. If you don't need me handling Troth, I know you can think of a thousand ways to utilize my skill set."

Maxwell thought about it for a second. He weighed the effects of a possible shoot-out at his estate, the reality he probably wouldn't survive, and the realization that no good could come of it. Then, he thought of Sampson and the tools the man possessed. Having a man like him on his side could only help the cause.

"Okay, Daniel, tell me what you want in return for both of us walking out of here alive and tell me exactly how I can insure your loyalty—that you won't come back and do this again?"

"I don't want much, Mr. York—just tell me everything about Project Stasis and who Troth is talking about when he talks about the senior partners. Then, give me a job to do and a blank check to do it and we'll both be happy."

York considered what Sampson said and asked. "So, that's it, hmmm? All I have to do is hire you?"

As cunning, proficient, and deadly as Sampson was, York thought he had figured him out and knew what made him tick. It was so unsophisticated that it was actually scary—the former major was a man in search of a mission. He was putting himself up to the highest bidder—a pure capitalist—and as soon as Daniel Sampson had a mission and proof of loyalty through payment, the man would probably die trying to accomplish that mission, at least that was how Maxwell York figured it.

Sampson sneered. "Yup, that's it—give me the info and make it worth my while to work for you and this episode is behind us."

York replied eagerly, "Okay, okay. You've got a deal. Now, untie my staff and let's get down to business.

Chapter Nine

Sitting off to the side of the study, hunched over with an icepack held onto his bruised temple, Andrew did not look well. His usually neat hair was in disarray. The tail of his shirt was untucked and hung out sloppily from the waist of his expensive, pin-striped slacks. Two of the men who had been in the computer room, Maxwell York's other assistants, lingered near the liquor cabinet on the far side of the study. They were nursing drinks out of highball glasses and were reaching down to rub abrasions on their wrists—the areas where they had been secured to the legs of a table with zip-ties.

The other two assistants, a man and a woman, remained in the computer room. They were busy initiating communications with the rest of the MYB, Ltd., the company's network of offices around the world, and other associates. After they had contacted Boston and ordered the back-up security crew coming in on a helicopter to abort, they had to inform the other partners everything was secure. The communications disruption had set off alarms all around the world and had automatically triggered counter-measures against any threat or security breach. All of that had to be reversed.

Maxwell York had been speaking, lecturing actually, for quite a while. In such a relaxed posture, he was an exemplary display of an elder statesman passing on wisdom to a pupil. For his part, Daniel Sampson was relaxed—as relaxed as he could be—sitting on a tan, soft leather divan directly across from York. A half-full glass of brownish liquor sat on the coffee table in front of him, untouched.

York continued his oration, "There are seven-billion people in the world and most of them are incapable of producing anything; yet they use up valuable resources that could be more efficiently utilized. Think about that, Daniel. They produce nothing but using up everything. Look at places like India, Bangladesh, Haiti . . . people living on top of people and most of them are beggars. Look at the people of Europe, they are nothing but wards of the state, reliant on the public nipple for sustenance, rioting in the streets when they don't get government handouts. Africa? What country in Africa has a gross national product as big as Texas? None of them—not one on the entire continent. I think we can make things better."

At that point in York's diatribe the old man's focus had turned inward, as if he was talking to himself, but speaking aloud the thoughts and beliefs he had held inside for a very long time. Instead of interrupting, Sampson sat quietly and listened. But, even as he tuned out, waiting for the details he wanted to hear come up, he recognized a lot of what York was telling him from discussions with Troth. Maxwell York was unknowingly confirming much of what Sampson had already learned.

As York continued, his voice went from strong and accusatory to a much weakened tone, almost sad. "Now, look at the United States—worthless, unskilled laborers demanding pay and benefits for tasks that could easily be done by machines. There is no craftsmanship, there is no ingenuity. The workers are all stuck in the industrial age, half of them not even aware that the information age has matured to the point that manual labor is a useless waste of human energy." Turning his attention back to Sampson, York went on, "You saw the riots in Greece when their bonds collapsed and the government was forced to stop paying their citizens to sit around and do nothing? Eventually, the same thing is going to happen everywhere, even on these shores. Pretty soon, the only jobs available will be in the service sector. How many people will be able to afford anything on minimum wage? Almost half of the country wants Social Security, food stamps, free medical care. Who needs those people? They're all useless parasites!"

York paused and took measure of the man sitting in front of him, gauging his reaction. Seeing none, he continued, "Americans, well, in every developed nation for that matter, are unwilling to learn new trades, they're unwilling to take chances. The world is leaving them behind. Because they are unwilling to take care of themselves, they have all become superfluous and serve no purpose—and they deserve to be treated as such. With robotics and computerization there's simply no need for seven billion people." He drew out the number in slow, emphatic syllables.

Sampson noted a devious grin form on York's face when he stopped talking. Apparently, he was not secure enough or maybe he was simply unwilling to come out and say what would logically come next—what was clearly on his mind.

Trying to prompt him into continuing, Sampson wryly prodded, "What about the so-called professional trades, the political class? What about the advance of technology for the future?"

York actually smirked. "There is no use in at all for lawyers, politicians, bankers, and traders of worthless paper. What do any of them, of us, create? And what about computers and technology? How much faster of a computer do I really need? What can someone do with it besides find more ways to be devious or destructive?"

His voice got louder and his speech became more rapid. These were topics he had thought about quite a bit and reached conclusions on but seemed to have a shortage of outlets to discuss his thoughts, his compulsions, his pet-peeves. He went on in a rush with more rhetorical questions, "Tell me, Daniel, do I really need a car that goes faster or is ever more ostentatious? Are they going to design and build me a better yacht or a private plane that goes faster than the speed of sound? For what? There is nothing more people need in this world than what we already have—but not everybody has it and that, my friend, is the problem."

"I am the ultimate conservative, Daniel—not the blow-hard, attention seeking Republicans. They are just our puppets, bought and paid for to distract the masses with foolishness. What I'm talking about—what I mean by being a true conservative—is for me and my kind to regain our glory of our forefathers and then maintain the world exactly as is right now. We will preserve our way of life for ourselves and our children. That's all Project Stasis is."

"The way the world is right now, Maxwell? Isn't that funny? You know the wealth is concentrated in a few peoples' hands—the super-rich like you and your kind running everything? What you're talking about is what? Neo-feudalism, isn't it?" Sampson was not totally ignorant of history or world events, even though other people's suffering meant absolutely nothing to him.

"Yes, eventually," York replied casually. "But first, we have to take things in stages. This stage is what I like to call, "inverted totalitarianism."

Sampson looked at York with a confused expression. "What the hell is that?"

"It's what the people of the Occupy Wall Street protest and others like it around the world are fighting against—they just don't know it—or don't know what to call it. Simply put, it's big business as dictators instead of people or a person. We're using the collective power of banks and corporations to subjugate the masses. We've buried everyone in debt in the name of capitalism and have them willing to abiding by our social contracts. Now, all we have to do is change the nature of the social contract, and offer them relief from their obligations in return for subjugation of their will."

101

"Actually, the next stage will be a very painful process but then it will get easier. First, the birthing pains, the people begging like newborns for nourishment and comfort. Then comes abundance—because it is the will of the willing; the weak, hungry masses, to be fattened up before they are led to slaughter . . . Who better to lead them to serfdom than the glamorous corporations they so adore? It's about economics, Daniel, not about politics.

"And, thanks to the Unites States Supreme Court, that's more true than ever. When the Court decided corporations are people, too, with the same rights and privileges as any other citizen, that was when the game changed. It's people like me who really control all of the corporations and now we don't even have to hide our motivations or political bribes anymore. The politicians don't have to pretend they are working for the people. Everyone knows they work for their biggest donors, and that's us."

Still driving for more details, Sampson asked, "So what happens to people like me? What happens to schlubs like the barber, the baker, the candlestick maker—you know, all the workers you think you can replace with computers and robots?"

York nodded, appreciating the opportunity to expound upon his ideas, not realizing Sampson was citing things he learned from the secret recording. "Well, when the time comes, we're not really going to need the army, per se, at least not like the military is now . . . We're going to need more of a policing power to enforce the rule of law, our rule of law. There will be no need for any sort of conventional war between nations once all of the land is divided up. An honorable, fit, military man like you, though, you'd be the type of man who would train others to maintain our laws and our order. Haven't you noticed how we've already started to militarize the police forces across the country? Haven't you noticed how our wars are being fought more and more by drones—computerized machines? Look at the tactics the police have use to subdue protesters, look at the weapons. They are using purely military tactics. The armed forces will become our police and they will be the driving force behind us. Yes, we will need people such as yourself because our police will be all the force we'll ever need. They will be our enforcers—kind of like the police are being trained now—and they, like you, will get their just desserts."

"As for your other question, what do we do with the marginally skilled? Unless someone can rebuild a broken robot that cooks or can program a computer to tell a robot how to better farm wheat, there isn't much use for them, is there? The question then becomes, how does one get rid of these parasites, these useless people who exist to suck the world dry of resources? The only rational way to do it, Major, is by using creative destruction. Let the weak and powerless die off so the strong and powerful can rise up even stronger than ever. Creative destruction will stop the endless battles for resources, the fight for wealth, and insure a highly capable population. I'm telling you, this world will be a much better place if we let the old ways and the old expectations simply die off to be replaced by the new."

There, Sampson thought, he had finally come out and said it—creative destruction was the old man's way of articulating the mass liquidation of a few billion people. Although Sampson knew that was where York was going with his vision, he still wanted to hear it come out of the old man's mouth.

Maxwell York was actually glowing as he spoke, on the edge of some sort of adrenaline high, it seemed, as he went on, "We'll retain the best workers, the brightest minds, and the best technologies to insure the continuation of our lifestyle, the lifestyle we choose to live. Those are the ones who will procreate en mass. The rest of them, the unskilled, the stupid, the desperately poor, soon, their propagation will cease."

"Don't you see it, Daniel? We don't need all of these damn people! Think about it, really, what do we really need? Food, shelter, comfort, travel, entertainment. No more wars, no more starvation, no more poverty, there will be more than enough resources for everyone. What more could one possibly want but to want for nothing?"

Sampson was not exactly shocked by the megalomania and he knew where the conversation was going. But, he remained patient and waited for the punch line. Soon, he'd be able to get down to business—and what that business was depended on how York answered the next few questions.

"How did you plan on doing it, on getting rid of the ones you don't want or need? What, nerve gas and a lot of really big incinerators? I think that's been tried before . . ."

"Don't worry, Major, just like me, you're going to die when it's your time to go—as long as you manage to not get yourself killed, that is. There's maybe two, three-decades before people will see the fruits of our labor—but they will start to notice the changes before the end of the decade."

"What do you mean? No mass executions this year? No concentration camps to determine who to save and who to kill?"

York shook his head at Sampson's pathetic attempt at sarcasm. "No, Daniel, I'm not Hitler—there will be no mass-scale liquidation and, much unlike Hitler, this is not about race or religion, it's about the ability to contribute to society: doctors, inventors, scientists, engineers, artisans, even sports stars will be enabled to reproduce. I don't care where they come from, what they look like, or what they believe, only that they have the capacity to contribute in some way. Actually, when the time comes, nothing like a pandemic or mass extermination will happen—at least not

104

caused by us. As you know, something on that scale would be a logistical nightmare. Can you image the carnage all over the place, making entire cities and regions uninhabitable?"

Daniel quipped, "Yeah, I remember Steven King's book, 'The Stand' and what a mess that virus turned out to be. We wouldn't want that now, would we?" Sampson knew it sounded preposterous ingratiating himself into the scheme, but he figured by sounding slightly maniacal himself, he would keep York off balance.

York called him on it immediately. "I don't think you're taking me seriously, Major. The change in population, it will be subtle, gradual—nothing on the massive scale like you're insinuating. You think I don't have the capacity to do what I say?"

"Well, I'm not sure. See, you haven't really told me anything yet—a lot of theories, a lot of platitudes, but no fucking substance, man." The edge in Sampson's voice and narrowing of his eyes exposed a growing impatience. "Tell me exactly how you're planning on doing it and maybe then I'll take you seriously."

"I can't tell you because . . . because the science is beyond you." The words came out of the old man's mouth with a tinge of arrogance. "I know you were a decorated officer and that you are educated, but what exactly do you know about genetics? What do you know about statistics and population growth projections? Ah, but, Daniel, I'm getting ahead of myself here. Neither you nor I will be alive to see it. What you asked about was Project Stasis and now you know . . . the rest of it is simply a vision of the future."

"Maxwell, you know I know better, so don't lie to me . . ."

"I'm sorry Major, I am getting very tired. It has been a very eventful day. If I may?" York turned to face his assistant. "Andrew, I need you to download the files and projections from Hamilton Genomics." Turning back to face Sampson, he continued, "The only way to achieve our goals—the only way to make what we want possible is to monopolize the markets in a vast array of natural resources. What we want and what we get will sustain our kind into the future. What's wrong with that? Nothing! It's capitalism at its best. I don't know why you're even bothering to ask me about this—Troth already told you enough to put it all together, now didn't he?"

"What does it matter what Troth told me? You control him you—you're one of the men he calls a 'senior partner'."

"Yes, I do believe Troth told you way too much about us . . ."

Andrew Stevens looked lost. Totally out of character for him, he rudely interrupted, "You want me to give him the files from Hamilton Genomics. But . . . but Mr. York . . . we don't even know . . ."

York scowled at the interruption and answered gruffly, "Just do it Andrew, it's too late for him to stop it. None of you seem to understand, it really doesn't matter who knows what anymore. No one can stop what's already happening."

As he said the words, Maxwell York looked old and tired—much older than just a few hours before. The commotion of the day, all the talking and drinking, and the physiological drain from the adrenaline crash had really taken its toll on him. It was a big deal for him to have visitors—one of them being a known hit man, psychopathic killer no less.

York was at his limit, but pressed on the best he could. "In fact, Andrew, give Major Sampson the background files and the files associated with our gold bug problem. I've decided to ask him to—no, I mean, give him a mission—if he's willing to take it."

106

"Well, that depends, Mr. York. What's the mission?" Sampson's ears had perked up and his eyes widened. It was an involuntary reaction to being given a goal to achieve. Having a challenging objective was the only thing that kept him relatively sane.

"That's very simple, Daniel. There is a gold mine somewhere in the far north regions of Canada that's producing an unusually large amount of very high quality gold ore."

Sampson smiled, he knew where this conversation was going and it sounded like an answer to his main question even before he asked. "The stuff they were smelting in Pennsylvania, right?"

"Precisely. I want to know exactly where that mine is, how they found it, and what technology they're using to extract it. We've tried to back-track the shipments of ore, but they are careful and up in the Arctic, apparently, there's simply no place to hide for someone who is doing the tailing. Our satellites can't pinpoint even a trace of mining activity anywhere that far north. The point is, you're going to have to go it alone and track down that mine under some pretty hostile conditions."

"That shouldn't be a problem . . . but how do you know there's a lot of gold at that particular mine—or that it's so pure?"

"It's all in the files, Major, the shipments we were able to track, the tons of gold they sold to the South Korean Central Bank . . . the banks they have opened using gold credits backed by gold. That could be a big problem for us. You're a smart man you'll be able to put it all together." York's voice was starting to fade fast as the exhaustion drained his energy more and more.

"What are you going to do with the information I get, go after the gold yourself?"

York answered with difficulty, "I know Roland Troth told you . . . because, because I heard him tell you . . .

107

before long, paper money won't be worth a thing. Soon, the only way to buy something will be with gold. We already control the majority of the mining companies in the world and most of the world's reserves. If they have the capacity to alter the world's supply, I have to know."

The old man had let one other little piece of information slip, Sampson realized. Not only was Roland Troth's staff compromised, but York also had the man's Greenwich mansion bugged. That was something he would have to file away and maybe use to his advantage at some later date. "So that's it, huh? I tell you exactly where that mine is, how they found it, and how they're getting the gold out, right?"

"Right. But there is one more thing Major Sampson, one minor detail I need you to take care of to seal the deal between us."

"Yeah? And what's that?"

"I want you to find out what Troth is planning to do about the natural gas project he is supposed to finish. Find out why he's meeting those people from Pennsylvania— and then I want you to do what you do best . . . make Roland Troth disappear. I looked at the man eye to eye. I don't trust him."

Sampson didn't hesitate. "Okay. No problem."

Roland Troth had been a big help to him, getting him a new face and all, but there were no meaningful bonds. Words were just words—they meant nothing. Sampson, therefore, had no problem with liquidating Troth—if that would gain him the support sponsorship of even a bigger fish—one of the biggest in the pond.

He rose to his feet and stared directly at Andrew Stevens. "Snap, Snap, Andrew! You heard the man, go get those files for me so I can get the hell out of here and get to work. And, while you're at it, cut me a check for about $10 million. I'm going to need some pocket change." Sampson's tone was grossly flippant.

"Sure, why not?" Maxwell York agreed, shrugging. Money did not matter at all to him—in his mind it was just worthless paper and was accumulated for the purpose of being spent.

"Fine," said Andrew, as he turned and walked into the computer room, still holding the ice pack to his tender temple. A minute later, he returned carrying a thumb drive, handed it to Sampson, and walked a safe distance away. "Everything you need to know is there. I didn't cut you a check but I did give you access to a numbered account in the Cayman Islands with instructions . . ."

Sampson interrupted him, "I know how to access numbered accounts. Just make sure your boss over there never lets it go dry . . . I'm holding you responsible, Andrew."

Andrew nodded to acknowledge, but it was obvious he was still smarting from Sampson's earlier attack. The hate oozing out of him was palpable, but he was trying his best to retain his composure—not out of professionalism but out of fear. Maxwell York just sat back, seemingly amused at the attitudes being displayed. The other two men in the room simply averted their eyes and tried to be as invisible as possible.

"Is there anything else Major Sampson?"

"Yeah, one more thing." Sampson walked up next to Andrew and stood close, leaning in even closer. He spoke softy, "The butler, Stewart, he was really helpful. He's tied up on the roof with your three sharpshooters. You'll have to buy them new guns." Nodding at York, he went on in all but a whisper, "If he sends anyone after me, if he lied to me, or if that account dries up, I will come back and I will cut him and you to pieces. Do you understand?"

Andrew had no time to answer. Sampson's hand was so fast no one even saw it move from his side to the sheath strapped to his thigh or the dagger flash through the air.

The strange thing was, as both men watched the action from across the room, they noticed that Andrew did not react at all like they thought he would—at least not at first.

A second passed and then there was a sudden, intense burning sensation on Andrew's left earlobe. It actually felt like someone had held a lit match up to it. He reached up to find out what was causing the pain and realized that his fingers were wet and his cheek and neck felt warm. When he looked at his fingertips and saw red, he knew in that instant Sampson has cut his earlobe off.

"Ahh! Ahh! He cut me! He cut me!" As he screamed, Andrew fell to the ground, collapsing on one knee and cupped his damaged ear with his bare hand. The blood continued to flow and he continued to scream.

When Andrew finally stopped screaming and they managed to check the bleeding of his cut left earlobe, they all looked around and discovered that Major Daniel Sampson, USMC, (Ret.), was gone.

Chapter Ten

"Susan, did you talk to your kids yet today?" Michelle's voice came through the speaker was strained, but she was not in a panic.

"No, not until later, why?"

Tommy and Susan were driving down Third Street in Williamsport, the big black Ford towering over the compact cars around it. Susan had her phone in her hand, on speaker, so both her and Tommy could talk and listen. They had just pulled out of a shopping center where they had picked up some items for their trip to Greenwich.

"So you haven't been at your computer, you haven't checked the encrypted e-mail and attachments from Costa Rica?"

Only the computers in the Mario's house were able to receive and decrypt sensitive items sent from the villa in Costa Rica.

"No, why?" It was Susan's turn to look upset. "Michelle, are my kids okay?"

"Yes, yes!" Michelle responded quickly, "Sorry about that, I didn't mean to scare you. As far as I know, Chris and Lisa are fine—this has nothing to do with them."

"Then what the hell are you talking about, Michelle?" Tommy asked, his deep bass voice did not intimidate either woman. They were used to his masculine tone and took no offense.

Michelle shot back, "It's from Carlos! He's been busy down there analyzing a bunch of stuff and he's come up with something you have to see."

"What is it?"

"Just go home and read your e-mail before you go on your asinine trip to Greenwich. It's like the two of you are walking right into the spider's web. What the hell is wrong with you?"

Having no answer, Tommy and Susan looked at each other and shrugged. After making plans with Michelle to either talk or send text messages to each other no less than once a day, Susan hung up and Tommy took the next right turn, heading towards home.

As they talked and planned for the trip, there was nothing else they could do to insure their safety—besides, they didn't think Troth was so insane as to ask them to come to Greenwich and then do something stupid to them with others knowing where they had gone. Getting himself out of illegitimate stock trades was one thing; getting out of a kidnapping or a double murder charge would be something else altogether.

Trying to lighten the mood by talking about something other than Roland Troth, Susan asked, "Tommy, do you think Michelle was right?"

"About what?"

"About us never paying attention to her."

"She said that?" Tommy deadpanned.

They both laughed and continued talking until they pulled up to Mario's house. But, based on the way Michelle had asked her if she had spoken to her kids, an irrational fear right on the edge of paranoia lingered. Susan tried to keep it hidden the best she could.

Once inside the house, she rushed over and grabbed a laptop off of the top of the desk in the study and carried it over to the family room. Both she and Tommy sat on the comfortable leather sofa in the familiar environs of Mario's favorite room. Even though he had been gone for months, Tommy could still feel his best friend's presence in the room and thought of him every time he looked out at the huge deck, in-ground pool, and the gorgeous valley below. The view from that room, Susan's favorite as well, took everyone's breath away. On this occasion, the gorgeous vistas did not get one second of her attention.

112

Clicking on icons and typing instructions, Susan navigated the pathways of several secured sites so she could connect with Costa Rica without having everything she said and did monitored. It had become second nature for her to use the once-hidden high-speed networks that bypassed the usual carriers and their heavily monitored routers and switches. Almost all of the commercial lines out of country were subject to being recorded by the NSA, Homeland Security, the CIA, or some other alphabet agency she never even heard of. The trick was finding the fiberoptic trunk lines that weren't open for commercial use.

If it wasn't for Carlos and Helena watching her children—and keeping them safe in Central America—she never would have needed to learn the tricks of the "other" internet or navigating through the many international pathways of communication. She never would have mastered how to initiate high level encryption/decryption techniques or the tools to make sure no one could trace anything back to her. Susan may have been intellectually lazy, but she was anything but stupid. She learned what was necessary to communicate with Carlos in secret. His location, and even his existence, had to be kept secret because Carlos was not on the best terms with the government of the United States. As far as the feds were concerned, Charles Rivera-Ortega, AKA Carlos, had been dead a very long time and it would not be a good thing if the wrong people learned he was still alive.

With every passing minute, Susan was in a mini-panic to see and hear her babies. The one trigger Susan had that could set her off was concern about her children's safety. When she worried about them and their welfare, at times, it made her lose her focus and even become irrational. Protecting Chris and Lisa could turn her into a mad woman in order to save them. Reading the e-mail from Carlos had completely slipped her mind.

The connections were made via a very circuitous route and the computer in Costa Rica was activated to announce the incoming data stream. At the same time, the system at the Central American villa answered the link's request for an electronic handshake and decryption mode. The screen in front of Susan flickered and came back on with the image of Carlos framed in the larger of two windows. The other view was a much smaller image displaying what the camera at the top of Susan's unit was streaming to Carlos. She clicked off her own image and enlarged the feed from Costa Rica as big as it could be.

"Carlos? Can you hear me okay?"

"Audio and video is perfect, Susan. How are you?" His trim face and swarthy skin came in crystal clear with only slight delays in refreshed pixilation that occasionally caused his moving lips and thin mustache to blur.

"I'm great, Carlos, are the kids okay?"

"They're fine. As a matter of fact they are waiting to speak with you. Shall I call them?" Carlos's English was perfect, but his speech was slightly over-enunciated and shaded with a slight Spanish accent.

Susan breathed out a sigh of relief, knowing for sure her children were okay. Sitting beside her, Tommy patted her shoulder with true understanding. He knew Susan's kids meant everything to her.

"Yeah, Carlos, in a second. First, what's up with this e-mail and the attachments? We haven't looked at what you sent yet."

Carlos shook his head and the look on his face was easy to read. "So typical," he joked. "Just look at the faces I've isolated from a few news clips last summer and you're in for a little surprise."

"Why? Who are we looking for?"

"I think I've got the connection we needed between some of the guys who kidnapped Tommy, the guy you said confessed to killing Don, and Roland Troth . . . well, at least if your descriptions were accurate."

Susan and Tommy spent the next hour filling Carlos in on the latest developments and what their plans were. He, like Michelle, thought going to see Troth was a mistake—but understood their desire to try and reach some sort of resolution. Carlos also hoped what he had found gave them a little more ammunition, something else they could use for leverage.

Another hour passed when Susan finally got to see and speak to her children. Both Chris and Lisa were growing so fast in so many ways—seeing how much they changed from day to day made Susan want to cry. After expressing her love and making promises, once again, that they would be together soon, Susan finally tore herself away and let her children go so they could go finish their homework.

In his former life, Carlos had been an accountant. He should have been a private eye, Susan thought. The e-mail explained what he had done and the attachments displayed the results. After Tommy detailed how he had been kidnapped in Pittsfield and what he saw—and Susan described everything she had experienced—Carlos had been able to put together some preliminary profiles of the people who were involved. From there, and from following the news stories that went on and on after the Williamsport bombing, it wasn't that hard to connect the three men at the farm in Pittsfield with the ex-military men who were blamed for the attack in Williamsport.

Although the media outlets had mysteriously gone black about the details of the bombing long before they should have, the necessary resources and archives on the internet gave Carlos many paths to follow. He left almost all of his other duties and responsibilities around the villa undone and worked continuously through the summer trying to find answers.

Researching the information he had combined with many guesses he made, led him to a series of unclassified records concerning the hiring of civilian personnel to handle various military tasks in Iraq. Following that thread, eventually he was able to find a concrete link between the men who they figured did the bombing and a bankrupt military contractor called AMPERS.

By going to a special website that saved old web pages in an archive, Carlos searched back in time and found exactly what he was looking for, something even the best search engines may not have been able to find. Dating back to about a year after the start of Operation Iraqi Freedom, AMPERS, Inc. had published publicity photos of some of their corporate officers. Although pictures of the actual mercenaries were not available—as if seeing their images required some sort of top secret clearance—seeing the CEO and reading where he had served before he retired from the military turned out to be the lead Carlos needed. Using the name of that firm, Carlos dug deeper, like following a trail of digital bread crumbs.

It was from a tiny article in the archives of the Wall Street Journal where he was able to link AMPERS to the private equity arm of Troth Hard Assets and Resource Fund. As soon as he saw that nexus, Carlos knew he had hit the jackpot.

Taking the head shot of Captain J.T. Snyder, U.S.A. (Ret.), CEO of AMPERS, Inc., and scanning it into a facial recognition program was something that would have led to a fruitless search just several months before. But, the rapid development of hardware, software, and their expanding capabilities, made what he did next possible. Borrowing tricks Don had taught him about stealing CPU cycles from idle computers around the world, he started searching every picture ever published on the internet since 1992 looking for a match. The thousands of computers he had hijacked were instructed to scour every single image on every single site and send back results only if the probability of a match was greater than 90%.

A week later, the results pointed to two images that matched J.T. Snyder. One of them was a reproduction from the front page of the Wall Street Journal. It was the day Roland Troth's wife was killed in a helicopter crash earlier that year. The facial recognition program indicated that one of the men posing as Troth's body guard was actually J.T. Snyder. From there, everything came together like the straight edges of a jigsaw puzzle.

The video feed of Troth coming out of his building in Greenwich the day his wife died was seen all over the world. Carlos remembered seeing it and searched several news sites for the footage. As soon as he found the clearest footage, he isolated all of the bodyguards' faces and tried to match what Tommy and Susan had described to the images of Troth's bodyguards.

That was what Susan and Tommy were staring at still sitting in Mario's family room.

"Holy shit!" Susan gasped, "That's the asshole I shot!"

"Are you sure?" Tommy asked, his eyes wide and anxious.

"Yes, I'm sure! I'll never forget him."

"Come on," Tommy directed, "bring that along and let's go to Greenwich."

Chapter Eleven

An invite into La Moglie Fedele, "The Faithful Wife," was unheard of for the likes of Major General Adam Smythe. La Moglie Fedele was an exclusive club that catered to only the richest, most well-connected men in the world. The walnut paneled walls, Colonial furniture, and ancient Persian rugs attested to the clubs longevity. Cuban cigars and snifters full of Napoleon brandy attested to the refined taste of its members. The lack of members with a net worth under $5 billion and the exclusion of women attested to its exclusivity. The club did make provisions so members could sample any sexual delight. All that was necessary was a walk up the elegant spiral staircase to the second floor and a "contribution" of no less than a $1,500 to La Moglie Fedele.

At the insistence of Senator O'Connell, a political operative of the first order, General Smythe had to set aside a block of time for a personal meeting. The senator had been quite specific the meeting couldn't be dished off to a subordinate. Although the location of the meeting was original, Smythe believed the topic would be the same as always, buying weapons. Being pressed into the meeting, no matter where, had Smythe in a foul mood.

Sitting next to the General in a matching black leather chair was Senator Butch O'Connell, the ranking member of the club's rules committee and the most powerful Republican in the Senate. O'Connell was a self-proclaimed evangelist. He pulled in the Christian Conservative votes with his fire and brimstone rhetoric and by being the biggest war hawk in the upper chamber. At the same time, Big Butch, as his friends called him, was a foe of abortion. Rape, incest, health of the mother—it didn't matter—there should be no abortion because it was just plain wrong to kill people.

Besides the senator's political contradictions, the word around the Capitol was that Butch, the iconic Bible-thumper, had some odd sexual proclivities. He liked to have his whores dress up like Catholic School girls so he could "properly" punish them for following the wrong faith.

Unhappy about being summoned, yet trying to act civil, Smythe greeted O'Connell cordially and spent the appropriate amount of time making small talk with someone he believed to be the most grotesque specimen of American politics. The senator acted no better than a slimy huckster selling snake oil—at least that was the General's impression when they had met many years before. The association between slime and O'Connell always stuck with him.

"Okay, Senator, let's get to the point—what exactly are you're trying to sell me?"

Amused at the supposition, O'Connell's response was animated, "I'm not tryin' to sell you anything, General."

O'Connell body language was relaxed but his face expressed mirth. Talking to a figure who was not afraid to get his hands dirty did not phase him in the least. As intimidating as General Smythe was, O'Connell was not shaken.

"Let's just say I'm aware of some of your concerns about NDAA and I thought I'd invite you here and, ah, explain a thing or two to you about the new division under your command."

General Smythe all but shouted, "Who the hell gave you permission to explain anything to me about my command?" If there was one thing that set Smythe off, it was a presumptuous civilian trying to tell him how to do his job. On top of that, the sound of O'Connell's southern drawl was repellent to his ears.

"I understand how unconventional this is."

"Unconventional my ass! This is downright criminal. You think I'm going to let some scurrilous, rank scumbag like you give me orders, you gotta be out of your mind!"

"It'd be best if you kept your voice down, General. Give me a chance to explain and you'll understand where I'm coming from."

"First of all, Senator, you don't give me orders—unless you got more stars on your shoulder than me. Watch how you talk to me or I'll mop the floor with you."

Butch O'Connell was accustom to dealing with self-important cretins, but Smythe had his head completely up his own ass. "You're right, General. Approaching you this way was inappropriate. I hope you can pardon me for being so forward, but you were chosen for this—you're the one we picked to protect us from an insidious scourge plaguing this nation. All I am is an ambassador, an ambassador from some concerned patriots."

"Chosen, huh?" Smythe was circumspect in his response, "What do you mean, by whom, Senator O'Connell?"

Seeing he had his attention, Butch pressed on, "My, ah, let's call 'em, sponsors, know what you did in Pennsy, ordering the A-10's to take out the terrorists. That was a gutsy decision."

"How do you know about that? That's beyond top secret and there's no way in hell you have author—"

The Senator held up the palm of his hand so calmly the smoothness of the gesture silence the irate General. "You've gotta realize, people a heck of a lot more powerful than I can find their way around and discover things; so, let's drop this assertion of prerogative. Let's just say I'm here so the people who know everything you've done can maintain plausible deniability."

All the General could do was nod his affirmation.

"The fact you had authorization to use force to stop terrorists doesn't absolve you from violating Posse Comitatus."

Stunned, Smythe shook his head and asked incredulously, "What the hell do you mean? The C-I-C himself ordered me to stop those thugs using any means necessary. Besides, the provisions of the Patriot Act II authorize the use of force."

"Not by the Air National Guard, no sir. I know because I wrote that law personally. Fact is, that's why the National Defense Authorization Act was amended, to allow whatever kind of force you chose to use. Too bad the passage of the NDAA was after the fact. Now, I'm not here to condemn you or threaten you—I'm here to commend you and let you know there are people who recognize you've got balls—and because you got balls, you were especially chosen to head this new division and that's why you're here."

"What you're saying is, because I wasn't afraid to order those planes to fire—you think I'm the right one to command a division of men to shoot American Citizens when they disrupt some political event or stop traffic?"

"No, General, that's not what I'm saying."

"Are you aware that most of the men turned over to my command by J.S.O.C. are veterans? That most of 'em have done multiple tours in Iraq and Afghanistan and they've seen more combat over the past ten years than any other American soldiers ever?"

"Yes."

"And you want me to put those men on the front lines against civilians? American civilians armed with rocks and bottles? Are you and whoever the fuck you represent off your collective rockers? Those boys will slaughter 'em just on principle."

"Well, no, that's not what we want you to do—you've got it all wrong. Matter of fact, General Smythe, we want the opposite."

"What the fuck are you talking about?"

"Your special forces division is going to protect the real Americans. We need your men to prevent a revolution."

O'Connell was only partially lying, but he saw General Smythe already knew what he was talking about—he too had read the reports about the internet traffic and growing seditiousness. O'Connell got Smythe to open his mind. Now, he had to get him to accept the reality of the situation, the complete truth would come later.

"The only way there's going to be a revolution is if we stomp on the peoples' rights. Up until now, I believe you and your people got things all wrong—backwards even," Smythe spat.

"General, do you support the Constitution?"

"Do I support it? I swore an oath to defend it!"

"Do you think the Constitution changes with the times or should it be read as the Founding Fathers intended?"

"Senator, now you're going off into politics. That's not for me to decide, or for you to decide—that's why people vote."

"True, but are you satisfied with who's doing the voting? A bunch of socially conscious hippies and eco-freaks electing one socialist after another? They're taking away our God-given rights and giving them to others."

"Again, you're talking policy and politics. That's not my concern. I follow orders and do my job to the best of my ability."

Butch O'Connell shifted in his chair, and put both feet down flat on the plush carpet and leaned forward. "What kind of a world do you wanna live in, General?

What kind of world do you wanna leave behind for your kids? You got kids, don't ya?"

"What the hell kind of question is that?"

"An important one after I tell you about Project Stasis, you're gonna have to make a choice. As my favorite President, George Bush, said, 'Either you're with us or you're against us.'"

The General stood up and all but shouted, "I should have you arrested and sent off to a black site."

"Sit down General—unless you wanna talk about the people you had killed at Gitmo."

"How the hell do you know about that?"

"Because of Dr. Liebman, he's with us. How do you think Major Burkley got out after the Article 32 hearing? Dr. Liebman let someone bigger than you know what really happened and—"

"I . . . I didn't know . . . I had no idea Burkley was cut loose." He was stunned at the reach of whoever the senator was representing.

"He wasn't released—not in the way you think—but that's none of your concern. Now, you wanna hear more, or do you wanna call in your black helicopters and agents?"

The General sat down heavily in the overstuffed leather armchair. He leaned forward and ran his meaty right hand through his thinning gray hair. "Okay, okay. What is Project Stasis?"

The basic overview of the plans—a future with a ruling class and, in the distant future, a much smaller population—were laid out over brandy and cigars. In the alcove where they sat, no one disturbed them and no one came near unless O'Connell pressed a button to summon a uniformed waiter. The objective was to give a man who had been a loyal servant to his country for decades a chance to jump ship and come on board with the movement. Major General Adam Smythe had proven his mettle with the job he did at Gitmo. What the most elite of the elite partners wanted to know was if the General had the balls to go for broke. If he took the initiative and followed the path he was being led to take, the General would pass the second test that would eventually earn him a seat at a much bigger table.

"I don't know, Butch. Something just doesn't feel right about having so much power and the ability to let loose our war dogs on a whim."

O'Connell kept the tone of his voice low and leaned closer to Smythe, "You've already been compensated for protecting our interests, Adam, so don't sit there and act like you're squeaky clean. Sure, there may be some collateral damage; and yeah, there may be growing pains—but think of the outcome. Money will be no object for you and you'll be the one in military control, making sure no one steps out of line. I don't know what the hell else you want from us."

"I never said my hands were clean, but isn't this going too far? Wouldn't we be subverting everything we stood for"?

"You're wrong. If you're thinking this won't save the American ream, maybe it was a mistake to bring you on board."

"No, Butch, I'm not saying that—"

"So what exactly are you asking for?"

"I want you to tell me what's intended for my division—for right now. What am I gonna have my men do—who are we going to unleash them on?" Smythe's words came out with sincere emotion.

"Is that all that's bothering you?" O'Connell exhaled in relief. Then, with a wry grin, he continued, "Your new division is supposed to be a rapid response team—like a Mike Force when you were back in 'Nam—if I tell you what your first mission is, It'll ruin all the fun."

"Butch," Smythe groused with familiarity brought on by liquor, "stop being an ass and tell me what the hell you want me to do."

"You know, I said all along we should have brought you in sooner so this wouldn't happen. I'm telling you, Adam you've gotten yourself upset over nothing. Heck, I should get you demoted just for wasting my time—"

Smythe leaned even closer towards O'Connell and whispered harshly, "How can you call this nothing? Stop playing with me, Butch, this is serious."

O'Connell leaned forward and put his cigar down in the ashtray. With a serious look on his face, he obliged, "Okay, Adam. You and I have a connection going back to VMI, and neither one of us takes that lightly." He flashed the distinctive gold class ring so the General could see it clearly—just in case he had forgotten. "Because of that bond, I'm taking you at your word . . . you're with us and you're not going to run for the hills after I explain things to you, right?"

"Butch, as long as you don't ask me to have my boys kill thousands of innocents for nothing, I'm with you all the way. But you have to convince me . . . you have to make me absolutely sure that you and your people—"

"Our people," the senator interrupted.

"Our people, aren't going to ask me too—"

O'Connell put his palm up and sat back looking completely relaxed and composed. "Listen, Adam, soon, there may be an incident in the Middle East. Your men were reassigned stateside to keep 'em away from that conflict. We need 'em here in case things get out of control, to protect our security interests right here on our shores. We're not doing this to kill other Americans."

Smythe was thrilled by what he was hearing and couldn't hide his enthusiasm—and he needed to know more. "How, Butch? How?"

"You're going to secure the Strategic Petroleum Reserve in Louisiana along with the oil transfer and storage station in Cushing, Oklahoma. Once secured, your men may have to make a path for the Keystone Pipeline and protect the men who build it."

"From whom?"

"From home-grown eco-terrorists and these anti-capitalists, who do you think?"

"That's it? But, why? Why use these men? Isn't that overkill?"

O'Connell swirled and sipped alcohol from the snifter before answering. Then, he dodged the question. "Forget that for now. Instead, let's talk money. It'd be a smart move if you took the cash you made in Gitmo and buy oil futures. My broker said there'll be a lot of action— for sure—I just can't say more."

"Why? I don't understand."

"You're not the sharpest crayon in the box, are you General? No wonder you stayed in the military. I'll lay this one out for you, but this is it. After this, just take whatever I tell you as gold." Butch lowered his voice even more and continued, "It's not just a threat that the world's oil supplies are going to be disrupted. When the price of gasoline triples, how do you think the great citizens of this nation are going to react? How long before they attack our natural resources? Now, if I'm right, the next time we talk, I hope you've got a whole new perspective."

Smythe could not bring himself to speak. He knew exactly what Senator O'Connell was talking about—the same exact conditions that brought on revolutions around the world.

It all became clear to him. He was being asked to protect democracy, capitalism, and their way of life. He decided at that moment he would do it. He would do his job and lead his troops honorably.

Chapter Twelve

In the late 1800's the railroad tycoon, Commodore Cornelius Vanderbilt, had several obscenely opulent mansions constructed along the East Coast. The most famous of the family mansions was in Newport, Rhode Island. A much lesser known, yet still gorgeous chateau was located in Osterville, Massachusetts, on Cape Cod.

With five-hundred feet of waterfront on Oyster Harbor adjacent to a deep water dock, the privately owned estate was the perfect place for Sampson to obtain the transportation he needed so he could rendezvous with his suppliers. Stealing the 44-foot cabin cruiser and navigating to a large ship waiting near the easterly channel past Nantucket was not difficult.

The ship waiting for Sampson was a decommissioned U.S. Coast Guard cutter rechristened, "HELLBENDER." It had been fully restored and retrofitted with modern engines and repainted in an unexceptional, commercial blue schema so as not to attract attention. The big ship resembled a research vessel with deck full of scientific apparatus. Below, however, most of the berths and cargo bays had been converted into exhibits of the latest samples of military weapons, armor, and electronics. Some gear on display, for sale to anyone willing to pay a small fortune, was considered "top secret" and typically forbidden from even being seen by the public.

The rendezvous with Sampson off the coast of Cape Cod had been arranged days earlier and, luckily, the arms dealer's floating military hardware store was already in the area. The dealers sold to the former major regularly. Since he was one of their best customers, they had no problem making arrangements to pick him up.

The former Navy men operating HELLBENDER held the ship idling near previously selected buoys. That was to be the primary waypoint. Several crewmen were posted as sentries watching for their customer and watched the traffic on the water until they saw the right signal from an approaching "guppy."

After Sampson boarded the ship, it took him a few minutes to explain to the captain—someone he had known for many years—why he no longer looked like the man they were expecting to see. The drastic change in his appearance, which wasn't all that uncommon in their line of work, required Sampson to answer a few personal questions and display the one thing the captain recognized as exclusive to the Daniel Sampson he knew—a one-of-a-kind, USMC tattoo on his chest. Once he cleared the captain's scrutiny, Sampson had plenty of time to examine, test, and choose from a large selection of new gadgets the dealers had on display.

The Quartermaster "Q" from Ian Flemming's James Bond novels would have been drooling over some of the weapons and technologies available. There were rifles that fired multiple projectiles; light-weight, shoulder-fired rockets with unbelievable ranges, accuracy, and blast capacities. The latest infrared sniper scopes were much smaller, lighter, and were equipped with self-adjusting range finders accurate to within three-millimeters.

The armor on display reportedly could stop a .44 magnum at close range. The black vests and pants were extremely thin and light. The material used was made out of the same proteins found in spider's silk, which was manufactured by genetically modified goats that excreted the super-strong proteins in their milk.

The most impressive items, though, were the electronics. There were miniaturized devices used to pinpoint the precise location of cell phones. Detectors had been merged with the ability to track the phone user's actions or listen in on the calls. All that was needed was a cell's number and whoever was using it could be both tracked or monitored anywhere in the world. Previous generations of the same technology required several cabinets of equipment. It was all packed into a device the size of a notebook.

They had hand-held body scanners that looked right through clothes to the flesh, chemical scent detectors able to sniff out chemical weapons, and a device to remotely steal all the data from any other portable electronic device. For crowd control, there were mounted and hand-held microwave units to induce minor burns and low-frequency sound units to rattle skulls with subsonic waves. The gear was developed with the billions of dollars allocated to the defense industry for national security. The decade had produced devices prior generations thought possible only in comic books.

While on board, Sampson was also able to confirm his usual resupply and provide his hosts with the necessary funds to settle his tab. The items he needed would be ready for him to pick up on shore. After securing new identification, perfect in every detail right down to the magnetic strip on the back and the RFID tag imbedded in the front, he was able to kick back and do some very important reading while the ship conveyed him beyond Nantucket Bay to the Connecticut coast.

*****

It was hard to understand why Maxwell York had Andrew to provide him with what should have been sub-rosa computer files. It wouldn't have surprised Sampson at all if the memory device given to him was completely blank—a diversion tactic used by York to buy time and to get Sampson out of there as quickly as possible. But, when he plugged the thumb drive into the port of the laptop and started reading the files, he understood why York was so quick to divulge the details about Project Stasis.

Most of what he found was public information about people and events that had driven the United States, Europe, and Asia into financial and political malaise. Even though he was not all that familiar with the law, very little of what he perused struck him as illegal—at least not in the conventional sense. The vast majority of it was old news. But, the files included a unique, descriptive, running commentary on the world's affairs, He skimmed over the details, absorbing the overall themes, and tried to figure out exactly how everything was related. The files read more like a dissertation on corporate shenanigans than some vast conspiracy.

The next set of documents were what Sampson found to be most interesting. They laid out affiliations like genealogical charts. The graphs illustrated connections between individuals and how they either directly or indirectly controlled corporate boards. Almost every one of the Fortune 500 companies was either, managed, owned, or controlled by a very small group of people. For someone who had fought for his country, who had at one time believed in the system, Sampson was chagrined to see the same names controlling vast fortunes across many industries across the globe. It was another confirmation of what he learned when he started associating with Roland Troth—the game was fixed and the fix had been in since before they were born.

The charts, trees, and graphs actually did not clearly state who the most important players were—the "higher-up" both Troth and York had alluded to as senior or senior partners. But, the most influential could be inferred by how they were strategically placed to influence different spheres of politics or industry. In the political realm, by following the links to those who had the most responsibilities with the least recognition told the entire tale. The collective had been able to reach deep into almost everything, everywhere and control politicians with either campaign contributions, donations to PACs, or promises of lucrative jobs.

There were major players across the globe and there seemed to be a lot of autonomy. There were areas of responsibility under the control of factions but the areas were not based on national borders, but by parts of continents. Sampson clicked open several files dealing with the foreign associates. There was an entire section on the Sicilian, Michael J. Papa, who funneled money from Egypt's generals and other African dictators into Italian investments. He also recognized the name Karl Hensch a former member of Stazi, the East German Secret Police. Hensch had run operations out of Tripoli and was a big time player in the covert operations business. The rest of the names, Sampson decided to skip.

The people Sampson guessed to be the most senior, he was not surprised to discover, read like a who's who roster of descendants of former monopolists and robber barons. Also part of each faction were many names somehow connected to the noble families of European descent and relations of the Russian Czars. The most prominent families mentioned were described as descendants of the bankers and financiers who funded Europe during many financial upheavals and centuries of war. The Rothschilds.

Through bond deals, the Rothschild family had come to own—in all but name—the Bank of England. In the early history of the United States they pushed for and advanced the ideals of the Federalists. They also pressed for, and eventually got, a strong central bank in the United States. As part of the secret history of the United States, it was the Rothschilds who were behind the War of 1812. At their urging, England declared war to force America to secure its debts with gold. Once the United States pledged the collateral to the Rothschild family, the British withdrew. Oddly, England signed a peace treaty and asked for no concessions from the defeated Americans. With such a history and wealth, the Rothschilds may as well have been royalty.

Sampson noticed that the descendants of the Rothschilds, or their representatives, either had seats on the boards of the world's biggest banks or they were connected to every one of the twelve Federal Reserve District Banks. Some were even on the Board of Governors of the Federal Reserve itself. After scanning the charts and interconnections between them, he thought he understood the hierarchy of the cabal he was studying and seen how their intentions were passed down the line. They simply kept it in the family.

The system was set up so that most, if not all, of the participants were made aware of common goals or directions but there were very few clearly articulated objectives. It reminded Sampson of the Inner Party in George Orwell's novel, 1984. Orwell had broken society down into three distinct tiers: Inner Party, Outer Party, and Proletariat. What Sampson was reading would have been the roster of the Inner Party, the group Orwell had described as the ones who knew the truth, who dictated everyone else's lives. In the novel, Sampson thought Orwell never really explained how the Inner Party came to power and that he was living what the famous author had left out.

Reading further into the body of other files, everything was laid out perfectly. Like clockwork, one industry after another would move operations offshore to chase cheap labor, and then move again to even cheaper labor markets—leaving hordes of workers behind in not one, but several nations. The people left behind would be buried in debt, hopeless, and desperate. There was a direct link between money, labor, and the ability to expand profits quarter after quarter, or as needed. The corporate moves allowed for cheap labor costs, for sure, but the malleable nature of exchange rates allowed for unfettered currency manipulation.

Sampson was better able to comprehend how and why almost every company in the United States was hoarding cash—to the tune of $2 trillion. They were waiting for the next crisis so they could swoop in and buy out all of the smaller players who would be close to collapsing and begging for relief. That would further concentrate the upper-tier's power and influence for pennies on the dollar.

Sampson got a profound enlightenment seeing how the many independent mortgage brokers and the banks in the United States worked together to inflate the housing market and then made a mad dash to the regulators and politicians once the bubble burst. The key composition explaining it in detail was a file containing a thesis written by an economist. After he read that, Sampson had to fight the urge to go hunting bankers.

As the professor explained it, no one was really losing or paying for the bailouts because it was all vapor. When the government disbursed the bail-out money to the banks, that was borrowed money. The government borrowed money created by the fed. The money did not come from taxes collected on the transfer of actual goods or services, but was simply created out of thin air. Without true economic activity, the mere creation and transfer of money was nothing but a masturbatory exercise that only hurt people with no access to the play money being created. The barriers of entry into the world of the rich was money which gave the wealthy the means and the ability to pull in even more money while everyone else starved.

The information was not some big secret, but, just like Sampson, no one outside certain circles seemed to realize what was going on. If they read the research paper he just read, he thought, the American people would puke and clean it up with the worthless paper they called money.

He completely understood why the likes of Roland Troth were trolling around the economic wastelands scarfing up all of the property and resources they could as cheaply as they could. They had created the conditions for the growth of despair amongst everyone else and were happily reaping what they had sown—what they had planned to do all along. When people finally figured out what was happening it would be too late.

As far as any real structure and organization went, and as far as the plans York and those like him had, that was it. "Damn," Sampson thought to himself, "Just when it was getting good!" He still didn't know exactly what was coming for the business and political realm or when. Andrew may have had snookered him and not given up all files York ordered be turned over.

One folder remained—a folder filled with files from a biotech company. It was the key to understanding the long-term, final phases of what York and his partners had planned. Then, Sampson remembered, there were the other details, parts he overheard in the recording of Troth's meeting with York. There was something about robots and computers and no need for manual labor—and that other stuff about York's offspring. However the rest of that fit in, those topics were things he would have to get out of Roland Troth once he got back to Greenwich.

That would have to wait. Sampson was exhausted and his eyes hurt from reading so much. He needed to get some sack time before they reached his destination. Minutes later he was fast asleep.

******

Sampson disembarked at Groton and quickly made his way to a discrete warehouse a few blocks west of the docks where the USS Nautilus was on display. There, he followed the usual routine to pick up the supplies and new

134

gear he ordered. His suppliers were very organized and kept their inventory up-to-date. It was important in the illicit military-hardware trade to have in stock not only the latest products but also the popular specialty items, even from decades past. So, they stockpiled discontinued goods, especially what they deemed, "best of class."

The specialty items Sampson needed were from the former Soviet Union. The Kalashnikov AK-47 built in Russia—not a recent knock-off from some third-world country—was the weapon of choice for where he was going. Unlike other weapons, the old Soviet-made AK's were especially hardy under Arctic weather conditions. The Soviets also made the best bunny suits—the warmest, white camouflaged combat gear—in the world.

Everything he ordered was waiting for him inside of the cargo bay of the warehouse. After he was scanned for weapons or tracking devices, and his new identity verified, the surrounding area was surveyed for any hidden law enforcement personnel. As soon as the all-clear sounded, he was electronically buzzed into the cargo bay. No one else around and he didn't look for anyone. The gear he ordered on the ship was already packed in a blue Chrysler minivan and the vehicle was fully fueled up and ready to go.

From the warehouse in Groton, Sampson drove the unobtrusive vehicle over a scenic route to Old Greenwich, where he would meet up with Roland Troth at his cozy little 20,000 square foot mansion.

Chapter Thirteen

The most interesting feature of the Seven Rams IPO was a trial run of a gold-barter system. It was to test the viability and legality of actual money in digital form instead of fiat currency. Paper dollars held value only because other people believed it did. There was nothing backing up the currency. The project was something Michelle had bandied about in her head for years and it was being implemented through the bank holdings of the Seven Rams Gold Trust. They could not call what they were issuing "money" or "currency" because that would run afoul of the law. Instead, it was touted as an experimental system of barter based on credits.

Through their banks, currency could be converted at the current price of gold into an account as gold credits. Like the old gold certificates, the value of the outstanding credits would be backed by gold bullion and held in security at the trust's depository. There would be no actual currency or coinage issued. The gold credits would be tracked and monitored by a computer network. The credits would be convertible into either gold or back into currency based on the up-to-the-second price of gold.

The Gold Credit System, if it worked, was set to transform a major swath of the country once known as the Rust Belt. It would be the only place in America that—if desired—people could transact business using a true gold standard instead of fiat currency. The territory where the credits could be used was only restricted by logistics, an area that would expand as more merchants signed on and received the needed equipment. Although there were no immediate plans to go national, the possibility was there.

The biggest challenge in implementing the Gold Credit System was not getting people to use and accept the credits, since it was just like using a debit or credit card.

The hard part was getting the infrastructure in place to handle the transactions. The software was written, the computer severs were in place, and the people were being educated. But, the process of getting the actual machines to securely handle transactions into the retailers' hands took time. They all believe the credit system would probably work if they could avoid legal troubles with the authorities.

The Gold Credit System was one of many projects backed by Tommy, Carlos, Susan, and Michelle to help the people hurt by Roland Troth. In fact, they were using money they earned by besting Troth to pay for the venture's operation. The project was also in response to the major banks and the fraud committed on ten of thousands of mortgages in the area. Profits from the system were earmarked to buy back mortgages and mortgage backed securities from the banks and stop the money vampires from hurting more people.

Based on the initial response from Williamsport to Harrisburg to just east of Pittsburgh—where they had already started implementing the Gold Credit services—the demand was going to be enormous. A few of the country stores had already started pricing products in gold credits and would not accept dollars. Having to plan for a gold credit rush was inspiring.

Michelle and her staff were often interrupted by gold bugs. They spent an inordinate amount of time fighting off institutional investors who were clamoring for a piece of the action. The country was in turmoil. Every week there was news about people protesting and demonstrations turning violent. The situation had deteriorated to the point where rumors about the National Guard taking to the streets in the major cities and imposing curfews were rampant. With so much going on, including the American debt crisis and the Euro Zone falling apart, the markets were bouncing around like superballs and everyone was on edge looking for a safe-haven. Gold was the commodity panicked people piled into during the most tumultuous times and this was no different. Michelle would not let any private equity firms or hedge funds buy in and she set a ceiling on the amount any one person or institution could convert. Still, the staff fended off literally hundreds of requests for information from big-name investors.

Crunching numbers was not Michelle's favorite activity. Her doctorate was not in accounting or finance. But, getting the financials in order was of paramount importance. Administration of two complicated trusts was a task she had taken on voluntarily but now she was starting to regret it. Because Carlos was sequestered in Costa Rica and Tommy and Susan were on their stupid little adventure to Connecticut, she couldn't lean on the other directors of the two trusts for help. The Seven Rams Gold Trust and the Clearmont Geology and Mining Trust had one CEO and she was it. Michelle felt like she was burning out with so much responsibility dropped in her lap. It was both exhausting and very stressful.

She was not completely alone, though. There were others, very capable managers, running the day-to-day operations. But, Michelle was the chief executive overseeing it all and the one responsible for getting everything in place for the IPO. She had to deal with the regulatory pressure imposed on the bank. It was a relatively small but rapidly growing bank with branches in two countries. Fortunately, they had adequate capitalization and a foothold in areas where the economies were driven by mining and drilling. The bank also had a growing customer base because people were clamoring to join in and be part of the newly created Gold Credit System.

Then, there were the mines located in several different continents and the rights to mines in other countries. Each country had their own regulations, tax structures, and arcane royalty demands. The administration of the mines caused plenty of problems and the trusts spent almost as much money on lawyers as they did on manual labor to deal with export licenses and fees owed to the territories for the mineral rights.

The foundry in Pittsfield had several divisions of its own. Luckily, they had an excellent manager in Zeke for the smelting operation where the gold ore was refined. He was a man they could really count on with no doubts whatsoever. The manufacturing arm at the foundry was where they designed and made complex, specialty drill bits for the unconventional mining that made them all filthy rich. Their designers were a mix of engineering and technology professors from Carnegie Mellon, RPI, and MIT. The technology part of the operation used to be the primary concern of Donald Clearmont —the son of the trust's founder—and Donny's input was sorely missed. Interns under his direction designed robotics, computer controlled devices, and computer simulations. The whiz-kids who were trained by Donny had played major roles in the success of both trusts. It was sad, Michelle thought, how hard of a time they had getting new interns because the last batch had been slaughtered. The taint of the bad fortune would haunt them for years. It was even sadder though that her dear friends, along with some of the interns she knew, had been murdered.

Still dressed in work clothes from the building site, a flannel shirt, faded jeans, and work boots, she did not look like the typical executive controlling billions of dollars worth of assets. Yet, everything she did had just as much impact as many Fortune 500 CEOs. The stress of the day showed mostly around her eyes, the only area of her clear, caramel-colored skin that hinted at her true age of fifty-something years. But, burning the candle at both ends was starting to take its toll.

Michelle was staying at the same house where Susan had been staying, Mario's old place. It was convenient for everyone. Besides, his place was gorgeous and comfortable. Sitting at the desk in the study, she clicked on the save button and then clicked an icon to open another spreadsheet. The columns and rows of numbers on the screen represented the financial statement of the Clearmont Geology and Mining Trust. Two different accounting firms had submitted the figures after conducting independent audits.

Getting the trust's books in order was an immediate concern because of their commitment to changing it into a public corporation partially owned by the employees. A lot of regulatory filings were required before going public and, in this instance, it was even more complicated than usual. They had to redistribute shares from the original twenty or so surviving families of that trust to thousands of employees.

As soon as she was done with the numbers, she had to fly to New York and meet with the investment bankers underwriting the IPO. That, she figured, would be a much more pleasant experience because she'd be staying in a penthouse they owned on Central Park West and she'd have plenty of time to go shopping—at least that was what she hoped. If the protesters and police would only stay south in the financial district, everything would be just peachy.

The final pieces of information she was waiting for were the estimates of proven gold reserves and what they believed was recoverable. As the future CEO of the publicly traded Clearmont Mining Company, the reports filed with the SEC had to be verified and signed by her. That was the most delicate issue to be resolved. Before she would endorse the filing they had to independently verify the values of gold the geologists believed they controlled.

As soon as Zeke gave her the latest updates and readings, she could log off the computer and get some rest.

Since mineral assays and technical analysis of radio-wave refraction patterns were far from her area of expertise, she relied on Zeke and his men to decipher what the independent geologists and mineralogists had found. Michelle had not seen the latest estimates of recoverable reserves and she was growing tired of waiting for Zeke to call with the number of troy ounces they had to claim. Once she made those entries, they would finally be able to set the IPO price and file with the SEC.

She tried to calm herself down and be patient and realized Zeke was just being extra careful; taking his time, as was his way. But, the wait for his call was driving her nuts. There was simply too much to do to sit around and twiddle her thumbs.

No longer willing to wait, she decided to call. If Zeke hadn't finished reviewing the final reports from the geologists, she was going to raise some hell. He had to give her something.

"Yeah?"

"Zeke? What's going on?"

"Waddya mean, what's goin' on? I'm workin', dammit!" Even though old Zeke was a life-long northerner, his speech had a style and rhythm as if he was born south of the Mason-Dixon line.

"I know you're working, Zeke! I'm sitting here waiting for your call and the proven reserve numbers—"

"I know what you're waiting for, Michelle," Zeke's tone continued to be gruff and even caustic. "What the hell you want me to do, these numbers are all wrong."

"What do you mean, all wrong?"

"Screwy, as in they can't be right. They don't make sense worth a god damn and I don't know what the hell I'm supposed to tell ya—'specially since y'all kinda rushin' me and all."

She felt like she was banging her head against a very dense wall. "Just tell me why you're so sure the numbers are wrong."

He pushed air out through his cheeks in frustration. "Because if what these gosh darn charts say is even close to right, we've got as much gold on our hands than the Central Bank of China!"

"Oh, come on, Zeke, stop exaggerating."

"I'm not exaggerating, miss, I'm telling ya like it is! What we've got is enough to scare me—and I'm not just talkin' provable reserves, I'm talkin' recoverable!"

"What are you basing this on, the assays? And where are you talking about, which mine?"

"We're talkin' Canada and the reports say it's coming in on the wave scans at between 2,000 and 2,500 feet below the depth we're already at. This other vein is sittin' almost right below the vein we're already mining."

"You're fucking kidding me!"

"Nope. Let me read it to ya so you can hear for yourself. The report says, 'Imaging wavelengths reflected back signals for large deposits of quartz. The frequencies were altered and redirected to the target. The wavelength echoes returned with the signature for gold.'"

Zeke cleared his throat and continued, "Now, to double check the mineralogist said he ran a gamma wave scan and, sure enough, it came back gold—and lots of it."

"How much?" Michelle's voice was shaking when she asked. The vein they were already working, although hard to reach, was one of the densest, riches finds in the world. If there was even more gold under where they already had their unique mining and drilling operations up and running, the profit potential would be enormous. "How much, Zeke?"

"Ahhh . . . Michelle, we're not on a secure line, I . . . I don't think I should say, at least not over the phone."

"Oh my God, Zeke, don't be such an ass! Once we go public, everyone's going to see exactly what we have."

"That's what I'm saying! For our own sake, maybe it's not such a good idea to tell anyone exactly how much we're sitting on. Maybe we shouldn't go public . . ."

"You're kidding me . . . .it's that much?"

"Ahhhh, yeah."

*****

What Zeke had told her was huge news and immediately made her reconsider the IPO. Unfortunately, that was not a decision she could make on her own. A glass of wine and a hot bath had not helped to settle her anxiety. Michelle finally made up her mind that to get things done right, she needed support—a lot more than Susan was able to give her at that moment. Once her mind was made up, nothing was going to deter her from trying, no matter how many objections she was going to have to overcome. With purpose in her steps, she walked back to the office, sat down, clicked an icon on her computer, and made the required encrypted connections to Costa Rica. As soon as Carlos's image appeared on screen, and they ran through the polite formalities, Michelle went at him with a rapid string of questions.

"Are the kids okay?"

"Chris and Lisa are fine, they just miss their mother."

"How is Helena?"

"She's in Heaven, Michelle, you know she loves those kids."

"Carlos, she took a deep breath and pushed on, "is Darla okay?"

"He responded with a sad look on his face. "She's not handling being away from home all too well, but she's doing better."

"Did you teach her how to shoot—like you were supposed to."

"Yeah, she knows how to handle a weapon."

"Does she understand why that was necessary?"

"Not really, Michelle. She's not that interested in the news. As far as shooting goes, though, she's a natural and she's worked hard. What's going on there? How is Susan?"

Michelle ignored his question and pushed on with what she had to say. "Carlos, listen to me, I want you to leave the kids there and bring Darla to New York as soon as possible."

"Are you kidding? You want me to risk coming back to the states?" Carlos's eyebrows lifted in surprise.

"Haven't you been watching the news? This country is going nuts, besides I have some big news and I really need your help." Michelle was doing her best to sound strong, but the vibrato in her voice gave her away. Anxiously, she prompted, "If you're going to come, there's no better time than now—just hire a private jet and fly into Teeterboro . . ."

"But the kids?"

"Chris and Lisa will be just fine with Helena—she knows how to take care of herself and she wouldn't let anything happen to those children—you know that. Plus, you can call Don Jorge ask him to stay over. I'm sure he'd love that."

"Okay, Okay, I can come and I'll bring Darla with me, but what's the rush?"

Michelle paused and bit her lip to stop herself from crying. Relenting, she let it all out, "Carlos, I need your help. I can't do this alone . . ."

Chapter Fourteen

"In 2011, in Arab nations of North Africa, there were many civil protests and the protests evolved into revolutions that unseated several dictators. This has been called, 'The Arab Spring'. Simply stated, large segments of common citizens rose up and threw off the shackles of tyranny—at least that was what the world was told."

Sitting back in his recliner, Maxwell York held the IPad several inches from his face and squinted. Despite eye surgery a few years before, his vision was failing and he had difficulty focusing on the newfangled screens. As old as he was, he knew he couldn't make some things work as they once did—nor go back in time—no matter how much money he had.

To any one of the assistants watching York, it looked like business as usual. Their boss appeared engaged, reading the latest summary of reports and messages Andrew was parsing and routing to the device in York's hands. None of the young, ambitious assistants knew their taskmaster was taking a mental vacation.

York thought to himself ruefully how the financial particulars of this or that deal were dry and boring and how none of it held his interest. Instead of filling his brain with the details about the cost of insuring sovereign bonds in the failing European Union, or buying some new missile technology, he was ignoring what Andrew was electronically pushing to him—even though the data was what was asked for. Instead, York was watching a webcast of a seminar from some Libertarian think-tank. Speaking was a Harvard economist by the name of Hayes. The Professor continued:

"The politicians praised the movement as one of the most powerful manifestations of democracy in a generation. In Libya, NATO even gave military support to the rebels so they could topple Muammar Qaddaffi who was eventually captured, killed, and his corpse desecrated by his own people. What was sold to the citizens of the United States was that the Arab Spring was a struggle for liberty—the innate desire for democracy. However, what the citizens of the so-called free world didn't know was they were being fed a lie. The fact is, the civil discord was based on something other than the desire for democracy or freedom of choice. What led up to the Arab Spring was the result of economic dislocations-monetary manipulation planned and started right here in the United States."

Maxwell shook his head in resignation. No matter how hard they tried to conceal their tactics, someone was always able to piece it together. Most, like Professor Hayes, missed very significant details, but the man was close enough in his theories to cause a stir—if anyone was paying attention.

"Andrew, can you come here, please?" York's tone was not loud or angry, but commanding. He always retained an air of authority that made others pay attention.

Stevens walked over to where his boss and mentor sat, still amazed the old man was acting as if nothing had happened, as if that insane freak who broke in hadn't assaulted them, held them hostage, and then slipped out like a ghost. Reaching up and touching the bandage covering the side of his head, where his earlobe used to be, he asked, "Yes, Mr. York, what can I do for you?"

Looking down at the IPad in York's hands, Stevens crinkled his eyebrows seeing the information he had been working so hard to cull and organize was not on display. Instead, there was a YouTube video of some man lecturing.

"Have you seen this?" York asked.

"No, sir." He was anxious to display he was always on top of everything, but, in this instance, he had no idea what York was referring to. Stevens simply acted like the good student and waited for details with keen interest.

"You see, Andrew, its people like this who are dangerous to us—the ones most likely to disrupt our cause. This man, this professor, has pretty much figured out how we were able to accomplish our goals in North Africa."

Andrew retorted, "With all due respect, sir, it's pretty common knowledge the Arabs revolted because of inflation. The prices for food, fuel, and things they needed, rose to the point where very few could afford to survive. It's only the American media outlets who aired the political spin."

"Yes, I know. That was by design, my friend." Proud of this achievement, Maxwell glowed as he bragged with the satisfaction of a conquering general. He continued, "The entire world is changing, entire nations are falling apart, and most Americans barely notice because they're too busy trying to get a job or figuring out how to pay their mortgage. What they don't see coming is going to bite them in the ass. Information, my dear boy, is what makes Professor Hayes so dangerous."

Andrew knew exactly what was coming and how most Americans had their head buried in the sand. He also knew York had to keep hidden for as long as possible and that was why the Occupy movement was a problem. Their antics had brought about awareness and made people like Professor Hayes much sought after. Andrew also understood why the lecture by Professor Hayes was so bothersome. But, the fact was, that ship had already sailed. People all over the world—those who could afford it—and even central banks were buying gold because they knew the dollar was going to shit.

The fact that Maxwell seemed upset about the disclosure of the truth—of what was really happening and what was coming—raised another question in Andrew's mind. "Sir, if Professor Hayes's expounding on the devaluation of the dollar is so detrimental, why did you have me give all the information to that maniac, Sampson?

Those files pretty much proves everything this professor is saying . . . who knows what Sampson will do with it."

Again, York smiled, pleased that his pupil had not shied away from asking a probing question about something that seemingly made little to no sense. "Andrew, you read the file on Major Sampson, didn't you?"

"Yes, sir . . . the summaries of his training and his activities in Southeast Asia, Nicaragua, and Bosnia-but I didn't read the actual reports."

"How about the psychological profile? You read that, didn't you? And the later entries when he was brought into Iraq by JSOC?"

"No, sir." Andrew admitted, "I assumed he was crazy."

York sat the IPad down on the end table and stood up. He walked over to the large windows in the back of the study and looked out to his immaculate garden and beyond to the majestic ocean.

"That man, Major Daniel Sampson, is a pure psychopath. He has no friends, he trust absolutely no one, and he would not hesitate to kill if he felt any threat to what he thinks he wants or needs. He can do it because he has absolutely no conscience."

York turned back to face Stevens and went on, "No one really knows exactly what makes someone like that tick. For some people like him, it's the thrill of the kill; for others, it's the ability to get away with it. But, for Daniel Sampson, the situation seems to be quite different. Ever since he joined the Marines as a young man, he's been trained and he's been studied and he's been conditioned so that his particular skills could be—let's just say—exploited."

"How did the Marines know what they had on their hands when he enlisted?" Andrew asked, completely engrossed.

"That's a story for another day, Andrew, but the point is, he was conditioned to operate under the parameters of Force Recon. Do you know what that means?"

"No."

"Force Recon's motto is, 'Swift. Silent. Deadly.' It means our friend has been through three decades absorbing the disciplines of how to sneak behind enemy lines, destroy fuel depots, weapons caches, assassinate foreign leaders, and to do it alone without being detected." Maxwell walked closer to where Andrew was standing and met his eyes with his own cold, blue orbs—using his stare for emphasis. He went on in a dry, unemotional tone, "Sampson assassinated generals and dictators because that was his job. Under orders from the CIA, he killed a business man and his children—so there were no heirs—just because he was a possible political threat to a president.

"So, you have to ask yourself, why did he do what he was told? Why did he follow orders and not go off and be a serial killer doing whatever he wanted?"

"My God, Mr. York, I have no idea . . ."

"He does it, he follows orders, because he doesn't know anything else. All he knows, the only thing that drives him is completing a successful mission. Major Sampson only becomes dangerous when he starts to think for himself and acts of his own accord. Then, yes, he's probably the most dangerous man in the world."

Andrew Stevens was stunned. "Aren't . . . aren't you taking a huge risk just by being involved with him? What if he comes back or someone else convinces him to come after us?"

"You let me worry about that, Andrew. I've got a pretty good idea how to control him."

"With all due respect, Mr. York, I still don't understand why you had me give him all of that data—and the files from Hamilton Genomics . . ."

"What do you think he's going to do with that information?"

"I don't know, sell it? Give it to Troth?"

"No, he's not going to exploit it in any conventional sense. He has absolutely no trust at all for any person or institution since the military abandoned him and almost got him killed. Daniel Sampson has been a free agent, so to speak. He's been honor-bound to no one for quite some time. But now, seeing everything we have done and what we have planned, he has a task, he's part of a mission greater than himself and that is how I'll control him. By turning over all of that data, I showed him something no one else has—and that's trust—that I trust him. Trust and honor are things he will respect and return."

Andrew felt his cheeks grow hot with anger as the memory of Sampson abusing him came rushing into his head, "Again, with all due respect, Maxwell, you're making my point for me! He is too dangerous to control!"

"Relax, Stevens. Once he realizes where the world is going and he sees that his bank account tied to us is never empty, he'll act at my direction and create his own reign of terror elsewhere."

"Why would you set someone like that loose?"

"Because by the time he comes back from the fact-finding mission in Canada, this country should already be in turmoil. What I want him to do for us is to be a distraction, something the media focuses on and follows endlessly as his exploits get bigger and more daring. I'll get him to do here exactly what he has been trained to do in third world countries for the past thirty years —and he'll do it because he knows nothing else."

"So everyone will be following by whatever havoc he's creating and no one will be paying attention to you."

"Now you're catching on, Andrew. Control the media and you control the minds."

Chapter Fifteen

In Greenwich, the leaves usually started to turn in mid-September. By the time October rolled around, the trees were a mixture of red, orange, and gold with more and more fallen leaves scattered on the manicured lawns. Teams of immigrants would come onto the properties with their riding mowers and rakes and efficiently make piles so the rapidly browning foliage could be bagged up.

The delay in Sampson's return, although necessary, had put off the recruitment of a new security squad. Troth thought it was too bad Sampson had not been with him for the helicopter trip back to Greenwich so they could speak. Hiring a new team was something they would have to do later, after meeting with Thomas Jones and Susan DiGiovanni. Once that was taken care of, they could go through the files of the old AMPERS employees and choose a new group of men who could be trusted.

The fact Sampson went downstairs with the equipment and had not come back up to discuss things was a little disturbing, but there was nothing Roland could do. As much as he wanted to plan and scheme—and find out everything Sampson had procured—he instead left his guest alone to do whatever preparations necessary. The sound of gunfire coming from the basement did not come as a surprise, since Sampson had given him fair warning, but the noise was still very disconcerting.

The finished basement of Troth's estate had several neat little surprises. Beyond the guest bedrooms and storage in the front portion of the basement, a well-stocked wine cellar and a two lane bowling alley occupied the back. The bowling alley was where Sampson converted the lanes into a quasi-shooting range so he could zero out the sights of his new weapons.

It was Sampson's suggestion that they stay secluded inside the mansion. He refused to take any unnecessary risks and didn't want to take the chance of being caught in a trap or out in the open in what had clearly become "Indian Country" as he called it in Recon. The city blocks around the Troth Capital Associates building and plaza seemed to be under siege. Greenwich was crawling with federal agents as one hedge fund manager after another had their office raided or files seized. The Feds were busy trying to make examples of those who were not playing by the rules—or at least make it look like that was what they were doing. It was all a show for the disquieted public who had lost billions and needed someone to blame. However, the people being charged with insider trading or wire fraud were the small fish—bait actually—for the media and public's consumption. What the hedge fund managers who were brought down lacked was the protection offered by playing along with the right people, the people in the know. Still, Greenwich was hot and crawling with G-Men—and that made the already cautious former special forces all-star even that much more careful.

Sampson did not concern himself with what was left behind in the old armory in Troth's building. All of that equipment could burn for all he cared because he just purchased everything he needed. A Remington 700 sniper rifle was sitting on a bipod to the side of the left bowling alley. Designated the M-40-A1, Sampson first used it in '74 and wouldn't use any other weapon for that kind of work. There were two Springfield Armory 9's broken down into pieces for cleaning and a fresh coating of gun oil. Several boxes of ammunition of different caliber sat open on a table next to neatly aligned rows of ammunition clips, some loaded with hollow point rounds for the pistols and others loaded with high-velocity shells for the AK's. Also on the table were paper targets that had close clusters of holes through the centers. On top of several targets was a laptop computer with a 15-inch screen displaying a document.

Sitting on a wooden chair right off of the maple-grained wood of the bowling lanes, Sampson had an AK-47 across his lap and was running a bristled brush back and forth through the chamber. At the same time, he was leaning toward the screen of the laptop. His eyes moved back and forth rapidly as he read every line of the document from a firm called Hamilton Genomics.

Admittedly, the science was way over his head, but because he had read the supporting documents, it was becoming clearer what the project entailed. If he kept on reading, eventually he would be able to figure it out—maybe not the "how" part, but definitely the ultimate goal. It was confusing as hell trying to keep track of the bio-technical mumbo-jumbo: retroviruses, recombinant DNA, bacterial membrane proteins, along with complex statistical analysis of projected human to human infection rates using different vectors.

He was forced to skim over the heaviest reading. The esoteric scientific language was starting to give him a headache. That was especially true for the section on the X chromosome and how alteration of several alleles inhibited multiple births. Sampson was rushed for time, so he only scanned many of the files. He realized there was no way in hell he was going to be able to absorb all he wanted and needed to know and was definitely going to need some help figuring it out. That would have to come later.

Tapping on the keyboard, Sampson felt a new sensation, a slight tingling he hadn't noticed before. To his surprise—and a lot sooner than the doctor had told him to expect—the feeling in his fingertips was starting to return. It was an awesome, almost emotional, phenomenon when he was able to squeeze several hairs on his chin and pull hard enough to tug them out by the roots. It felt so good to feel he had the urge to keep on pulling out hairs until his chin was bald. That kind of fine motor control was a great sign. Things were just going to get better, and that put him in a terrific mood.

An intercom on the wall buzzed and cracked—the 1980's technology and thirty-year-old wiring came to life. The noise was enough to break Sampson's concentration.

"Sampson. Sampson, they're here."

The Major put the weapon down on the floor where a blanket was laid out. He stood and walked over to the intercom. Pressing the "SEND" button, he announced dryly, "I'll be up in a minute." It took him less than five seconds to reassemble the semiautomatic, 9mm and another split second to slap the mag into place. He pulled the slide back to chamber a round. Sampson was more than capable of handling almost anyone in hand-to-hand combat, but with this particular visitor—a man who was the size of a NFL lineman—he didn't want to take any chances. That was not to mention the fact that Thomas Jones had already disabled several highly-trained, well-armed men from Sampson's squad. No one but Jones knew exactly how that had happened, but what Sampson had been able to learn was two of his best men, both former special forces, ended up being incapacitated and another one killed. His conclusion was that Jones was not a man to take lightly. Still, Sampson wanted to know exactly what happened at that farm and how his men were so easily dispatched by a civilian with no training.

Jones and DiGiovanni were the only two surviving members of a group that nearly destroyed the legendary Roland Troth and they were in control of two very powerful trusts with vast resources. Securing the land, or at least the rights to it, seemed to be all Troth talked about ever since Sampson returned to Greenwich because that was what Maxwell York wanted. To do so, they had to go through Susan DiGiovanni and Thomas Jones.

Sampson pulled the flannel shirt out from his waistband and slid the weapon into the pancake holster at the small of his back.

Roland Troth held the phone to his ear as he stood looking out through the large bay windows that faced the front lawn of his estate. He could see out to the spiked, black iron fences at the periphery of his property.

"Is it Mr. Jones who's driving?" he asked.

Turning his head to look at an old closed-circuit monitor recessed into the wall, he leaned forward and saw a uniformed security guard standing at the driver's door of a white Land Rover. Troth asked, "The woman, does she have identification?"

He paused again and watched the dim screen. The guard said something and then reached a bulky arm out to take what looked like a driver's license. In his other hand, he held a yellow, timeworn telephone receiver connected by a long spiraled cord to the guard shack. The shack was at the end of the long, cobblestone drive that gave access onto Troth's five-acres of property. After listening to the guard's response, Troth directed, "Yes. Okay. Let them in."

Except for deterring reporters and petty thieves, the temporary security guards were all but worthless. If a professional was coming to take him out—like Sampson had feigned earlier that year—Troth knew he'd be a dead man. That wasn't true now that he had the dangerous Daniel Sampson on his side and living in the house. He felt a sense of relief and satisfaction the night before when Sampson pulled up to the servant's entrance in a minivan. It was obvious by the way they struggled carrying the military lockers to the basement that the Major had been able to meet his suppliers as planned and obtain the gear he needed. Troth even saw a few of the wares, weapons actually. Sampson was showing off one of the handguns to the guard while they unload the cargo. The man even aimed and pretended to fire the handgun.

Daniel Sampson found Roland Troth looking out of the window. Together, they watched as a gorgeous woman stepped out of the Rover and brush wrinkles out of her blouse. Then, they were awestruck seeing a giant of a man unfold himself and step out on the cobblestones of the driveway. His huge, bald head was what they noticed first—but the massive size of Thomas Jones's arms and barrel chest were clearly apparent under the suave sports jacket and stretched sweater.

"Look at the size of him," Roland chortled. He couldn't take his eyes off the man he was about to negotiate with.

"Yeah. Big guys fall hard." Sampson wasn't paying attention to Jones. His eyes were stuck on Susan DiGiovanni.

Meeting with Jones and DiGiovanni was a last ditch effort to secure the many parcels of land Troth had lost to the Seven Rams Gold Trust earlier that year. Ownership of the property was critical so they could finish building the pipelines and a massive natural gas terminal in Pennsylvania. Somehow, the two people Sampson was probing had thrashed an extremely well-connected, elite trading firm on its own turf. With that history, if they couldn't come to some form of an agreement, Troth would probably take things to the next level and figure out a way to take what he wanted.

Sampson knew the secure access code he used to gain unfettered access to the MIN-OPS network was compromised. Maxwell York's cronies in Cape Cod would be alerted he was using the system, but that no longer mattered. York's directives were clear, and using a secret link to a government computer system, even one that was being monitored was not one of his concerns. Actually, it would be a good thing if York's staff kept track of what was going on in Greenwich—that was, Sampson thought, beyond what the other hidden devices monitoring the house already revealed to the crew in Cape Cod.

*****

Standing off to the side acting passively, but constantly monitoring the situation, he held his communications device low, partially watching data scroll up his screen while Roland kept on talking. Sampson, fortunately, was able to tune out Roland's vainglorious diatribes. He'd already heard it all too many times. What Troth was saying had no relevance whatsoever to what they had to do. It was all just a distraction while Sampson tried to put the resources he had to use. When the visitors first walked into the mansion, he was able to clandestinely capture their images. Patiently, he waited for the results.

Haven't you seen what's been happening in the world?" Troth asked as he leaned back and sipped tea from a small, delicate cup. "People much more powerful than you tried to alter our path and failed. What makes you think you'll be any more successful?"

Sitting across from the old man in the opulent sitting room, Tommy and Susan looked stiff, even uncomfortable. They politely held tea cups and saucers in their hands, arms resting on their laps, but neither drank. They had cautious looks on their faces and were as alert as a pair of hungry wolves on the hunt.

Once the pictures of Thomas Jones and Susan DiGiovanni were taken, they were transmitted to a MIN-OPS socket for facial recognition scanning and database searches for matches. The search was a longshot, but they may have missed something. The details coming up were not helpful and drew only part of Sampson's brain power. More of his attention was directed at taking a measure of his opponents.

158

Jones, a massive, well-defined, black man, was handsomely dressed. He had sharp, dark eyes and an intimidating bald head. A former lawyer, he spoke deliberately, making each word count. The most interesting details they knew about Thomas Jones was that he was once a U.S. Attorney and his phone records revealed he maintained contact with a lot of players—judges, lawyers, and federal agents who were still in the game. That, combined with a massive amount of wealth, made the former football player exceedingly dangerous. Just through observation, Sampson thought Jones's irascibility was something he could use to his advantage.

Then, there was Susan. In her mid to late thirties, Italian-looking, she had a voluptuous, curvy body of a much younger woman. Based on prior research and data they already gathered, she was a relative nobody. Their sources confirmed that up until a few months ago, Susan DiGiovanni had been a young widow living in an upscale North Jersey neighborhood. She was making just enough money to pay her bills. The complete absence of intelligence reports made it clear she was not a player—at least not until her name popped up as being present at the foundry in Pennsylvania. Beyond the massive changes in her financial circumstances, there was nothing of any interest in her background.

Continuing to tune out Troth's voice, Sampson surreptitiously examined the woman's reflection in a mirror and then peered down at the device in his hand. The screen refreshed periodically as the cloud continued searching for hits. Sampson knew it would make things easier if they could find something, anything, to gain a tactical advantage. Seeing nothing useful, he caught Troths eye and covertly signaled to him with a nod that there was nothing.

Susan tried to keep an eye on the guy standing off to her left. He was leaning against a wall near the door frame, the only way out of that room. The dark-haired man looked like he was in his late forties or early fifties and was dressed casually. His posture, with his arms folded up, was anything but open and friendly. The way he held himself was right on the edge of being hostile. Beyond that, she thought there was something off about him: the way he carried himself, or the not-so-natural look of his facial features—or maybe it was the flesh-colored gloves he wore on his hands. Whatever the case, the presence of Troth's head of security, Dan, gave her pause.

Troth continued talking like he was dealing with simpletons. Although his body language was tense, his eyes were big and lively, dancing back and forth between Susan and Tommy as he spoke. "When was it? The summer of 2010 or 2011, when the first protests in lower Manhattan took off? You know, Occupy Wall Street? But, what was their message? Really? What were they trying to prove with the signs, the drum beating, and chanting their silly slogans against inequality and injustice?"

The Vice President of Troth's firm, Gerald Jacobs, was standing near the bar. He looked like he was listening but, Tommy noticed, in a distracted way. He was a thin man and would not stop fidgeting, running a hand through his gray hair, or adjusting his wire-rim glasses. Jacobs was the only one in the room dressed in business attire; a gray, pinstriped suit. At the same time he looked like he least belonged—a bum dressed up in an expensive suit.

The gun holster on Jacob's side was easy to recognize, because of his dealings with FBI agents and U.S. Marshals, Tommy immediately recognized the man was packing. Under his left arm, the bulk of the holster stood out against Jacob's thin frame. Wondering why one of Troth's VP's had a weapon and why he was acting so nervously had Tommy ill at ease. He could only pay scant attention to Troth's words. As soon as he caught Susan's attention, Tommy nodded slyly in Jacobs direction. Then,

160

he briefly formed the fingers on his hand in the shape of a gun. Judging by her nod, he was sure he successfully alerted her that Jacobs was armed, and hopefully how jittery he seemed.

Troth's voice suddenly took on a new variation, as if he was nearing the conclusion or making a point, "Sure, they raided the public square so their voices would be heard—and I think it's clear to all of us that their inspiration was the Boston Tea Party, the American Revolution . . ."

As rigid as she was in the presence of Roland Troth, Susan started to get more and more uncomfortable. Besides seeing the gun Tommy pointed out under Jacob's jacket, something else felt strange. But, she couldn't put her finger on what she was feeling. It was nothing obvious—actually it was quite subtle and more of a sensation than anything. Whatever it was, even though she wasn't sure of the cause, she was sure something just wasn't right.

Then, out of the corner of her eye, she caught him. He was using a reflection of her image in a mirror on the wall at an odd angle, but she caught him. Dan kept on turning his head and checking her out. Susan just knew the guy was former military—a detail that seemed out of place in such a luxurious locale—but more than that, her womanly intuition was setting off all kinds of alarms. Yes, she was sure of it. The security guy kept on looking her over, but he wasn't doing it in the crude, obvious way like Troth had done when they first came into the house. Instead, Dan's ogling was surreptitious, in a way he thought she wouldn't notice. The fact was, Susan's sixth sense was fully engaged and tuned in to his attentiveness. It was uncomfortable enough to make the hairs on her arms stand on end.

Susan was deathly afraid of Troth, but her attention stayed on the security detail. She instinctively knew the guy by the door was the most dangerous man in the room and, as slyly as she could, she tried to make sure her eyes were directed at him while pretending to focus on Troth.

Troth was droning on: " . . . the changes those public demonstrations brought, the revolutions, they won't happen again because Americans are too comfortable. Don't you agree?"

Tommy cleared his throat and leaned his huge frame forward, his big bald head glowing from the chandelier lights above. "Mr. Troth, I don't see where you're going with this. What does any of that have to do with you attacking us and threatening our well-being? That's what I want to know." Further emphasizing his point, he set the tea down and squeezed his huge hands together, working and flexing his hands.

"Well, let me tell you, Mr. Jones, the common cause of the protesters was unequal wealth distribution, right?" Troth leaned forward himself so that his face was very close to Jones, trying to signal he was not intimidated. He went on, "The point is they figured it out. We, the one percent, and we control eighty percent of the world's wealth, probably more. The more we concentrate our wealth, the more we consolidate our power."

"Yeah, so? Get to your point? " Tommy uttered intensely.

"What happened from New York to Los Angles? The politicians had the police raid and dismantle the encampments. There was violence; hundreds, maybe thousands of arrests. They broke the back and crushed the will of the people who stood against us. Think about it— the politicians did it for us; they did what we told them to do, stifled dissent. If those nobodies rise up again, they'll be crushed again. And, if you keep on fighting me, Mr. Jones, the same thing will happen to you. I don't think you realize what you are up against. Don't you know how much power it takes to do what we've already done?"

"Yeah, Troth," Tommy responded indignantly, "I know the kind of influence you have, corrupt and rotten to the core. But with me, you're not fighting against a bunch of nobodies in a park. I'm a billionaire just like you, and I have my own resources."

"Do you really think crushing you and getting exactly what I want will be any more difficult than crushing them? Trust me, Mr. Jones, it won't. You have no idea who you're dealing with, well, maybe I'm wrong about that. Maybe you do know . . . you did have a few partners at one time, didn't you?"

Troth's words were an tacit admission that he did have Donny and Mario killed. It took all of Tommy's willpower to stop himself from reaching over and snapping the old fuck's neck. No one had ever threatened him and got away with it—and there was no way he was going to let Roland Troth bully him into anything. At the same time, he knew there was more to consider than just himself, his hurt, and his own welfare. He had other people to think about: Darla, his boys, Susan, her kids, Michelle—shit, all the people in area Troth was targeting. A rash move and he may not get out of that Old Greenwich mansion alive—and that wouldn't be a good thing for the people who needed him.

He sat back into the soft, plush padding of the sofa and used all the self-control he could muster to calm himself. "Okay, Troth," he spit the man's name out from between his lips like a curse, "what do you want from me? What's it gonna take to get you to leave me and mine alone?" his repressed rage was still evident in his voice and on his face.

Troth relaxed, smiled, and sat back into the deep, silk-covered cushions of the chair. Calmly, he asserted, "Ah, finally, let's get down to business. Okay. I'll tell you, I'll tell you exactly what I want—I want all of the property around the Pittsfield Foundry. Plus, you'll have to concede the mineral rights and the right-of-way for my pipelines on the property you stole from me."

"Hey, Troth," Susan spoke up for the first time. Her voice was strong and uncompromising. "Why don't you go fuck yourself?"

Chapter Sixteen

By observing them, Sampson realized the visitors had Troth figured out. Their reaction was coming from a place of control and they knew exactly who was responsible for their unsettled lives. Nevertheless, Troth was acting as if he had not heard Susan's vulgar response. Instead of changing tactics, Sampson noted, Troth went down the same road and said almost the exact same thing he had just said, emphasizing it as a demand. Despite the outburst, Sampson couldn't help himself from studying her.

There was something about Susan DiGiovanni—something he was drawn to. He kept on looking down at the phone and scanning the room but was compelled to look at the mirror he was using to watch her. Seeing how demure she was when she came in made him wonder even more about the summer's events and how she fit in. She seemed to be more of a leech who got lucky and inherited some substantial resources. There was nothing about her to discern how disruptive she could be. However, there she was, sitting like a princess, right in the middle of everything, and sounding like Snooki from the show, "Jersey Shore." The woman intrigued him.

Susan's rapid ascent into billionaire status made him wonder for a second if she was the Black Widow type. Then, he mentally smacked himself back to reality, and probably would have laughed out loud if he was alone. It was a member of his hit team who killed an heir to a fortune who bequeathed everything to her. Sampson savored the fact that he was personally responsible for killing the second man whose estate she controlled. In essence, he was the one who made her one of the wealthiest women in the world.

To Sampson's chagrin, however, Troth loved the sound of his own voice more than anything. It would have been more interesting to hear their side of how they brought the hedge fund to its knees, beyond the basic details about the collapse he already knew.

*****

In the market tussle that all but destroyed Troth's hedge fund, three banks were literally snatched up from right under his nose. It got so bad, the hedge fund—Troth Hard Assets and Resource Fund—was forced to liquidate assets to meet margin calls and cover short positions. The worst part, though, was that by losing control of the banks, Troth lost control of the property he needed to finish the natural gas projects. The banks held paper on the land needed to build exclusive pipelines in the Marcellus Shale formation.

Troth's firm had launched a multipronged strategy to isolate the geographical region from the rest of the country. They had used political ties to get lawmakers to restrict where any new pipelines could be built, putting up huge barriers for competition. When the housing bubble burst, the firm manipulated markets and caused an even more severe recession, driving the housing market even lower. They took advantage of the major banks failing and government bailouts using complex derivatives to gain ownership of mortgages and then forced foreclosures on as many properties as they could. That way, Troth's firm could buy hundreds of thousands of acres of land needed to build the pipelines for pennies on the dollar. If they had been able to pull off the scheme, the natural gas drilling and pipeline monopoly would have been gigantic.

Up until that point, everything had gone perfectly and it looked like the Troth's fund would attain a monopoly able to net a trillion dollars of profits over fifty years. Then, Troth and his firm overreached.

Trying to force Tommy Jones and his partners into selling their property in Pittsfield, Roland Troth ran into a hornets' nest. The Seven Rams outwitted him and bought the banks Troth needed right out from under him—and they came very close to bringing down Troth and his hedge fund in the process.

*****

"I want all the property around the Pittsfield foundry and, I want back the property you stole from me."

"And, I want you to go fu—"

Tommy cut her off. "Susan, that's not getting us anywhere. Troth, you called me for this meeting and I've been sitting here listened to you go on and on. You don't have to tell me you're special or part of the elite—how else would a cold-blooded killer like you get out of jail as fast as you did?"

"Cold-blooded killer? What are you saying, Mr. Jones? I've never harmed anyone in my life!"

Susan couldn't help herself—she blew out a wet, slobbering raspberry. "Oh, isn't that rich, Troth? I know exactly what you are. As a matter of fact, I know you a lot better than you think!" Her Jersey-Girl accent was in full force. Pulling up the laptop she had brought in with her, she continued her rant in a sarcastic, harsh tone, "Here, I've got something to show ya—it's what the kids today call a 'mash-up'. I made it on the way here don't you just love modern technology?"

Not waiting for a response, she activated the computer and guided the pointer, tapping and scrolling. She turned the screen toward Troth. "I think you recognize this man, Paul Josephs. He used to work for you. Before you had him killed, he came to us and told us about you and everything you did."

Seeing the face on the screen, Troth scoffed and leaned back further, turning his head. "Didn't you read the reports? Even the Attorney General of the United States

167

knows Josephs was out to get me. He was responsible for what you're talking about, not me."

The image on the screen drew Sampson's attention. It was a freeze frame and he recognized the setting. It was the office where he had burst in and shot Josephs in the head. The kill had to be only minutes later. Sampson was so shocked to see the image it caused him to take a few paces forward. He wanted to know if the raid itself was recorded, and if so, how much of it. The last thing he needed was taped evidence of one of his assaults. Even though he had been fully camouflaged, there were ways others could use details to pin the killings on him.

"Show us the rest!" Sampson commanded from the side of the room. No longer standing against the wall, he was slowly moving closer to where the others sat.

Everyone stopped and turned to stare at him. His voice was deep and commanding and they were startled by the sudden outburst.

"I said, play the whole thing, I want to see the rest."

"I'll tell you how it ends," Susan all but spat out in his direction, unfazed. "One of Troth's men—or should I say your men—kills everyone and blows the head off of a young girl who had her whole life ahead of her."

When she had said "your men," the hairs of Sampson's neck stood on end. Either she just assumed he was in on it—because he was introduced as the head of security—or she knew he was involved. Either way she was right and that was not a good thing.

She went on. "This isn't the raw footage, just a few snippets so you know what we have." She tapped on the screen and clips of Paul Joseph's confession played like a newsreel but his emotion was real and clearly captured with each statement he made:

"There is a hit team outside right now."

"Roland Troth is the one responsible for all of this."

"I'm doing this because Troth is going to have me killed."

"He's using CBO's, mortgage backed securities, and inside information to make sure he's on the right side of trades."

"Roland Troth is going have a natural gas monopoly . . ."

Another voice, off screen, asked Josephs a question, "Who ordered Donald Clearmont killed?"

Josephs responded, "Roland Troth."

"That means nothing!" Roland roared, "Paul Josephs was nothing but a disgruntled employee."

The clips were enough to prove Susan and Tommy were in possession of evidence that could put Troth away forever. At the end of the first part of the presentation, she had edited together several charts detailing specific evidence about currency trades, trading partners, and deals that led right back to Troth's firm.

It was clear by Troth's expression he couldn't believe what he was seeing. His eyes also betrayed him, jumping back and forth nervously from one face to another. The evidence Josephs had provided about the trades— details Sampson was supposed to stop from ever being revealed—was critical. The trades proved Troth had manipulated the stock market and profited profusely. The electronic trail was something Troth couldn't weasel his way out of.

Panicked, but doing his best to maintain his composure, he protested, "That won't hold up, what court of law would consider that evidence?"

"Do you think that's all we have? Really?" Tommy asked in a tone dripping with indignation. "You're right though, a court may not let the interview come in as evidence, but there is plenty on here for the feds to retrace your steps and crucify you."

Troth asked, "Where is the original? Who else has seen it?"

"Oh, now, don't you worry about that Roland. I've got a friend up here in Greenwich. We stopped by his place before coming here. You see, if I don't go back Special Agent McCord of the FBI promised he'd review what I left with him." Tommy smiled a huge smile and his extra-white teeth sparkled in the light when he tilted his head. "Agent McCord is a good friend of mine and he won't look into this unless . . ."

Gerald Jacobs had been standing on the other side of the room, silent but fidgeting. The more he heard from what he was unwillingly witnessing, the more he had the urge to bolt. He didn't sign on with Troth to get involved in these kinds of illegal activities, and he never expected to hear what had heard. Making some slick trades on inside information, that was one thing. But these people were talking about murder plots, buildings exploding, and other crazy accusations. Jacobs felt trapped. There was a lot he could manage, a lot of anxiety and pain he could take—but going to jail was way beyond his bounds.

In a shaky, nervous voice, Jacobs asked in the direction of Tommy and Susan, "Why would you do this— I mean come here and, negotiate? Why didn't you just turn everything over to the police and be done with it?"

"Well, isn't it obvious?" Susan asked with a scowl on her face. "Because there are things we want to do the law may frown on." Her tone was meant to look threatening. "You see, Mr. Troth here has been known to get himself out of sticky situations so we didn't want to leave anything to chance."

"And," Tommy added, "maybe this way we can come to terms without involving the government, if you know what I mean. By letting my friend hold onto the evidence, it kind of guarantees us a fair—"

"—And safe—" Susan chimed in.

"—and safe, negotiation."

Susan tapped on the laptop's keys one more time. The screen went to blank for a second and then came back on showing a news clip from after Troth's corporate helicopter crash that killed Troth's young wife along with his second in command, C.B. Ross. The clip ran right up to the part when Roland was shown walking out of the Troth Capital Associates Building surrounded by his security team. The guards, all neatly dressed in matching blue, expensive suits, were marshaled in a protective pattern.

With a lilt in her voice, Susan teased, "I guess this was just a warm-up for the perp-walk you took a little while after this happened, huh. The next time you made it on TV coming out of that building, you were surrounded by FBI agents, remember?" Her eyes became big and excited.

Susan had used editing software to neatly enlarge and arrange the faces of the security detail surrounding Troth on the day of the helicopter crash. She cropped out the background, and, using the magic of software image rendering, had cleaned up the still images nicely until three large, close-up faces were displayed.

"You obviously know these men, Mr. Troth and Dan, or whatever your name is. This one," she leaned over the screen to see what she was doing and pointed, "his last name is Suarez. The second one is Francis, and the third one was Michaels, but he's dead."

Susan stopped and watched the men's eyes, gauging them, trying to see if there was any recognition. Neither one of them reacted in any obvious way. Dan displayed absolutely no emotion. Even though she didn't get the response she hoped for, she was still thrilled with the work Carlos had done, enabling them to spring one big surprise after another on Troth.

Troth was the first one to speak. "So, what do you want?" He sounded defeated.

171

Tommy cut in, "Do you know where these men are?"

"Today? Right now? No."

"Well, when was the last time you saw them? We know from the news clip it was after they worked for AMPERS, and for a while they were your personal bodyguards."

Sampson got another shiver when the man mentioned the name of the old military contracting firm. He didn't know how much Jones and DiGiovanni knew, but it was clear they had gone to the trouble of unraveling the past—which made them extremely dangerous. Worse than that they had gained a huge tactical advantage in the negotiations. Sampson knew when he was being flanked and immediately started to plan his counter-measures.

Tommy continued, "The last I saw these fools," he indicated the men displayed on the screen, "was when I shot 'em."

Troth piped up, "And you have the audacity to call me a killer—yet you shot my men? I never shot anyone . . ."

"So, you admit they worked for you, right?" Susan asked with a sharp tone.

"Yes. So what?"

"Do you admit you ordered them to kidnap me in Pittsfield?" Tommy shot back.

"No, of course not! Anything those men did, they did of their own volition or on the orders of that fraud Paul Josephs."

Susan jumped right back in, "So you're also denying the fact that you ordered Donny Clearmont killed and that Mick Michaels killed him at the Metropolitan Corrections Center?"

How the fuck could she know that, Sampson asked himself, now fully on high alert and mentally gearing up for action. If they knew those specific details, there was no telling what else they knew. Not having nearly the same amount of resources he had at his disposal, they had been able to pull everything together and gather the evidence to connect it back to Troth on their own. If they could do it, so could the authorities.

Sampson immediately recognized there was a potential threat to everything York was doing. Waiting to eliminate Jones and DiGiovanni until Troth finished negotiating the land deal made no sense. As the others in the room bickered, Sampson faded a little into the background, typing in a text message to Maxwell York's assistant, Andrew Stevens.

"Stop! Enough of this!" Troth shouted in a weak voice. It was loud enough to stun everyone. They sat silently, looking at him. "This is getting us nowhere. You say you're here to negotiate, so negotiate. What do you want from me?"

Susan cut in, "I want to be left alone, I want to know for sure that my children will be safe—no matter what—and I want to know what it'll take to make that happen.

Troth relaxed and sat back. "I agree, to a point, that there is no need for hostilities between us and I believe it would be beneficial if we worked together. As partners, I assure you, you would have nothing to fear from me."

"Be more specific, Troth, what do you mean by partners? How does that guarantee our safety?" Tommy cut in.

"I'm aware your firm is going public, preparing to file for an IPO."

"Yeah, so?"

"Mr. Jones, Ms. DiGiovanni, I'm not after you—or your children. I don't even know you. What I'm after is what you possess and control which happens to be what I need. Behind such structures as public corporations, there is a measure of safety. You'll have a board of directors and shareholders behind you. You'll no longer be in a position where your elimination would have any real impact. However, we would have to strike this deal before you go public."

"This is crazy! You're a ki—" Susan blurted out before Tommy pulled her by the arm to settle her. She was disgusted by the idea of working with Troth—and sitting in the same room with that maniac was starting to freak her out.

""Let the man finish, Susan," Tommy counseled. He wanted to hear exactly where Troth was going and what he knew.

"Thank you Mr. Jones. As I was saying, I'm especially interested in the banks and what you are planning on doing with credits backed by gold bullion. Maybe we can negotiate a transaction where we team up. In return for shares of your bank and the rights on the property you control, I'll give you shares in the pipeline I'm building. That way, we'll have the best of both worlds."

"That sly old bastard," Sampson thought to himself. A combination of the gold resources and the gas monopoly would elevate whoever controlled both to the top of the food chain. Troth was making a play to break away from Maxwell York and carve out his own niche of wealth and power.

Just then, Sampson's communication device vibrated. He tilted the phone up and looked at the screen. It was an encrypted return call from Maxwell York.

Turning so the others could not hear, Sampson answered in a hushed tone, "Yeah? Speak."

"This is Maxwell."

"I know who it is. Are you able to hear Troth?"

"Yes. The son of a bitch is planning on a coup and cut the rest of us off at the knees."

"I thought that was where he was going . . ."

"Listen, and listen to me good, Major Sampson. I want you to kill them all now. Do you understand?"

"Roger that, I'm out."

Sampson slid the phone into his pocket. He reached calmly and slowly around his back with his right hand. His movements were slow and measured. As he moved forward toward the others, he simply acted like he was listening, leaning forward as Troth continued to be peppered with questions and negotiate a deal.

The words, along with all other sounds, faded out of Sampson's consciousness for a microsecond. He mentally pictured the moves he would make and exactly what he had to do. The moment he visualized the attack in precise detail and formulated several possible escape routes, his eyes narrowed to a squint and he went into the zone.

He pulled the 9mm out from under his plaid shirt and shot Roland Troth point blank in the back of the head.

Chapter Seventeen

The Old Greenwich estate of Roland Troth was not the most beautiful, nor the grandest, in the area. However, it was one of the most secluded. To the west and south of the fenced-in acreage around the mansion was a winding stream. Although little more than a shallow gully further towards town, the ancient waterway had once carried deep, strong currents and gouged out a steep ravine along the woods heading north. The ravine created a small natural barrier in that direction. On the northeast side there was undeveloped property and a magnificent Georgian mansion. It had been unoccupied since the late 1990's— when the previous owner sold it. No one knew who the new owners were. Even though the large stone estate sitting on ten acres of property was empty, the lawns and gardens continued to be tended by a local landscaping service. The set-up was perfect as far as Troth was concerned. The lack of neighbors and the tract of forest provided him with seclusion he desired.

Running past the trunks of the large oak trees, Susan did not notice how beautiful the landscape was. Having just scaled the iron fence and scratched her side on the spiked top of the barrier, she didn't care about the colorful leaves or the majestic trees she was sprinting past. She didn't notice the large branches creaking and swaying in the breeze. The only conscious thought she had was getting away as fast as her legs could carry her.

She ran with all of her might, dodging large, round trunks in a blur. The taste in her mouth was acrid and made her want to wretch. The smell of burned gunpowder filled her nose and was as strong as it had been when everything had gone to hell. Stopping to catch her breath, she closed her eyes for a second but only remembered fragments of what happened.

She had been sitting across from Troth, looking at him, arguing with him, when it looked like his head simply exploded. Blood, brain matter, pieces of skull flew off in every direction. Stunned by the sound of the report, the sight of Troth's head, and the sensation of warm ooze covering her face, must have made her black out. What had happened next was a fog and she had no clue how she got out alive. She didn't remember running through the house or finding an escape route. The fear she was about to be killed must have overwhelmed her mind. She simply ran for her life.

Susan's lungs burned and she coughed, trying to spit the sour taste out of her mouth. But, she was unable to spit because her mouth was so dry. Reaching up to push the bangs out of her eyes, she felt the clumps and stickiness of drying human biological residue. Somehow, that made some memories of what she had just experienced—what she was unconsciously trying to suppress—rush back into her consciousness. As the memory of Troth's head coming apart, she started to vomit. Her stomach empty, she kept on heaving until her body could no longer take the strain and she fell to her knees, exhausted. Tears streamed down her cheeks and mucus hung from her chin.

Trying to get herself together, Susan used the bottom of her blouse to wipe her face clean. Once again, she tried to clear her throat and spit to excrete the sour taste of bile on her tongue. She then focused on standing up and starting to run so she wouldn't have to think about what she had witnessed. She ran wildly, not knowing where she was or where she was going. She just ran.

She was in shock and in a panic, unable to act rationally or stop and think things through. Blinded by terror, Susan did not see the edge of the ravine or the rocks in the dry stream bed. The next time her right foot came up for a stride it came down on nothing. She fell and tumbled hard onto the mud and rocks below.

*****

"You can go home now you won't be needed for the rest of the day."

"Are you sure everything is okay, sir? I coulda sworn I heard gunshots." The guard from the home security company was standing in the guard shack near the front gate gripping a walkie-talkie. In his other hand, he held the old yellow phone to his ear. A van sat right outside of the gate decorated with the logo for Richter's Home Security and a series of orange gumball lights on the roof.

"Yeah, don't worry about it, that was just me down at the range showing off my toys to our guests. Listen, just take your partner and go—I'll make sure your supervisor never knows—oh, and there'll be a nice bonus for the both of you." Sampson was standing at the side entrance of the house, looking back and forth from the monitor to the guard shack and van parked outside of the gates. He just needed the rent-a-cops to leave so he could finish cleaning up and make a clean get away. After that, he could control exactly what happened in Greenwich. But, if the idiots didn't leave immediately, he knew he'd have to go outside and kill them.

"All right, sir, we're goin' but I just don't wanna get in trouble or lose my job."

Sampson shook his head at the slovenly fool's desperate pleas to spare his meaningless job. "Don't worry. If your boss fires you, I'll give you a job right here working for me." Seeing the look of relief on the man's face on the monitor, he knew that had done the trick.

Less than a minute later, the van pulled away and the two men from Richter's Home Security were gone. Two down, three to go, Sampson thought. He walked back through the kitchen into the hallway and took the stairs two at a time down to the basement. In the right lane of the bowling alley, two maids and a man-servant were tied up. They were sitting back-to-back with their wrists bound behind them. He did not deliberate, think about what he was doing, or say a word. At that point, Sampson didn't care about leaving witnesses behind or that they could identify him. What mattered to him was time. He needed time to find the woman, set up a diversion, and get out of the area before anyone was alerted. If he had enough time to get away, no one would ever catch him.

In several quick moves, Sampson cut the house staffs' throats. They all died quickly and painlessly. Then, he packed the gear he needed into army surplus duffel bags and carried it upstairs.

Tommy Jones groaned in agony. Earlier that year, when he was kidnapped and shot in the knee, he had not felt this much pain. Rolling over to his side and trying to pull his legs underneath him, he experienced a kind of hurt like he'd never felt before—but he had to stand up. He had to for Susan's sake. His face was covered with blood dripping down from the long gash on his head where a bullet had grazed his skull. His head ached from either the concussion of the bullet or from when he dove off the couch and hit his head on the floor. Shaking his head back and forth and opening and closing his eyes seemed to help him focus.

As his head cleared, Tommy remembered the guy pointing a gun at him—after shooting Troth—and pulling the trigger. He saw the assault in his mind's eye in super-slow motion and realized he had failed to move quickly enough because he couldn't believe what was happening. The dive to save his own life was pure instinct and he knew he was lucky to be alive. But, then his heart ached remembering how he heard Susan screaming at the top of her lungs. There were a few more shots, the sound of a window breaking, a door crashing—and then Troth's head of security was on him.

After the gunshot knocked him silly and Tommy found himself on the floor, he tried to stand up and get a hold on the man attacking them, but the guy was strong and wiry like a steel band. For a while, they had gone at each other like animals, or so it seemed, but it didn't last long. Even though he had at least 100 pounds on Dan, there was no way to get a grasp—the man moved like a trapped wolverine in heat. Before Tommy knew what was happening, Dan had him in some sort of freakish martial-arts hold and popped his right elbow completely out of joint—rupturing the fluid capsule. A second later, even as Tommy hollered and bucked his body in agony, the guy put him in another weird hold and twisted. The pressure was intense and exact, separating Tommy's left shoulder with one thrust. Howling in pain and on his knees, he could do nothing but fall helplessly onto his forehead, holding the weight of his torso up with his neck. That was when Dan got behind him and stomped on the back of his neck.

At first, the sensation that spread made his arms feel like they were tingling, and then as if they had been set on fire. The next blow to the back of his head knocked Tommy out cold.

Unable to use his arms, but surprised he was not paralyzed and could move his legs, Tommy struggled with all of his might to straighten his distended right arm. His elbow had swollen to twice its normal size, but if he could get his arm to unlock—in a more human-looking configuration—he knew he'd be able to move it. The same was true about his shoulder he just had to force it back into socket—no matter how much it hurt. He gritted his teeth and tried to focus his thoughts on Susan—he had to help Susan—and he popped his shoulder back into place, screaming and grunting through the pain.

Sampson was standing at the doorway, watching the show. He stood silently listening as Tommy struggled, fighting through the pain, trying to move his arms. Finally, when the huge man on the floor stopped swearing and shouting, Sampson calmly walked up behind him. With a look of admiration on his face, he said, "I can't believe you survived that! That's just nuts," and shot Tommy in the back of the head.

******

She did not know how long she had been unconscious or even how she ended up on the ground. The sides of the concavity she fell in weren't steep and, as her eyes came into focus, she could see the brownish sprouts of dead weeds at the border of the depression. Susan lifted her head and managed to get up on her hands and knees. Standing, the reality of her situation started to come back in little flashes of memory: Tommy diving to the floor; her panic, bolting from the couch, sprinting down a hall, not knowing where to go or how to get out, seeing a door, running to it. The gunshot, another one, pulling the door open, running, running, running.

This wasn't happening, it couldn't be. "Oh, yes, it is!" her brain screamed at her. "Get moving!" Her legs didn't move, so her brain screamed at her again, "Run, you stupid bitch!" Finally, she started to run, following the stream bed north.

Still not knowing where she was going or how to get there, her legs just kept on picking up her feet and putting them back down. The trees closed in around her as she moved further into the woods as continued to put distance between herself and where she had fallen—or was it Troth's mansion she was running from? She couldn't remember.

There was a bend and the course of the stream turned to the west. When she came around the turn, she saw a small country bridge and a lane up ahead of her. That made her press harder, knowing that the road, no matter how small it was, had to lead somewhere. Her legs started pumping up and down a little harder and she lowered her head in a sudden burst of energy.

*****

The traces of blood from the bottom of her shoes showed the direction she ran. After he finished off Jones, Sampson followed her tracks to the kitchen. There, he saw the broken window pane in the door she must have whipped open in her panicked escape. Since he had not heard the sound of an engine, he knew she was on foot. So, he decided not to chase after her because he knew she was easily tracked. The woman couldn't have gotten far and she had a long way to go before she could get help. If she did happen upon someone, it would still take time for them to call the cops and for the cops to dispatch a unit. That gave him a small window to do what he had to do.

He went back to the sitting room and searched Thomas Jones, locating the keys for the Rover. Then, walked outside to determine what direction Susan had gone when she ran. The newly raked lawn clearly showed her tracks pressed into the grass and her path lead towards the woods. He pulled out the military communicator and dialed up the code for a connection into the MIN-OPS network, quickly retrieving the latest surveillance satellite images for the zone centered on 41ø 4' North by 73ø 38' West. Using digital zoom and automated mapping grids, he located the area around Troth's property, calculated the time that had elapsed, and the woman's most likely route. Once he knew where she was with reasonable probability—and where she would be—Sampson got in the white Rover and headed toward a small dirt road and an old wooden bridge at the edge of the woods.

*****

With her heavy breathing and the sound of her heart thumping in her ears, Susan did not hear the SUV when it pulled up and stopped on the bridge. Even though it was a cool autumn day, sweat poured down off of her damp hair and blurring her vision. Easing up her pace, she looked up she saw the white Rover. "Oh, my God, Tommy! Thank God! Thank God! Thank God!"

She couldn't see him in the driver's seat, but who else could it be? It was the vehicle they had rented from the airport because she recognized the odd looking luggage or ski rack on the roof. It didn't look like a typical SUV, so it had to be Tommy—but how did he find her? She slowed to a walk as she went up the embankment and over to the left side of the bridge.

The old structure was made of wooden beams and it looked like the boards could barely hold a person, let alone a large vehicle. But, there the Rover sat, unattended. No one was in the vehicle and no one was around. When she looked in and saw her laptop in the front seat, she knew for sure it had to be Tommy—and he must be out walking around, looking for her.

"Tommy!" She yelled, not exactly loud or confident at first. Then, she really put her diaphragm into it, "TOMMY!"

She walked around to the driver's side to see if the keys were in the ignition or maybe if she could see a hint of which direction he had gone. Seeing neither, she put her fingers in her mouth, turned to the woods and started to blast out the loudest whistle she could manage. Susan never even heard him or saw him coming. He stealthily walked up behind her and clubbed her in the head with the butt of his new AK-47.

After subduing the woman, Sampson drove most of the way back to Troth's estate, leaving the Range Rover behind and carrying Susan the short distance to his blue van. He bound her up to the front passenger seat with zip-ties and then loaded the rest of the gear he needed into the back of the minivan, along with a few select goodies from Troth's mansion.

Taking the time to clean himself up, he replaced the bloody, gloves with a clean pair. Then, he made a quick trip out to the shack so he could swap the old yellow phone in the guard's booth with a similar one from inside the house. He also looked around the guard shack and found the security company's paperwork. A log sheets denoted the unit number of the company's van. After he took the phone with the guard's fingerprints into the house, he left Greenwich and headed for the security company Troth had hired.

When he found the exact van the guards had used, he did what he knew would throw the scent off of him for weeks, if not for good. He also made it so the authorities could quickly determine who had killed Roland Troth and his staff with minimal effort. The entire time Sampson was busy planting evidence Susan remained unconscious. She looked like she had nodded off and was simply sleeping, which raised no suspicion. Soon, after he finished setting up several locations for maximum interference, he was on the road with a still unconscious Susan at his side.

Chapter Eighteen

"Why are you wearing gloves?" The silence in the van was suddenly broken. Her voice was weak and it sounded as if her throat was extremely dry.

The inside of the minivan had been quiet for quite a long time and Sampson was surprised to hear her. It was long past when she should have woken up from the trauma-induced nap he gave her. The alluring sound of her womanly voice caught him off guard. He quickly recovered, "To protect my hands from infection."

"The gloves look gay."

Unsure if he had actually heard her right, he turned and gazed over at Susan. She was sitting slouched in the passenger seat. Her legs were secured to the rails under the seat with zip-ties and her wrists were bound and linked to her ankles with several more of the coupled, stiff, plastic bindings. He turned his attention back to the road and noticed a sign for the New Bedford exit. "Do you need to use the head? Are you hungry?"

Susan sat up straighter and tried to reach the back of her head with her hands. Unable to reach far enough, she tilted her head forward and rubbed the top of her scalp. "Why the fuck did you hit me? Asshole!"

Sampson didn't answer. He looked at her again, his brows raised and he shrugged. "Well, do you have to go or not?"

"How do you expect me to go to the bathroom like this?" She extended her hands as far as they would go, displaying they were bound.

"I'll make accommodations. So, what's the verdict?"

"I don't have to go, but I'm thirsty as hell." To emphasize the point, she cleared her throat.

He reached back and pulled forward a red and white plastic cooler. Looking from the road to Susan to the cooler full of ice, bottles of soda, and wrapped sandwiches, he asked, "What do you want, regular or diet?"

"How about a shot of rum? I need something to dull the pain . . ."

Sampson pulled out a regular soda and handed it to her. There was just enough slack in the bindings for her to open the liter bottle and tip it back for a sip. Once she satisfied her thirst, he flipped a hoagie in her direction. The heavy roll with slices of meat and cheese poking through the lettuce was wrapped in plastic. It landed on her lap and she picked it up, maneuvering the soda bottle between her thighs so she could use both hands.

"Is there mayo?" She asked as if it was the most natural thing in the world to be tied up in a minivan, eating a sandwich.

Her poise was unexpected. "No." He answered dryly. "How do you feel?"

"Like someone whacked me in the back of the head. How do you think I feel?" The cola made her feel a little better and the hoagie looked really good, so she started to unwrap it.

"Susan, right?" He glanced at her again, seeing if she minded him using her first name. When she just looked at him and bit into the hoagie, he went on. "If you don't remember, my name is Dan."

"I remember."

"What's your connection to the Seven Rams Gold Trust? No one's been able to figure out what you do."

With food in her mouth, she chewed, swallowed, and asked, "Who the fuck are you?"

"I just told you, I'm Dan."

"No, you ass, I don't mean what's your name, I mean, who the fuck are you?" Seeing a flicker of embarrassment on his face at her use of invectives, Susan was grateful for the wild day of her youth. Despite a proper upbringing, hanging out with a rougher crowd as a teen had given her an edge and she had the ability to call on that toughness at will, using it to her advantage when it suited her. The expletives befuddled people and put them off balance. She looked at Dan and sipped more soda.

Sampson quickly donned a different expression, trying to look as if he hadn't been disconcerted by her language. "Right now, I'm either your best friend in the world or your worst enemy—depending on how you answer my questions."

She sneered. Wryly, she responded, "Yeah, I saw how friendly you can be. What did Troth say to get on your bad side?"

The opportunity to find out exactly what she had seen and what she knew fell right into his lap. "He was going to kill you and Tom Jones—"

"Oh, my God! Tommy! What did you do to him?"

"I didn't do anything to him!" Sampson turned and looked straight at her, eye-to-eye. He went on earnestly, as if he was telling her the truth, "That guy standing behind your friend—"

"Gerald something," she interrupted. Remembering the man with the gun and Tommy pointing it out to her, her voice quivered with dread. "what about him?"

"He shot Tommy in the head before I could take him out—" Sampson tried to say this with sadness, but Susan couldn't tell if he was acting—she was too busy screaming.

"Nooooo!" she wailed in grief. "Oh, my God! Oh, my God . . . Noooo!"

As she cried and wailed and shouted out with hurt and sorrow, Sampson kept on looking over at her. Although he could not relate to the deep emotions she was expressing with her tears, he knew she was not putting on some sort of act and could sense the authenticity. He didn't say anything for quite a while and just let her cry as he drove. Eventually, Susan calmed down and was reduced to sniffling and sobbing. Occasionally, he would glance in her direction and see huge tears stream down her cheeks. The sobs, gasps, and snot dripping from her nose— unattractive features a self-conscious woman would never let anyone see—were things she did not hide. If she knew exactly who he was or saw exactly what had happened at Troth's house, Sampson figured she would never have allowed herself to be so vulnerable.

Replaying the exact details of the attack, he saw with his mind's eye how Susan had looked up at him with confusion as Troth's splattered blood and brains dripped off of her face. Like she was coming out of the gate at a track meet, she had bolted out the door and was gone by the time Gerald Jacobs and Thomas Jones hit the floor. He remembered hearing sounds somewhere behind him in the house, but he hadn't heard her footfalls when he went to the basement or when he finished off Jones and sanitized the scene.

From his perspective, there was no way in the world she could have seen him do anything other than shoot Troth. She wouldn't even have known he was the one who knocked her out except for the fact he already admitted it. Still, he had to explain why he knocked her out and why she was fastened to the seat. Judging by her reaction, he figured she bought the line about killing Troth because Troth was going to kill them.

For the longest time, Susan seemed to be lost somewhere in her own mind, though, thinking, mourning, maybe planning what to do next. For a long time, they drove in complete silence. Sampson had no clue exactly what was going on in her head, but what he did know was she probably would have been a lot more on guard, aggressive, maybe even on the attack if she had seen anything. Because of her passivity, he believed she had no idea he was the one who killed Tommy. Her grief, instead of rage, put his mind a little more at ease.

Susan didn't know how much time passed before she regained her composure. Hearing that Tommy was dead initially shocked her—but then the same dreadful thoughts kept on circling around in her mind peppered with sadness and grief. "Not again" were the words popping up in her head as she remembered losing Donny and then Mario. Now she had to grieve for Tommy. For what? What was it all about? Property? Gold? Natural gas? All material possessions—stuff that meant nothing to her. She would have given up all of the gold in the world to have those three men back. They didn't deserve to die, yet Roland Troth had them killed. But, Troth was gone—wasn't he?

Maybe it was over. Maybe she was safe, and her kids were finally safe. She wanted to believe it was over—she wanted so badly to believe there would be no more killing. What brought her back was the thought that the end of Troth meant the end of danger.

Sniffing and wiping her nose, Susan asked, "Troth is dead, right?"

"Yeah, he's dead."

"Are you sure?"

"Yes, Susan, I'm sure."

"So, maybe now that the motherfucker's dead, the people I love will stop getting killed."

Sampson sat still, paying attention to the road but listening carefully to her vent. He could hear and feel the rage in her voice, but he also detected hope. At the first hint that she was a threat to him, though, he'd have to kill her. He hoped she didn't put everything together because, despite her emotional liability, he liked having her around. The more he was around her, the more relaxed he felt. Even though they had just met and had barely spoken, Susan DiGiovanni made him feel things he could never remember feeling before.

Rubbing the streaked makeup from her eyes and cheeks, getting herself together more and more, Susan asked the obvious question, "Why am I tied up?"

Sampson answered, "Because I still don't know who you really are or who you work for. I don't mean to be an ass, but a lot of people have been dying around you lately and I—I didn't want to take any chances." The hesitancy in his voice could have won him an Oscar.

"This coming from a guy who just shot the man he worked for?"

Smiling wryly, he answered, "Good point."

He pulled the dagger out of the sheaf attached to his left leg and motioned for her to extend her hands toward him. Sampson cut the thick, white plastic ties with one quick swipe.

Then, he deftly flipped the dagger over so the hilt was facing Susan and handed the dagger over to her. As she reached out and took the knife, he shrugged and put a look of regret on his face as if he was saying he was sorry. He wanted to get her to trust him, and, by handing her a deadly weapon, it was as if he was passing off control of the situation to her. Giving her control, or seeming to, Sampson hoped she would relax even more and eventually come around to believing everything he said.

He watched her use the sharp blade to finish cutting herself free and was happy he had been able to avoid explaining any further why he knocked her out and tied her up. If she would have pressed for details, he might have been stuck. He had engaged her in a confidence game and was pleased she was, at least for the moment, playing along. Getting her fully ensnared depended on how well everything went over the next few hours.

The next time he caught her eye, he asked, "Everything okay? Do you want me to find a hospital so we can get your head checked out?" Sampson's voice dripped with concern, but he hoped like hell she would decline the offer.

"No. I'm fine. What did you hit me with, anyway?"

"A rifle butt to the head. I didn't think it would do that much damage and disabling you gave me a chance to find out more about you."

"What are you a caveman? All you had to do was ask!"

"Like I said, no offense, but the people around you have been dropping like flies. From what I've been told, their demise has been pretty good for your pocketbook."

"That is pretty offensive, and I really wouldn't blame you for thinking that if you didn't work for Troth. If anyone knows how the men I knew died, it's him and probably you." Suspicion was starting to creep into her voice.

"Wait a minute, wait a minute. You got it all wrong, lady. Yeah, I worked for Troth, but until you and Jones came here today, I had no idea what he was into. As far as I knew, you and your friend wiped out Troth's security team and, just like everyone else, I believed that other guy was the one. That's what the government has been saying, right? Besides, Troth wasn't charged with anything, was he?"

Sampson paused and took measure of her to see if his words were having any effect. She remained silent, so he went on. "Susan, you've got to believe me, actually it was you and Jones who convinced me Troth was the one who started this mess. I just joined up with him because he lost his entire security team and I swear to you, I had no idea what he was doing . . ."

"Explain how, Dan! Explain how you didn't know, how you just joined up with Troth. How do you just join up yet have the balls to shoot the man in the head like you did?" Susan still had the commando dagger in her hand

and she noticed his eyes flash back and forth from the road to the dagger, as if he was afraid of it.

"Okay, I'll tell you—but this has to stay between us. Before I started working for Troth, I worked for someone else, an associate of Troth who was paying me to keep an eye on him. It was my real employer, actually, who wanted to know what he was up to."

"And you just happened to hear something that made you mad enough to kill him?" she rolled her eyes for effect. "Who died and made you judge, jury, and executioner?"

"It's none of your damn business what I was hired to do. What's going on is bigger than you, bigger than me. I thought you'd be smart enough to figure that out."

"I have figured it out!"

The tension of their outbursts caused them to retreat back into silence. Even though they were connected by a weird set of circumstances, they were still strangers. The mutual withdrawal to neutral corners, based mostly on discomfort, gave them time to collect their thoughts and calm the situation. Susan was slowly regaining her faculties and starting to focus a little better on the situation at hand. She knew that in dealing with the man next to her, she had to choose between treading carefully or going for broke. It wasn't the first time she'd been in that type of situation, but the last time had not turned out so well.

Throwing caution to the wind, she asked, "Are you a hit man?"

"I'm not gonna dignify that with a response. What the hell do you think?" Sampson looked at Susan and then suddenly his eyes sparkled with amusement. It was clearly a signal to her she hit on the truth, but he was unwilling to come out and say it.

"That was a non-denial—denial if I ever heard one," she declared.

Susan had no idea what the hell she was going to do next. She just found out Tommy had been killed and she witnessed Roland Troth getting his head blown off—yet there she was calmly sitting right next to the killer. The copious amount of stress over the past few months must have warped her brain because she knew the reaction she was having was way off. In the past, she would have done whatever she could to get help, to notify the authorities, to somehow have the police come and lock them both up until everything was sorted out. At least that way she would be safe and would be able to get back to her children. Now, the furthest thing from her mind was contacting the authorities. She didn't know who to trust or who the right people to contact would be. Maybe it wasn't just her that was out of kilter, maybe it was everything.

After learning all she had learned over the past year, she knew the world was a lot different than she had imagined. Her choices were thus limited to relying on Michelle and Carlos or believing in a complete stranger she knew for sure had just blown off another man's head. That detail was not something she could hold against him. Troth had been responsible for a lot of heartache in her life and was her sworn enemy. And, under a different set of circumstances, she had done the exact same thing. How could she condemn a man as a killer when she herself had killed?

Because she happened to be sitting next to Dan and had no other way out, there was no choice. For the time being, she'd play it the best she could and use the most alluring of her womanly charms. She'd seduce the son of a bitch. That way, she hoped, he wouldn't kill her, at least not immediately. And, as long as she kept him interested, it would give her time to think of what to do next.

It had not slipped her memory how Dan was eyeballing her when they first went into Troth's house, or that she busted him snatching glances of her in the mirror.

But, she couldn't be too obvious about the seduction part. She'd have to play the bitch first, at least for a while. Susan knew instinctually that Dan would smell a rat if she went soft on him too quickly. Plus, with a man like that, he'd probably be even more turned on if she presented a challenge to him. Strangely, the thought of seducing a probable hit-man did not bother her all that much. It made her wonder if getting knocked in the head had scattered her brain even more than usual.

Sampson pushed on. Ignoring her prior sarcasm, he tried to gain her trust. "Listen, Susan, I'm telling you the truth—after Troth's men were killed, I got sent in to watch him because the people who control him thought he was losing control."

"People who control him? Yeah, right! What are you talking about? You want me to believe there are people more powerful than Troth?" She looked over at him and examined his expression. She couldn't detect falsehood and, as implausible as what he was saying seemed, her intuition wasn't setting off any alarm bells.

"Okay. You don't really believe me and I don't know if I can trust you. How do I know *you* don't work for Troth?"

"I guess you weren't paying much attention to the meeting Tommy and I were having with your boss . . . oh, yeah, you were paying attention—you heard enough to kill the man!"

"Yeah, okay!" Sampson sighed, acting like he was frustrated. "We're not getting anywhere like this. Let's do a little tit-for-tat here. If you give me something, I'll give you something and maybe we can learn to trust each other."

Susan's eyebrows knotted up. "What do you mean? I don't understand."

"I'll ask you a question and you have to answer and tell me the truth. Then it's my turn."

"How am I going to know you're telling me the truth?" Susan eyeballed him with suspicion.

"How am I gonna know you're telling *me* the truth?" he repeated in a mocking tone. "I'm going to ask you things I know a little something about. If you lie, I'll know. You can do the same thing."

"Okay, I'll play your stupid game—but on one condition."

"Yeah, what's that?"

"You let me use your phone so I can call a friend and have her get in touch with Tommy's wife. I've got to let them know what happened and that I'm okay."

Chapter Nineteen

One stoplight towns in western Pennsylvania were charming places to visit or drive through—at least that was the way it used to be several decades before. Located at ancient rural trading posts or logging villages near rivers, the towns no longer served a purpose. There were no occupants for the large downtown buildings and many towns were too small to warrant police or fire departments. With no jobs, children moving away to establish careers, and no entrepreneurial opportunities to speak of, the tiny burgs had been in decline for a very long time. So few residents remained in the once robust townships, they were all but barren.

Stanton Frazier had driven through many similar places over the years. But, to his surprise, the tiny town of Pittsfield was quite different from what he expected. Cruising down Main Street, there was traffic. Cars and new pickup trucks motored up and down the strip. More annoying, and even quite dangerous, many gravel and cement trucks bullied their way across town almost taking up both lanes. What could be called the downtown area was also bustling with foot traffic. Small mom and pop shops were open and seemed to be doing brisk business. A big, ancient building in the center of town, City Hall and the Post Office, had constant activity.

A car double-parked in front of a store actually caused a minor traffic jam in a town with a reported population of under three thousand. Stanton knew why things were different there than every other shithole, decrepit town in the middle of nowhere. Pittsfield was gearing up to be the center of gravity for two necessary commodities.

He pulled the metallic gray Chrysler 300 into a parking space that opened up right in front of him. The walkway leading up to the City Hall was less than twenty-feet away and the Sheriff's Office, he knew, was in the basement of the same building. Based on the calls he made, the sheriff himself was supposed to be in. Frazier got out and walked slowly toward the side entrance where an old metal sign painted in blue with a big gold star pointed to the office he was seeking.

The Sheriff's Office looked like something out of either an 1880's or 1980's movie set, depending on one's perspective. Wooden desks and chairs, possibly antiques, sat on a bleached-out oak wood plank floor. The iron gates and bars enclosing the two holding pens were accessible with enormous brass keys that hung next to a long, high dais. An antique gun cabinet securely accommodated several modern weapons and was safeguarded with a steel bar and Master locks that looked strangely out of place. The computers on their desks were big, boxy, and attached to huge CRT monitors. Like the phones and dusty fax machine, most of the equipment in the office had been rendered obsolete. Frazier couldn't help but shake his head in disappointment. No law enforcement agency in the country should be so poorly equipped. One relatively tiny grant and the Pittsfield Sheriff's Department could have the latest, most effective law enforcement tools ever invented—and it wouldn't cost the town one plug nickel!

No one was in the front office to greet him when he opened the door and stepped inside. However, moments after Frazier took measure of the office two men in dark blue uniforms opened a door and walked out of an office behind the dais. Following them was a man in a plaid shirt, jeans, and work books. The flecks of gray in his red hair were the only indications the thin, freckled, youthful appearing individual was a man and not a boy.

The man extending his hand, "Hi, I'm Randy Babcock—you must be Director Frazier . . ."

"Assistant Director, FBI." The two men shook.

The two uniformed deputies nodded respectfully but did not speak. They moved to their desks while Sheriff Babcock extended a hand to direct Frazier into the office.

"Sheriff, I'm glad you could meet me on such short notice."

"Well, to be honest with you, we're usually not here until later. Me and my men work at the foundry, this sheriff's gig is just part time."

Frazier leaned back and crossed his thin legs. "Not much crime out this way, huh?"

"Sure isn't—but times seem to be a-changin'. A lot of people coming into town, lots of strangers looking for work now that the foundry's expanding."

Stanton made a mental note about the foundry, knowing it was a big part of Thomas Jones's operation. The fact it was expanding was relevant to the extent that laws were usually broken by someone. Making it into a federal offense was another story.

Randy continued, "So, what exactly is it that I can do for you, Assistant Director?"

"I guess it'd be fair to say since things are changing it isn't so quiet around here anymore."

"Like today? Yeah, I haven't seen traffic like that in years."

"No—like earlier this summer at that farm . . ."

Leaning forward in his chair, Babcock responded," "Wait a minute, wait a minute . . . hold it right there, sir. If you'd have told me that was what you wanted to see me about, I could've saved you a trip—I don't have anything to say about that."

Frazier uncrossed his legs and leaned forward, staring intently into the sheriff's eyes. "And why exactly is that, Sheriff Babcock? Do you have something to hide?"

Babcock's face turned bright red. "Are you kidding me?" The sheriff was so upset he couldn't remain seated. He stood up quickly and started to pace. "What is it about

198

you pricks from D.C.? Don't you people talk to each other?"

"Calm down, Sheriff."

"Calm down? You just accused me of hiding something and the last time I talked to the Feds, they said to do the exact opposite!"

Stanton held his palms up. "Slow down, Randy, slow down! What do you mean by 'the Feds?' and what do you mean they told you to do the exact opposite? I don't understand."

Babcock rubbed the light-colored hairs on his chin. "It means that I was ordered—threatened actually—to not talk about what happened with anyone because it's a matter of national security."

"Ordered by who?"

"I can't tell you that either, national security."

Frazier shook his head as if trying to clear it. "I don't think you understand, Sheriff—I can have you charged with obstruction of justice if you don't answer my questions."

"Oh, ain't that just goddamn wonderful?! On one side I got the military tellin' me to keep quiet, on the other I got the FBI telling me to talk!"

"Who in the military, Sheriff? Tell me who so I can call them and so you know its okay for me to hear your side?"

"My side? What the hell do you mean my side? I had nothin' to do with what went down at the farm!"

"Well, that's what you're claiming, but how do I know that's the truth? How do I know anything you're saying to me right now is the truth? Make me a believer Randy. Make me believe your story and I'll leave you alone."

*****

Stanton Frazier had taken his time driving up to Pittsfield. Now, driving back toward his home in Arlington, he had time to digest everything he had learned. Squeezing a small-town dick like Sheriff Babcock was a breeze. Getting the information he wanted only took promising the rube he wouldn't get in trouble and telling him no one would know where the information came from. One tiny threat and one small promise and the sheriff rolled right over. As soon as Frazier had flashed his bona fides, Sheriff Babcock couldn't wait to throw years of loyalty and friendship out the window.

Frazier mulled over the details in his head. It was Thomas Jones who shot the two men in the barn and it was Susan DiGiovanni who killed the man in the house. Everything was covered up—kept hush-hush under some national security shit because the men who were shot were once with some special-ops team. But, why had there been a blackout about someone being killed? If the dead guy was a veteran, wouldn't they celebrate him as a fallen hero? Obviously there was a lot more to the story and whoever was doing the cover-ups had some colossal juice backing them up.

He had heard enough based on what Babcock told him to have both Thomas Jones and Susan DiGiovanni locked up forever. Even if they had the best lawyers and best justification in the world, they would still be charged and tied up in court for years. The problem was, as Frazier saw it, as soon as he brought the charges, whoever went to such great pains to cover up what really happened would come after him. That was something he couldn't afford to happen and that meant he had no choice but to contact Roland Troth and find out what the hell was going on. How could Troth both want Jones taken out of the game and be protecting him at the same time? That was, of course, if Troth or one of his cronies was behind the cover-up. None of it made any sense unless it was the military itself pulling all the strings and obscuring all of the details. If that was the case, Stanton definitely wanted to get as far away from the situation as he could.

His mind started to spin, mulling over the tangled web his life was starting to become. There was too much going on and too many asses to kiss to please everyone. The next chance he got, he was going to tell Troth it was over, time for him to retire and let the chips fall where they may.

While daydreaming about his second retirement, he felt the phone vibrate in his jacket pocket. Frazier pulled it out and looked to see who was calling. It was from Constitution Avenue and 10th in D.C.—an extension in the Justice Department's upper floors.

"Hello? Frazier here."

"Stanton, this is James LeCroix."

"What's up LeCroix? Why are you calling me on this line?"

"It's business, Frazier. Have you heard the news?"

"No, I don't listen to the radio when I'm driving."

"Well, you're going to have a heart attack when you hear this one—and, guess what? I was directed to find you and fill you in."

Frazier was incensed and annoyed by the man's playfulness. "What the fuck are you talking about? Directed by who?" He hoped it had nothing to do with terrorists on American soil. Since he was the FBI's designated point-man for those types of events, any kind of action would keep him tied up in hearings for months. Doing that once in a career had been enough. Not knowing what it was about, the amusement in LeCroix's voice was annoying.

"I was ordered by none other than the Attorney General of the United States to locate you, Mr. Assistant Director, and assign you personally to a murder investigation in Greenwich, Connecticut."

"Why the hell is he assigning me to murders? That's not my purview! That's not even federal jurisdiction."

"Evidently, it is. Get in touch with Special Agent in Charge Frank McCourt in the Greenwich office. He'll fill you in on all the details—but it looks like you're going to be able to wrap up the investigation you're doing right now."

"What . . . what do you mean?"

"One of the vics is Roland Troth!"

Stanton Frazier shook his head in frustration. "I am not amused, you asshole!"

"Well, you should be," James LeCroix said while half-chucking. "Don't you get it, man, we're free. We're absolutely free!"

Not knowing what to think or believe, Stanton Frazier hung up the phone and tossed it into the passenger seat. He had to think.

*****

Two telephone conversations had been flagged for analysis by human intelligence. The system automatically picked up on words, phrases and even the context of the conversations and signaled HUM-INT to analyze data if specific parameters were met. The system also had a list of people and numbers to monitor. If both conditions were satisfied—a designated special topic with a designated person of interest—the call was digitally recorded and sent to a special computer bank for further analysis. At the same time, alerts were electronically sent out to any and all named parties or agencies whom had added or flagged a name or a topic on the filtering list. It was that person's or that agency's responsibility to listen to the phone conversation and decide what, if anything, should be done.

Andrew Stevens was the one who had flagged the names and numbers of the people whose calls were intercepted. Using the name of the Director of the CIA, and the daily password he established, he had access to everything.

Electronic notices for the calls were sent out and routed to the estate on Cape Cod. Both alerts connected the callers in multiple ways with multiple key words and topics. The selection matrix of the filtering program lit up like a Christmas tree. In the intelligence world's parlance, such a high rate of hits would be rated as a "four-sigma" for actionable intelligence.

Andrew listened to both calls; one originating from Michelle Alvarez-Rivera to the manager in Pittsfield and the other from James LeCroix to Stanton Frazier, who appeared to be driving away from Pittsfield. The call between a DOJ Assistant Attorney General and the Assistant Director of the FBI alerted Andrew those two would have to be monitored more closely. He logged a note to an affiliate in Greenwich. Stevens already knew Troth was dead because he had listened to everything from a bug transmitting audio from Troth's estate. The call between Michelle Alvarez-Rivera to the manager in Pittsfield was something else all together.

He pressed a few buttons and wirelessly transferred the audio he wanted to keep to his IPad. Then, he used a system administrator's override to cleanse the MIN-OPS network of any reference to the calls or the people involved. What was taking place was much too important to allow for any government interference. Once satisfied there were no traces of activity, he stood up from the computer terminal and hustled away to find Maxwell York.

He did not like the idea of waking York up, but he had no choice. As important as the news was, what he had to tell his boss couldn't wait.

"Mr. York? Maxwell?"

"Yes, Andrew. What is it?"
"It's done. It's over—Troth is dead."

Chapter Twenty

Two muscular men dressed in stylish, navy blue suits stood right outside of the mansion. The barrels of their sub-machine guns poked out from the bottom of their jackets. They also had matching wrap-around sunglasses covering their eyes and flesh-toned ear pieces with a short wire tucked into the back of their shirt. The taller man was smoking while the man on the left touched his chest and spoke into his cuff. "East perimeter, all clear, over." Off in the distance, Maxwell York could be seen shuffling along the walkway in his silk robe. His gray hair whipped back with the wind.

Standing in the security room inside the mansion, Stevens looked over the newly installed bank of monitors. The old system of cameras and motion detectors had failed miserably. Sampson not only made it onto the estate, but right into the house with no one knowing a damn thing. Andrew was going to make sure nothing like that ever happened again and that Maxwell York was safe.

He turned to the new head of his security team, a short black man with a barrel chest, bald head, and a neatly trimmed goatee and asked, "When will the instillation be done."

"Three days, tops, Mr. Stevens."

Carl Simmons was a former high-ranking employee of Blackwater. Although no longer employed by the firm, his connection to the military contracting community made it possible for him to draw from more than 2,500 former special forces members for individual assignments. The jobs Simmons took with private citizens were usually a lot less profitable unless special circumstances were involved. Carl's firm had a force of ten men handling the immediate concerns at the Maxwell York estate.

"Good. I don't want a mosquito getting in here without me knowing about it." He reached up and rubbed the place where his earlobe used to be and then turned to the valet. "Stuart, summon the crew for me, and tell Becky I want an update on her progress."

"Very good, sir." Stuart turned on a heel and left.

As Andrew and Carl watched, the monitors on the walls tracked Stewart's movements through the house, switching views as he went from zone to zone.

"This is going to work out just fine," Andrew said aloud, not directly addressing Carl.

Less than a minute later, Steve, Raymond, and Becky all cluttered into the newly converted security room. Stevens had watched them leave the computer room and rush over. They reacted the way he had hoped, promptly, with deference.

When they entered the room, he addressed them all. "As you know, we're moving onto a new stage and Mr. York has given me complete operational control. We'll be leaving here soon and your back-ups will be coming in to assist Mr. York. Things will be changing quickly, so we need to be on our toes."

It didn't take long for Andrew to walk them through the new security system and explain the set-up. The ID tags and motion sensors all made sense and even the discomforting presence of the stout, dour Carl Simmons went over smoothly once they became better acquainted.

Andrew explained, "After that maniac Sampson showed us how easy it is to infiltrate this place, we had no choice but to upgrade—so he actually did us a favor by pointing out how vulnerable we were."

Finally, Stevens led them all back to the computer room. Maxwell York was following his usual routine, walking through the gardens at the back of the estate, slowly making his way to his favorite spot so he could stare out to the ocean and think. As was their practice, York left Stevens in charge to handle things.

The three others were used to taking orders directly from Stevens as if they were coming from York himself—although on this particular day, the subordinates were surprised York chose not to do the briefing himself.

Andrew took the lead position in the room. With a serious, semi-scowl on his face, he looked sternly at his subordinates and asked, "Are we all ready to kick this thing off?"

They lowered their heads so Stevens could not see the look of trepidation in their eyes. They knew the time had come for the final stages, the execution of what had been planned for years, but none of them could bring themselves to accept it was really going to happen.

"Becky, did you bring what I asked for?"

Dressed smartly and with her hair in a bun, Becky looked every bit the businesswoman. She had a Masters in Finance from Wharton and a degree in Political Science from Duke and because of her intelligence and trustworthiness she was Steven's top deputy. With security and secrecy such serious matters, her duties often included tasks someone with much less education could handle.

"Yes, Andrew." Becky extended her arm and handed him an IPad. "The encrypted messages we sent out made the rounds and you'll see replies from everyone except for the partners in the eastern-most time zones. As far as D.C. goes, we got acknowledgments from our people in every cabinet department except for State."

"Who's our man at State?"

"Robert Easton."

"Call him personally." Stevens directed. "Steve, I want you to get in touch with First Vice President Reza Rahammami and Admiral Mohammad. Route it to Tehran through Israel."

"Okay. That shouldn't be a problem." Steve rubbed an acne bump on his swarthy face. "What do you want me to tell them?"

"Tell them Mr. York is moving things up. He wants the mining to commence as soon as possible."

"Are you out of your mind? We're not ready for that yet!" Steve protested. "We need at least another week, maybe two."

"We can't wait, Steve. You know we can't control everyone, everywhere—and if we wait that long there may be a leak. We have to use the element of surprise . . . well, as much as we can get. You just heard Becky, everyone's already on notice something is going to happen—it's up to them how they react."

"Andrew, this is all your doing isn't it?" Raymond asked icily.

Andrew held up a restraining hand, "No, Ray, this isn't my idea—Maxwell is the one who made the decision and that's why we're going to New York. We'll be staying at the war room on the Upper West Side to manage the situation ourselves."

In dissension, Ray complained, "What are the other partners going to say? What are they gonna do, Andrew?"

Stevens silenced the complaining chorus of his associates with a hard stare and tightened lips. "I've given the order and whether the partners like it or not, it's time to make our move."

Becky asked in exasperation, "I don't understand, what changed? Why are we being so rash?"

"It's not for you to question these decisions—but I trust Maxwell. Last night, I advised him we'd intercepted intelligence concerning a major discovery—a gold deposit in Canada that's big enough to disrupt the markets and upset everything."

"How big?" "Who made the discovery?" "Where?" "Is this connected to the Seven Rams Trust?" The three associates shot out questions, each tripping over the other for answers.

Stevens held his palms up to stifle them. "I know, You'll get a full report soon—let's just say York is motivated to get things started and get started now. If the amount of gold not under our control increases materially, that will upset our plans."

"If we don't control the currency, we don't control shit," Raymond commented to no one in particular.

Steve added, "So, what's the move—how do we get control of the gold?"

"Do we have to use gold as the currency?" Becky asked.

The confused and concerned subordinates kept on stepping all over each other when they spoke, trying to get answers. Andrew was doing his very best to respond but the questions quickly became debates and discussions between them.

"Are you serious?" Raymond asked incredulously, "I'd give it five-years, max, before everything fell apart if we tried to institute a fiat currency again—it has to be something tangible."

"So, use precious metals—but why not simply set price controls and use mandated gold reserves?"

Seeing they were getting nowhere fast, Andrew cut in brusquely, "Enough! We can't sit here and debate—we've got work to do."

So, what's York's plan?"

Stevens paused, reaching up to rub his chin. "Whoever guessed this is coming from that gold trusts was right. They were the ones who made the find and they're going public with the news within days. We can't let that happen. We've been following them ever since they disclosed the fact that they'd been hoarding gold and sold tons of it to the South Korean Central Bank, right?"

"Right," Steve responded.

"And, what do we know about them?"

"We know that they've been in operation for decades but weren't on anyone's radar screen because they were selling relatively small amounts of gold. Plus, they used offshore accounts and dummy firms to collect premiums and hedge using derivatives."

Raymond added, "We also know they took over the banks in PA They've got teams of lawyers all over the place to handle their businesses without breaking laws or getting any bad press."

Andrews turned to Becky and directed the next question to her. "What is it, then, that's protecting them and keeping us from controlling the operation? What's stopping us from buying out or simply taking over the major gold deposit they just found?"

Becky smiled, knowing the answer without any further prodding. "What they have with all of that organization and structure is the rule of law . . . They're protected because they're legit."

"So, if there's no rule of law, they can't control the outcome, or who takes what from them, can they?" Steve chimed in.

"Exactly! the plan is to induce a panic right now and force the government to implode. That way, we can alter the playing field and get control of that gold mine. After we come in as the saviors to the commoners, we'll restore the rule of law—but it will be our law and we will be in total control." Andrew explained the last part with a flourish.

"Why don't we just have the people associated with the trust eliminated and buy up their assets?" Steve asked.

"That would have been feasible a year ago—but now they're filing for an initial public offering and that complicates matters. Too many people are involved— thousands of bankers and lawyers—and if we did something so brazen, that'd tip our hand and, again, things will be out of our control. We have to make this happen on our terms with us guiding each move, every step of the way, or it won't work. Even though the main players, Clearmont, Mezzara, and Jones are dead, and there's still two or three principals. Yeah, we could kill them off, but not right now."

Raymond took the conversation back, "If we seize control—it doesn't matter what we do—if we are the law, we can seize their assets whenever we want, right?"

"Yeah, but from the PR perspective, there's already too much negative press and if anything like the seizure of property is traced back to us—before we have the legal authority to do it—the public wouldn't react well. Remember, we've got to get and keep the people on our side for this to work. Based on that, I agree we should act now," Becky chimed in.

"After we establish ourselves and get what we want, we'll restore some semblance of order and enforce our laws. You just have to have faith in the process." Andrew was all but beaming.

Steve looked concerned. He asked, "What if it doesn't work? What if everything gets out of hand and we can't restore order?"

There was no delay in Andrew's reaction. He laughed and said with irony in his voice, "It may not matter. Hamilton Genomics will probably wipe us all out with their genetic manipulations."

All of them stood silently and no one else laughed. The three facing Andrew Stevens immediately recognized the fact that he didn't answer the question Steve asked— and they knew he didn't have an answer. Losing control of a revolution, a revolution they were going to cause, was a tremendous risk, for sure. But, by bringing up the one thing that bothered them all the most—the biological engineering part of the plan, he managed to distract them from the prospect of failure.

They had little faith in what had been deemed "creative destruction" of the population, yet they were still involuntary participants. A failure of the genetic program was a grim prospect. But, what was done was done. There was no going back. The subordinates were caught in their own thoughts and just stared at their feet.

Wanting acknowledgment Andrew chided, "Come on, Raymond, Steve, don't tell me you're not afraid of what might happen—what they could do to us?"

"I don't know, Andrew, we've seen and read the studies . . ."

Becky added, "Well, does it matter? It's too late now."

"The wrong genetic mutations and the human race just might be wiped out—to me that matters." Raymond interjected.

"What do you propose we do?" Steven asked. His posture indicated that he was unsure of which way to go.

"Forget about it and do our jobs," Andrew replied, "We're not going to just sit back and let things happen. We have direct control of over $200 billion dollars in assets, liquid, and if everything works out the way it's supposed to, all of us will be part of something unprecedented in the history of mankind. With the backing of Maxwell York, we—the four of us—will be in control of America. What more could you ask for?"

"How about making it through the next few months alive?" Steve offered. "I mean, shit, we could be dead right now if Sampson came at us like it was a wild west saloon."

Just a mention of the experience made Andrew compulsively reach up and touch his ear. "Well, there's some good news on that front. Because Sampson accomplished his primary mission so efficiently by finding out where the mine is, and how they're getting at the gold, we no longer have any use for him. Mr. York has given me the okay to have that nut eliminated." Stevens pressed a button on the intercom and ordered, "Carl, can you rejoin us?"

"How do you know Sampson got that information?" Raymond asked.

"Ah, Raymond, ye of little faith as far as technology is concerned. Sampson was using a device designed and produced by one of the start-ups we funded. An undocumented feature of that magical little device is for a remote handler to turn it on and listen in a user's conversations without the user knowing."

"How did you know he wasn't going to pull out the battery?" "He did pull out the main battery, but there's an auxiliary one inside that can only be removed by cracking it open. Otherwise, it's activated when we want and becomes a roving microphone."

Steve asked, amazement in his voice, "So, you've heard everything he's said since he left here?"

"Almost everything—including Sampson getting the details on that mine you've been trying to locate from Susan DiGiovanni." Carl Simmons was the one who responded as he walked through the door. "We've been able to track him and monitor him after he resupplied. Then, we monitored his movements until the DiGiovanni woman made a call. After that, the signal faded. By then, though, we knew where he was and conducted surveillance from the air."

"And he didn't know about it?"

"He had no idea."

"Those drones are amazing, aren't they?" Andrew asked proudly, as if he personally had a part in inventing the UAV.

"So, where's he at and why is that woman with him?"

"It doesn't matter. I don't want you to be concerned about him." Carl responded. "Major Daniel

Sampson was once a part of the Marine Corps and he severed his country honorably, but now he's as good as dead."

Chapter Twenty One

Over the past few years, the FBI's Greenwich field office had been forced to make provisions for the press. The number of arrests and charges filed against hedge fund managers had gone through the roof, as had the number of media inquires. Special Agent in Charge, Frank McCord, hated the press and could barely stand the FBI's own public relations specialists—they were too close to the reporters and every one of them was vying for air time. McCord could never be sure if members of the media team were giving up confidential information about investigations just so they could land a consulting job with one of the networks. With so many leaks over the years, trying to plug the holes was impossible.

Time was up, though. The press was clamoring for details so they could get a sound bite for the evening news. He had to face the burgeoning room full of reporters. McCord knew he couldn't sit on what he knew much longer or else he'd start to catch hell from the higher ups. It wasn't beyond them to call and complain about delays. The jackals would push for information even if rushing things would hurt the investigation. Of course, they didn't care about that. All they cared about were details and it really didn't seem to matter if the details were right or wrong. Frank didn't work that way—not usually—but the intense pressure to solve this case was forcing his hand.

Roland Troth, the famous hedge fund manager, had been found dead on his estate. That would have been bad enough being that Troth was so rich and famous. But, adding in the fact that there hadn't been a murder in Greenwich since the Kennedy incident, and that the FBI had gotten involved almost immediately, had raised the magnitude of curiosity. What made things even worse was that inside the mansion, there wasn't just one vic, there was a massacre.

Three people who were on Troth's household staff were found dead in the basement. They were tied up and their throats slashed. Upstairs, where Troth had been shot in the back of the head, his firm's VP, Gerald Jacobs, had been shot twice, once in the chest and once behind the ear. Finally, there was the gruesome sight of Thomas Jones, a former United States Attorney. He was also McCord's old friend from their days together at the Pittsburgh field office. No one knew exactly what Tommy was doing at Troth's estate, but McCord had known Tommy was going there before he was killed. Besides being familiar with one of the victims personally, the fact that Jones had stopped by prior to going to see Troth raised all kinds of red flags and all kinds of questions.

When Tommy had asked McCord to hold onto the envelope, he never said what was in it. He only asked Frank to keep it safe and he'd be back to get it. Tommy Jones never made it back to pick up what turned out to be two computer thumb drives.

Invited guests visiting the Troth estate would not usually raise any suspicions. The fact that the white Range Rover he had rented from the airport was missing did. There was also evidence of Jones fighting back: the gash on his head and the dislocated limbs reportedly happened before the fatal shot to the back of his head. He was the only victim who had anything resembling defensive wounds. Then, there was what looked like a professional hit—perfect angle, perfect distance—on Troth, Jacobs, and the kill-shot on Jones. It just didn't look like Tommy was the intended target and the six murders sure didn't look random.

There was one other detail about the crime scene that kept on eating at McCord. A tea cup with lipstick on it was found lying on the floor in the room where Troth was killed. A woman who wore Revlon's Perfectly Pink lipstick was out there who either didn't see the person who busted up the place or else she was lying dead somewhere at another scene. If she witnessed the attack and got away, she would have sought help. Or, if she was missing, someone else would have reported it. McCord kept his eyes open for other agency reports, but none had turned up saying a woman was missing. If a woman was in that house and she was either hurt or killed, before long, she'd turn up. Otherwise, she had to be considered a suspect—whoever she was.

The Crime Scene Investigators had the cup in their possession and would be getting DNA, and hopefully prints off of it. Before long, they'd know who the mystery woman was, and, McCord hoped, they'd be able to find her.

McCord knew almost immediately he had to find out what was in the envelope—and on the two thumb drives Tommy had left behind. Once the Greenwich Police put the alert out about the murders and identified Troth and Thomas Jones as victims, he had several members of the tech staff take possession of the drives. They downloaded the contents onto a laptop so they could watch the compressed files. As soon as they saw the recording of Paul Josephs implicating Roland Troth for the terrorist attacks, McCord called the Director of the FBI. The Director put in a conference call with some bigshot at the Justice Department and McCord was ordered to take over the investigation from the locals. Since then, everything had been complete chaos. When Stanton Frazier showed up, McCord was to sign the drives over into his custody and maybe bring some sanity to the situation.

It didn't take long after the FBI took over the investigation at Troth's estate for media to catch wind of what was going on. Before anyone else in the office knew what was happening, the phone started to ring off of the hook and the circus hadn't stopped since.

McCord had to decide if he should link the murderers in Greenwich to the terrorist attacks to justify assuming jurisdiction over the case; or, if he should avoid that topic all together. He knew it would be better to let the bigshots in D.C. disclose the details about jurisdiction. He also knew someone in D.C. was setting him up as the fallguy. If anything went wrong with the investigation, they could blame it on him. The petty politicking had always disgusted him and this was just another case where the higher ups were positioning themselves for minimum responsibility but maximum credit.

Sitting tensely in his office, mulling over what to say to the press, Frank McCord looked out to the series of cubicles lined up right outside of his office door.

The phone on his desk chimed and he picked it up on the first ring. "McCord here."

"Frank, whatever you're doing, stop!"

"Tony, what the hell are you doing and where are you?" McCord barked at his number two.

"Listen, we picked up the security guards who were temping at Troth's estate."

"Yeah? Do they know anything we don't already know?"

"They lawyered up."

"Why the fuck would they do that . . . unless—"

"Unless they were hiding something. The funny thing is, when we first talked to them, they claimed to not know Troth was dead, that they'd been away fishing."

"So why'd they clam up on you?"

"Because of what we found in their company van— a very rare, very expensive painting."

"So, they were ripping Troth off and that's why they thought you were coming after them?"

"Exactly, and they put on a great act when we told them about the mess we found at the house."

"So, why are you calling me about this?"

The mirth in Scene Coordinator Tony Giambi's voice could be heard as he gushed, "Because when we searched the van and we found the fucking murder weapon!"

"The one that killed Troth?" McCord was in shock. "How do you know?"

"Well, we don't for sure, but there was blood and brain matter on it and the weapon is the right caliber. We've asked the Connecticut State Police to run the prelims to get blood types and DNA and to check it for prints. I betcha dimes to donuts the biologicals match the vics."

"Frank McCord cut in, "And if they do, this case isn't ours anymore and I'm fucked."

*****

It was a busy news day. As Stanton Frazier pulled off of I-95, he turned the radio on to see if there were any more crazy developments in Greenwich. The battery in his cell phone had died after so many exchanges between himself, Greenwich, and D.C. The last he had heard, they were off the case and the Attorney General in Connecticut had claimed jurisdiction. Still, he had to see Frank McCord and take custody of the two computer memory devices in his possession since Frazier was already on the road and wanted to clean up any loose ends in Connecticut, he figured he may as well be the one to handle the evidence and maintain the chain of custody.

The fact that two local men who worked for a private security company had been charged with the murders could have—but didn't—simplify matters. Supposedly, they were trying to steal valuables from

Troth's estate, but a lot of what Frank McCord told him about the crime scene just didn't seem to add up to a robbery gone wrong. On the first hand, Stanton thought, there were too many god damn dead bodies. On the second hand, the painting found in the Security Company's van wasn't all that valuable compared to other things that would have been easier to steal and hawk.

Frazier didn't know Troth very well. Even though he had worked for him for decades, their relationship was never anything more than business. The man was a snake and an elitist who had used his money and connections to make billions on Wall Street—using every piece of inside information he could to get ahead. He even had a few of his enemies set up and charged with bogus crimes—but, that was the extent of it. The fact that Troth was murdered could really be related to his crooked dealings—but that was something he would probably never know. Of course, Frazier could never forget, he was the one who sanitized the evidence dealing with Troth's men killing all of those people in Pennsylvania. With the dirtbag LeCroix, they were supposed to try and cover up any possible links as far as Troth was concerned. But, there had been nothing to smooth over other than the fact the men were employed by Troth. Frazier had read all of the reports and there was no evidence whatsoever that Troth knew what his men were going to do. The only evidence against Troth had to do with inside information, not murder. As far as Frazier was concerned, sure, Troth deserved to be locked up and stripped of all his wealth because he obtained it using illegal means, but he did not deserve to have his head blown off.

*****

Assistant Director Stanton Frazier cruised slowly down Maple Street and turned down Barker Avenue towards the new Greenwich FBI offices. Greenwich was teeming with reporters and he had seen news vans and satellite trucks lining the streets in front of City Hall when he had drove past. Luckily, the reporters were no longer staking out the FBI's offices. From what he had been told reporters had even established an encampment outside of Troth's property. They had been trying to breech the fence and get onto the grounds for exclusive photos of the crime scene. Nothing like this had ever happened in such a swanky town and it seemed that the talking heads were in a feeding frenzy over this particular horror story.

Once inside of the FBI office, guided away from the hustle and bustle of the cubicles into McCord's office, Frazier dispensed with all of the formalities. Having been a Special Agent himself, he was not so much into ceremony—and quickly got down to business. He took the seat opposite of McCord's desk while gesturing for the subordinate to remain seated.

"Okay, Frank, what are we gonna do with this mess?"

"I don't know, Assistant Director—"

"Please, just call me Stan."

"Okay, Stan. Listen, the Connecticut State Police have the scene locked down—that's their right—but there's a lot about this case that isn't adding up."

"Yeah, Frank, I feel the same way, but what do we have to bring this back to our jurisdiction? I'm gonna be straight forward with you here—and I just want your honest, profession opinion—do we even want to try to retain jurisdiction?"

McCord rubbed the grayish hairs on his stubble-covered chin. "Is this off the record?"

"Yeah, it's off the record."

"Personally, I don't want anything to do with a messed-up scene with all kinds of conflicting evidence.

There's just too much telling me—telling my gut—to run like hell from this one."

Stanton stood up and extended his thin, dark hand over McCord's desk. "I appreciate your honesty, Frank, and, I have to tell you, I feel the same way about this dog. The only thing is, aren't these the kinds of crazy cases the ones we signed on to crack?"

"Maybe twenty years ago, yeah. These days . . . I'm not so sure."

"I get your drift. Okay, give me those drives and I'll take them back to D.C. with me."

With a look of relief in his face, McCord put a clear plastic evidence baggie into Frazier's hand and slid the preprinted chain-of custody evidence sheet across his desk.

"As far as this case goes, I'm going to report back to James LeCroix at DOJ and let him decide, but I'll add my recommendation to let Connecticut handle it. In the mean time, just ask the locals to keep you in the loop and send you copies of any reports. And, by the way, do it politely, Frank. We don't need to ruffle any feathers."

"I hear ya, Stan. Anything else?"

"Yeah, one more thing. You were telling me there was evidence of a woman in that house and you had some biological evidence on her. Did that go anywhere?"

McCord stood up, escorting Frazier to the door and towards the lobby. "Yeah, but she's a ghost—not part of any criminal system. The State Police asked for an assist to run her DNA and prints nationally as a missing person/potential crime victim. No hits at all. On top of that, there haven't been any reports about a woman missing anywhere in the country."

"I guess that shouldn't surprise me and this woman is either running scared or she's with the killers."

Because of the amount of carnage, they all believed more than one person had done the killing—and hanging the crime on the two security guards was simply the path of least resistance.

"I don't think she's with the killers—we've got evidence of her running from the scene."

"What do the security guards say? Did they get her name when she came in?"

"They've said nothing. Like I told you, they lawyered up."

"Shit. You know what? You're right—this is their mess. I'm going to lay it on thick on that lawyer from Justice, LeCroix, that we should blow this chicken coop and move on."

"That's you're call, Stan. Let me tell ya, though, you won't hear about me calling D.C. complaining about it."

"Good. It's good to know you're with me on this."

"With you?," McCord chuckled, "I need to investigate a clusterfuck murder scene like I need a hole in the head."

"By the way, what was the woman's name?"

"Susan DiGiovanni. But, like I said, we've got bupkus on her.

Frazier rubbed the rough stubble on his chin. "Her again? Hmm, I'm going to have to find that woman."

"What was that, Stan?"

"Oh, nothing, never mind."

Chapter Twenty Two

They had been on the road for days. The unobtrusive blue minivan took a circuitous route all the way to Maine over seldom-used roads. They even traversed a few logging trails in the back country, making sure they weren't being tailed. Once they felt safe, Sampson stole a black SUV and they backtracked. By then, they had heard on the radio that the security guards were arrested and charged with six murders at Troth's estate in Greenwich. With no one on their tail, they felt safe enough to use more direct and heavily traveled routes. When they reached the border of Massachusetts they got back on the Interstate.

It was easy to make good time cruising through the Bay State. Off-season on Cape Cod meant almost no traffic, and once they were on the Cape, there were few people around to notice what appeared to be nothing more than an attractive middle-aged couple traveling down Route 6. Sampson refueled the vehicle and then they checked in at a small bed and breakfast right outside of Osterville.

While he carried up the items he thought he'd need, Susan showered and dressed in some extraordinarily expensive casual clothes they had picked up at a small shop.

During the drive, Susan and Dan had gone from hostility to an uncomfortable silence to polite chatter. That eventually evolved until the familiarity brought Susan a measure of comfort. She figured if he had wanted her dead, she would already be shedding rotted flesh from her bones. The more the comfort level between them increased, the more they engaged in their game that resembled, "Truth or Dare" without the dare option.

For every question Susan asked, Dan came back with one of his own. Even though they were both honest, each answer became increasingly candid. A closeness was also brought on from the sense of being on the run together.

However, the game they played was not symmetrical because the players didn't have the same objectives.

Sampson started out his friendly interrogation with softball questions, trying to put her at ease and get her to talk about herself. If nothing else, the tactic gained him favorable personality points. He asked her how old she was, where she was born, where she grew up, and where she went to school. Susan, for her part, answered honestly. But, when it was her turn to ask a question, she was much more focused on the situation at hand.

The last thing she expected was for him to be as informative as he was. In response to her questions, he told her all he knew about Troth and who the people behind him really were. He outlined the steps York's cabal had taken to corner the markets in natural resources and obtain as much property as they could. Because there were pieces of the puzzle he was intimately familiar with, he was able to paint a very clear, seamless picture while skillfully expunging his participation in the events.

He went on to link what he knew about the Federal Reserve, some politicians and the manipulation they used to gain control of property. When it came to the government, Susan had doubts, substantive questions about the veracity of what he was telling her. It seemed improbable that any such a group had the capacity to pull off something of such magnitude. To answer her doubts, he explained how everything worked, to the best of his understanding—how the regulators, cartels, oligarchies, and corporate directors were not organized like some mass secret conspiracy of elites. Instead, they were like a social clubs and where the higher-ups selected winners and losers. As Sampson had discovered and was explaining to Susan, the succession of CEOs and even success of companies was preordained. Successfulness would come quickly to those who followed "advice" given by an "acquaintance." The advice given as an order, but as friendly counsel bestowed

225

in cozy country club locker rooms or over dinner and drinks. Disaster would befall anyone who shunned the advice or those who followed their own paths. Even to someone like Sampson, who was not connected to those circle, it made perfect sense. The older members were able to quickly weed out the rebels or independent thinkers and retain the greedy, weak-willed sycophants to do their bidding.

It was through that process almost all companies and resources were actually controlled by the people at the top. Their power and wealth increased without having to divulge anything at all about the ultimate goals—other than it being a way to make the super-rich that much richer. As he put it, wrapping up his little lecture, no further motivation was necessary.

Susan seemed to buy into everything she was told because she knew what Dan was saying wasn't some elaborate delusion. Too many people had died, too much money was involved. The sky was actually falling. As they talked, she grew more confident what she was hearing was true because the same topics—at least the overview of the topics—coincided perfectly with what Donny, Mario, Michelle, and Tommy had taught to her—the long lectures she had endured when they were sequestered in Costa Rica. That she was able to recognize some of the names and events made the story that much more compelling.

As they progressed on their drive, his questions started to get harder for Susan to rejoin—not because she didn't know the answers—but because they touched on her emotionally raw nerves. What she was being asked to divulge was eminently personal. Sampson asked her to explain what happened to her husband. He asked about her children and where Chris and Lisa were staying. With only slight hesitation, she told him and she did not lie. He asked how she met Donald Clearmont and about his death in the Metropolitan Corrections Center. Susan wasn't aware he already knew most of the details, or that he was weighing each one of her responses toward her honesty. If she lied, he would know.

As painful as it had been for her to disclose the sensitive, emotional circumstances of her life, Sampson started to believe more and more that Susan was unique, a one in a million. He sensed she was a woman he could count on—almost trust—because she had not lied to him. It made her unparalleled in relation to everyone he had ever known and her bluntness affected him more than he cared to admit—even to himself. The last thing he ever expected, something he couldn't even put a label on, was that during their long drive together, he would start to feel something for her.

When she came out of the shower, Susan's hair was still wet. She was fully clothed in new jeans and a button-down red and blue striped white shirt under a green fleece. She had traded in her high-heeled black pumps—which had been destroyed during her run—for a pair of Doc Martin boots. It was the most rugged outfit they could find on such short notice.

Then, she noticed her big Gucci bag sitting on the floor next to the king-sized bed. She hadn't seen it in the van. That made her wonder how long Dan had spent in Troth's house after the attack. How could he have packed his stuff and found her stuff before leaving what he had described as a hectic shoot-out? Reaching for her bag and pulling out a brush and some make-up, she dismissed the thought and told herself she would ask about it later.

Sitting at the dressing table, she looked at her reflection and brushed her hair. The lines around her eyes and lips did seem deeper, or was that her imagination, she wondered? She heard the key in the lock and watched as Dan entered carrying Styrofoam clamshell trays and a paper bag.

"Susan, we've got eats," he announced cheerfully.

"What did you get?" As she asked this, her stomach growled.

"Steak and eggs or fried clams and french fries—and to drink, soda, coffee, and a bottle of Johnny Walker Red to drown our sorrows."

"Oh, you are an angel! Hand over the clams, big boy, and keep your hands at a safe distance!"

Sampson handed her the top tray and sat his own on the table. She cracked it open and inhaled deeply.

"Umm, these fries are headed right to my ass and I don't care."

He looked at her and deadpanned, "I don't blame 'em. I'd head right for your ass, too."

The joke shocked her. It wasn't the suggestive comment but the situation they were in. Ever since she regained consciousness in the van, and for the hours they talked, it was the first time he had really let his guard down or was even the slightest bit scabrous. Susan knew how attractive she was and wasn't fazed by men's inappropriate comments. But, that he even thought of her in that way, with so much else going on, took her by surprise. She looked into his eyes to try and divine where he was coming from. What she saw was amusement—not deception.

"My turn to clean up." Sampson grabbed a bag and walked to the bathroom. He started to strip, not bothering to shut the door.

She tried to avert her eyes and picked delicately at the food, her hunger somehow diminished. Trying to sound conversational, she asked, "Okay, so whose turn is it?"

"Whose turn is it for what?" He spoke and lathered soap over the thick patch of whiskers at the same time.

"To ask a question. I don't remember who went last."

She couldn't help herself. Out of the corner of her eye, and gradually, more candidly, she watched Dan's

228

naked torso; the way his taught body was put together, the way his muscles rippled as he moved his arms. Something she did not expect started to happen, she felt her body starting to react. Unwilling to go there, Susan consciously forced herself to look away and maniacally stuff several French fries into her mouth. Then, she took a long sip from the straw of the soda hoping the cold would help her stop sweating.

Sampson took out several disposable razors and started to shave. "I guess it's your turn—go ahead and ask your question."

"Okay, how can all of these CEOs and politicians work together and not get caught? I mean if everything they're doing is causing the economy to fall apart, how come no one stops them?"

He smiled in the mirror and looked back at her using the mirror's reflection. "Because who is there to stop them? Your question assumes there is someone in government who is trustworthy, and powerful enough, to take on the people who hold all the cards. Besides, no matter what anyone claims, they'd never understand what's going on. I mean, you could give them the connections between the bankers and other industrialists, the same people controlling everything, and they still wouldn't get it. Instead, the authorities would hold them up as paragons of success. Prosecutors could try to reconstruct the hierarchy—but they'd do it in their own image, because they've got no imagination. It's more like a multi-layered spider web than a ladder with one big boss at the top. Even Roland Troth didn't really understand the scope."

"How could that be? I mean, like, if there's no one person in charge how do they communicate?"

Sampson smirked. "That's another question. It's not your turn."

Susan clucked her tongue, rolled her eyes, and whined, "Go ahead."

"Okay, I'll give you a freebie on this one. It's not a homogeneous group like the Mafia. These people are nowhere and everywhere at the same time—they're legitimate business men and women, lawyers, politicians—and they're doing exactly what everyone expects them to do. So, how do the things they want done get done? Because they're all working for their own self-interest.

"If someone get support and financing to do nothing but get richer and richer, that's exactly what they're gonna do . . . that's all any of these people do—because the common cause is to let capitalism run its course. The endgame in capitalism is that there's a small group of winners and then there is everyone else. It's a zero-sum game. Get it? Good. Now, it's my turn. Who is that woman you mentioned, Michelle Rivera?"

"Michelle—well, she's this amazing woman, super smart, and she's basically running the entire business on her own." Susan had a unsteady look in her eyes, not knowing where to focus.

As she talked, he rinsed his clean-shaven face and checked the mirror for any spots that he missed. When she finished describing all of Michelle's attributes, he asked, "Who else is named in these trusts?"

"Isn't that another question, Dan?"

"Okay, you got that one—you're up." Casually, he dropped his boxers and stepped into the shower, sliding the glass door closed behind him.

With the water running, Susan raised her voice so she could be heard. "So how did these people get so powerful? I really didn't understand that part."

Hollering over the water, he answered, "They manipulate markets. They do things like create asset bubbles and then they pop them. When everyone else is selling to save their ass, the prices drop to the floor. That's when they step in and buy at a huge discount. They feed on other peoples' financial misery like locusts."

"That's what they did with the housing market and mortgages, right?"

Sampson turned the water off and ducked his head out of the shower, looking directly at her. He tilted head teasingly, then stepped out of the shower, completely naked and dripping wet.

Susan caught her breath and, acting indifferent, averted her eyes. She hoped he did not see her blush. Her cheeks were hot with embarrassment. Still, she was quite impressed by what she saw.

Reaching for a towel, he went on without missing a beat, "Susan, that's another question."

"Oh, come on!" She pouted. She was unable to avert her eyes as he pulled up his jeans and buttoned them closed.

He walked out of the steamy bathroom shirtless. His face was bare and, after getting cleaned up, he was even more handsome than she realized. Because he was standing, she could see under his chin where there was a scar that looked like he had work done on his face—it was too small and neat to have been caused by an injury. Looking at his fit chest and arms, she quickly forgot all about the scar. On his chest was a unique, detailed tattoo she recognized as something from the Marine Corps.

Susan stood and walked over the table closer to where he was standing, adding salt and pepper to his eggs. "Okay, Dan, it's your turn—ask away."

"Tell me everything you know about that big mine in Canada." Sampson picked up the cold T-bone steak with his hand and gnarled off a chunk.

Looking at him curiously, she answered, "I really don't know that much about it. Its north of British Colombia, somewhere in the Yukon, and it's right beside a big lake that's frozen most of the time. They can only work it something like 100 days a year."

Its isolation and the limit on working days explained why York's people were unable to find it. At the wrong time of year, no one would be up there. "How did they find it?"

"It goes back to the 1970's when satellites were mapping the surface of the Earth. I guess they bounced some kind of waves off the land masses and recorded the signals when they bounced back. The father of that guy I told you about, Donny, he figured out a way to find minerals off of the charts the satellites made."

"Is it like a big strip mine where they tear up the ground?"

"Why are you so interest in this mine? Besides, that's more than one question!" Susan protested.

"Well, I did ask you to tell me everything you know about the mine . . . I'm just asking follow-up questions. And, the reason I'm asking about the mine is because it's a big part of the mess you're in."

In his mind, Sampson loved the idea of getting the information he needed directly from her and save himself a trip up to the arctic. Just a few more details and he'd be able to give a full report to Maxwell York and without ever leaving the country.

"Good point." she responded emphatically.

"So is it a strip mine?" he asked again.

"No. They've been using a horizontal drilling system they learned from the oil and gas industry, but instead of bringing up oil, they're bringing up mineral cores."

"Like the ice samples the climate guys get?"

"I guess? I don't know—I never saw 'em."

"Wait a minute—that can't be right." He took another bite of the meat. He chewed a few times and asked, "Doesn't it take tons and tons of dirt to get just a little gold?"

Susan smiled. "Yeah, I thought that, too—like watching people in movies pan for gold."

"Right."

"What I was told was that's flake gold—or what they call placer gold. Placer gold is the stuff that the earth erodes and churns up to the surface. But this gold they found in Canada is rock gold, and it's in thick veins and each, like, 15 or 20-foot core they pull up has a lot of almost pure gold in it."

He whistled. "That's a lot of gold . . . but I still don't understand, veins of gold aren't in a straight lines . . . so how do they—"

"Please don't ask me to get all technical on you— but it has something to do with the special bits they use. They can somehow insert sensors into the many holes they make under the lake and bounce all kinds of waves in the bedrock. If quartz is found or a hard metal is down there, the waves bounce back a certain way—I think they call it an echo—and they map where the metal is.

"Why quartz?"

"Because gold and quartz are usually found together. That's where they drill. I honestly don't know anything more about it . . . but I do know they take the cores to another site for processing. The ore that's left isn't pure, so it's shipped to the Port of Newark and then trucked to Pittsfield to be smelted—but everyone already knows about that. Okay, my turn to ask a question."

Sampson smiled, knowing he had gotten all of the information he needed. "Go ahead, shoot."

"Okay, this is going to be an easy one. Were you ever married?" Susan's eyes met his and she knew the answer before he said it.

"No." He dropped the meatless bone back into the Styrofoam container and looked deep into her eyes. Suddenly, the animation left his eyes and he turned serious.

233

"Your question is this: What exactly happened at that farm in Pittsfield, Susan?"

She let the half-eaten meal drop from her hands onto the table. Her mouth hung open and she was clearly stunned, "How the fuck do you know about that?"

A cascade of images flashed behind her eyes. She smelled odors that were not there and exploding sounds that did not exist. The memory of her shooting and killing a man flooded her brain. Unable to block out the horror of that event, and the bitter pain of losing Tommy, was briefly freed from the bounds of repression. "I . . . I can't talk about it."

Tears of sadness spilled down her cheeks.

Chapter Twenty Three

Waking up in Dan's arms would not have been the worst thing in the world. No matter how strong and independent she was, having someone to hold onto and lean on would help ease the pain. Plus, from her perspective, the man was what she deemed a real hottie, someone she wouldn't mind scratching that itch only a man could reach. After losing her husband, then Donald Clearmont, and seeing so many people close to her killed, it seemed a complete waste of energy to deny herself any worldly pleasure. Despite her looks, the opportunity to engage in a meaningless tryst or similar emotionless erotic encounter had not presented itself in what seemed like forever. With a gorgeous stud right next to her in the same bed, the prospect of getting laid had improved significantly.

Dressed in nothing but panties and a t-shirt, Susan was comfortably tucked under the thick goose-down comforter spread over her body and the bed. Sleep had come easily because of her state of exhaustion and the psychic numbing of a few shots of whiskey. By morning, the emotions of loss—along with the memories of fear and horror—were successfully buried; once again deeply suppressed into her subconscious. What was manifest in its place was a deep need to be close to another human being. As she stirred, she felt the urges make themselves known through her tender, erect nipples and moistening loins.

Even though seducing Dan was her plan, actually sleeping with him wasn't what Susan intended. They took only one room because they didn't want to draw any attention. A middle-aged couple traveling together on Cape Cod getting separate rooms may have raised some eyebrows. Besides, the rooms had king sized beds, so no further thought went into the sleeping arrangements.

Still drowsy, and not yet connected to reality, Susan turned over and reached for Dan. In her mind, even if he dared deny her what she craved—at least she'd be able to cozy up to that manly, hard body for a few minutes. When she didn't feel his presence and reached over further, she realized his side of the bed was empty and opened her eyes.

Sitting up and wiping the sleep from her eyes, she looked around the room and saw a lot of strange changes had taken place while she slept. The dressing table had been moved from its original location and was sticking half-way out of the bathroom. The mirror that had been attached to it was now standing upright—leaning against the foot of the bed. Beside it was another smaller mirror at a severe angle, pointing towards the partially draped windows. The television was on, but the sound was off and flashing images were being reflected toward the windows. She could see the top of the dressing table had been cleared off, but from her angle, she couldn't see what was on the side hidden in the bathroom.

Waking up even more with every moment, Susan heard a light scratching sound coming from the bathroom and then the sound of something like pebbles falling on the tile floor. "What the hell?" she asked herself as she flipped the covers aside and swung her legs over the side of the bed. Cautiously, she crept on tiptoes over to the bathroom.

When she looked in, Dan was standing on the dressing table and had some strange device attached to a huge knife. Looking closer, she recognized what had once been a wooden hanger and a canvass belt. The belt was tied between the ends of the hanger and the hilt of the knife was looped in the middle. He was putting pressure on the end of the knife while using the contraption like a bow, sawing it back and forth. The point and blade spun quickly as the tip of the knife dug into the ceiling plaster.

"What the hell are you doing?" Susan asked.

236

Sampson didn't stop working. He knew she had woken up by the way her breathing changed. He also knew she'd be over to ask that exact question. He was almost finished drilling a series of holes into the bathroom ceiling with his commando dagger and wanted to get it done, so he didn't bother to look at her when he answered, "We need an alternate exit. We're being watched and if we walk out the door towards the truck, we're dead."

"You've gotta be fuckin' kidding me!" Susan cried in exasperation. "How is that possible." She turned and started to walk toward the window overlooking the area where they had parked on the street."

"Please don't do that, Susan!" The edge in his voice was to stop her from doing something foolish.

"If I don't look, how will we know if they're out there?"

Sampson shook his head, vexed. "Will you please trust me and stay away from the windows?" As he spoke, he jumped off the table.

She stopped and turned, "But, how do you know they're out there?"

"Do you know how they finally caught Bonnie and Clyde?"

"No."

"A posse lured them down a road, forced their car to stop and shot 'em up in an ambush. The reason they did that was because as long as Bonnie and Clyde were on the move, the cops couldn't catch 'em. We stopped and there's an ambush set up for us—I've seen it."

"Dan, are you comparing us to Bonnie and Clyde?"

"No—well, not yet at least. I'm just telling you I know they're out there and they're going to try to take us out before we go mobile."

"What do you mean 'take us out'? What the hell did I do—and who the hell are they? How did I get involved in this shit?" Susan wasn't in a panic, but she was getting there.

"I can tell from how they've set up the kill-zone, they're special forces, probably retired, working as private contractors. As far as who sent them, my best guess is the man I told you about—Maxwell York—or one of his associates. I didn't make a very good first impression with one of 'em."

Convinced that Susan was no longer going to look out the window, Sampson jumped back up onto the dressing table and went back to work drilling evenly spaced holes by hand.

"Why the hell would York want to kill you—I thought you told me he hired you."

"Maybe he changed his mind, that happens a lot, ya know."

Susan walked over to the bathroom door, unable to get in because of the table blocking entry. "So what are we going to do?"

"We're gonna wait until nightfall and use my little escape hatch. The houses on this block are close together, no more than five feet between the awnings. We'll get up to the roof and jump over to each house until we're at the corner and jump down from there, steal a car, and hightail it outta here. If we can manage to get off of Cape Cod alive, we'll be free and clear."

Susan looked depressed, "And then we'll live like Bonnie and Clyde until these goons ambush us, right?"

"No, Susan, we may hit up some banks, all right, but the only weapon we'll need is that brain of yours. And, no, they'll never catch us."

"Dan? Can you get out of the bathroom? I need to pee."

Sampson looked at the table and the door and shrugged. "You're gonna have to crawl in and we can't shut the door." He ducked, took one step and jumped down off of the table.

"You didn't think that one through very well, did ya?" Susan jabbed. She said it as she scooted up on the table.

"If you gave me two more minutes of peace, I would've been done."

He looked up to the hole he was making and then over to watch Susan swing her legs around and get off of the table inside of the bathroom. When she stepped toward the toilet, he noticed the firmness of her legs and the exceptionally detailed, sexy curves of her partially exposed buttocks. Before she turned to face him, he turned away and walked to the dresser on the other side of the room. Looking down, he grabbed the phone-like device he had been using in its disassembled state.

"How did they find us?" she asked. The sound of her voice bounced around the tiny bathroom before hitting his ears.

Raising his voice, he responded. "I'm pretty sure it was my fault. This device isn't an IPhone, even though it looks like one. It's NSA hardware that can tap into the government's spy networks. I think there's a transponder in it."

"Didn't you know that?"

"No. That wasn't listed as a feature."

"So you thought the NSA would tell you everything, huh?" The sarcasm in her voice was biting.

"I didn't get it from the NSA, this is a prototype— and I don't think anyone knows all the features. Besides, I had the battery out most of the time."

"Most of the time . . ." Her mother had always called her a smart-ass but Susan couldn't help herself. She immediately regretted her sharp tongue, but sometimes the wry barbs poured out of her before she even knew what she was saying. She tried to recover quickly by changing the subject, "Dan, I can't pee with you standing there listening."

"Don't be such a baby."

"Just turn up the volume of the TV, please?"

"Okay. Okay." Somewhere deep inside, Sampson wondered if what he was going through was what it was like to be married. The closeness with Susan was something very new to him. It dawned on him that he should sever the alliance forming with her before he had to kill her. As he grabbed the remote and started to turn the sound up, a very strange thought popped into his sociopathic mind. What he felt was something he never experienced before—he doubted he could kill her. Strangely, everything he liked about Susan was solidified in his mind as soon as he heard her relieve her bladder.

The volume of the television overwhelmed the other sounds and they couldn't help but listen to the broadcast. It was an emergency news alert and the anchor sounded frazzled.

" . . . indicate that Iran has, in fact, placed mines along the narrow channel in the Straight of Hormuz. Our sources tell us that, during the night, several civilian vessels left Iran and headed toward strategic points in the straight. The U.S. Navy tracked the ships and believed the ships were commercial fishing vessels. At daybreak, aerial surveillance re-acquired the location of the ships and infrared cameras on several classified unmanned-aerial vehicles detected the vessels lowering large metallic spheres into the straight. Since this overtly hostile action was observed, the Navy has been cautiously searching the area for mines."

"Our sources also tell us that SEAL teams attached to the Fifth Fleet were flown to the scene and engaged the suspected ships. They have, I repeat, they have captured and detained the crews of the ships and the suspects are, at this moment, in route to Bahrain for questioning."

"The Iranian government has just released a statement and proclaimed the seizure of ships bearing Iranian flags an act of war. The President of Iran, however, refused to confirm or deny if, in fact, the government of Iran had mined the straight.

"For those of you just tuning in to this special report, the Straight of Hormuz has reportedly been mined. This waterway, which connects the Persian Gulf to the Gulf of Oman, is two-miles-wide and much of the world's oil supply, up to 15 million barrels per day, pass through the straight on supertanker. As of now, all shipping in the Straight of Hormuz has been suspended until the exact nature and location of the mines can be determined."

"Now, for an update on the economic impact, let's turn to Jim Childs at the futures trading pits in Chicago. Jim?"

"Thank you, Brian. Without that vital supply from the Middle East, we can expect to see ever-increasing record prices for oil despite the President issuing an Executive Order this morning to open up the Strategic Petroleum Reserve. As of five minutes ago, trading in oil futures has halted for the day. Iran's mining of the Straight of Hormuz has put a strangle hold on the world's already tight oil supply and traders in oil futures bid up prices until they tripped the limit-up circuit breaker . . ."

Sampson turned the sound of the television back down and looked over to the bathroom. Susan was standing at the door with her head poked out and a worried expression on her face.

"Dan, does this mean what I think it means?" she asked, not hiding the concern in her voice.

"Yup," he responded dryly. "They just made their move and we're all in for a world of shit. Things are gonna get really ugly from here on out."

241

Chapter Twenty Four

Lucy, a 78-year-old widow, had been living alone and running the bed and breakfast by herself for four years. Up until that night, she had never had a serious problem with a guest. The men who had woken her up from a deep slumber bound her securely to the bed and, if that wasn't bad enough, one of them even put a rag in her mouth and tied a gag around her head—which had completely muddled the curlers in her bluish-gray hair.

Even though her heart was racing from fear, Lucy did not scream or try to move. The men who had subdued her had been so scary it behooved her to listen to them. They had promised if she kept quiet they would set her free as soon as they detained the bad people who had rented a room from her. She had no reason not to believe them. After all, watching the news that night and seeing the country go to hell in a hand basket, Lucy had little trouble believing terrorists were on Cape Cod and sleeping in one of her rooms.

Lying quietly and silently in the dark, she mentally chided her dead husband, Ernie, for not listening to her before he died. They should have sold the place and moved to someplace quieter and safer. She wished he was here beside her so she could give him a piece of her mind.

The squad advanced up the stairs in a row, six-deep. With practiced precision and stealth, they had not made a sound—not even a creak on the stairs. Sending in a six-man crew to assassinate one man in a private residence may have seemed like overkill, but their target was not just another man. They had to take precautions and be prepared for anything. Other than the six men creeping up the stairs, there were two other teams on stand-by secreted outside of the house along with two snipers covering the exits.

Dressed in black, the pointman of the column had electronic gear attached to his head and OLED lenses directly in front of his right eye—the latest advances in infrared no longer relied on the standard scopes and lenses. The pointman engaged night-vision to guide the team while the man directly behind him employed a thermal differential detector allowing him to see waves of body heat and movement through everything except thick concrete or steel.

The others snaking behind the point had their faces obscured with black balaclavas, cloaking their identities. No one observing their maneuvers would ever be able to identify them as long as they were not killed or captured. Each man was armed with their own personal Heckler & Koch MP-5s, modified individually to suit their taste. The weapons were locked and loaded and trained at all potential angle of attack. With the weapons suppressed, the men were not concerned about the neighbors hearing what they thought would be a few precisely placed shots into Major Daniel Sampson's forehead. What they were concerned about were the potential booby traps Daniel Sampson had set for them.

The pointman moved slowly and silently and slid as close as he could to the left of the door. The five other men discretely scooted over the top stair and across the hallway into position behind him. The stack faced the bedroom doorway they were about to enter, the last man turned slightly toward the hallway, guarding their flank and the stairs. Once in position, he squeezed the shoulder of the man in front of him who passed the signal up the line until the pointman knew everyone was good to go.

*****

Even at that late hour, the computer room tucked away inside of the estate of Maxwell York was more active than it had ever been. However, the usual group of proficient men and women who had been working there were gone. They had been replaced by an equally diligent staff of computer experts, bankers, and traders who were almost as competent and completely loyal to Andrew Stevens.

A similar scene of hyper-activity was taking place on the Upper West Side of Manhattan. An inconspicuous office building on 97th Street between Broadway and Amsterdam Avenue was the location of Maxwell York's well-concealed New York headquarters. With no sign out front and situated between a bank and an upscale boutique, no one who strolled past would have an inkling that behind the big glass doors with the big brass handles was one of the most optimally equipped trading facilities in the world.

The souped-up computers racked in the basement were connected to a trunk line and had the fastest, most direct digital access to everything—including direct links to the powerful resources on Wall Street and the Midtown banks. The crew working behind the scenes in Cape Cod were also linked into the Manhattan operation through their own socket—a private, encrypted connection enabling them to provide the New York team with constant updates of government activity.

Under the auspices of MYB, Ltd., Andrew, Becky, Stephen, and Raymond were busy on the top floor of the gold-shaded glass encased building. Since long before dawn that morning, they had been allocating resources—buying and selling commodities all over the world. There was no time to be wasted in their attempt to get the financial world to either bow down to them or bend over for them.

Stevens had managed to beguile his closest compatriots over to his way of thinking and successfully overcome their doubts and fears. The picture he painted for them was that of even more riches and vast power. But, what got them to act to the best of their abilities was the challenge to rock the other partner to their core and change the game forever.

On top of that, they all knew, because of the biological component of Project Stasis, their bloodlines just may come to an end. If their progeny was unable to pass on their genes due to the virus created at Hamilton Genomics, nothing they did really mattered. No one knew the long-term effects of infection or the possible permutations of the man-made viral strain. Although the goal was to reduce the population, it was just as likely that the virus would eventually wipe out all of humanity.

Maxwell York, who had suddenly taken ill, gave Andrew his blessing to do as he pleased and that was when the student finally became the master. The plan he conceived was put into action almost immediately with the alerts Becky sent out to most of the other partners. In the message, he warned of a major announcement they would be putting out and included was a suggestion to either dump or hedge their oil holdings. That move, in reality, was the exact opposite of what they should have done. Because none of the other partners knew the price of oil was actually set to double, they voluntarily put nooses around their own necks.

Andrew and his three allies intuitively knew what they were initiating was bound to happen sooner or later. Even if the elite powerbrokers of the world were able to control all of the world's wealth, and managed to eliminate large segments of the population, it would just be a matter of time before those left in control turned on each other. It would be just another feeding frenzy until the richest and the most powerful among the rich and powerful titans ruled them all. That was human nature and what the future held for any dreams of neo-Feudalism. A first strike strategy would put them at an advantageous position and overwhelm the others.

Using Maxwell York's vast resources to launch a preemptive financial coup against the others—the richest of the rich—meant keeping their intentions secret as long as possible, acting like they were doing York's bidding, and feeding everyone else as much misinformation as they could. Setting up and then cutting down their future competition was what the small, very ambitious group planned. As the action started, both the large war room in Manhattan and the computer room at the York estate on Cape Cod were burning the midnight oil.

*****

The men were crouched down with their weapons at the ready position. The point—who was crouched even lower in front of the door—listened for movement while he checked the door frame and knob for wires or any signs of tampering. A booby-trapped door was the only thing that was standing between them and a successful mission. The pointman saw no unusual markings or wires so he signaled the stack to stay alert for his mark.

Using the thermal detector to reacquire the exact location of the target, he signaled with his hand, indicating two people were in the room were ten paces in and to the left of the doorway. The point held up the hand-signal for the others to stand-by as he stowed away the optical gear and set himself for the take down.

The door was old and made of solid oak with a brass deadbolt lock. Since they couldn't cleanly break through the heavy paneled door, they had to use an alternate means of entry. With a delicate touch, the point pushed a cylinder against the keyhole. When he pushed a button, the canister inserted several tiny titanium feeler rods into the lock. An injector needle filled the shaft and tumblers with a liquid that hardened seconds after it made contact with air. As silently and smoothly as if he was holding the original key for the lock, he turned the device and the door opened.

*****

"Andrew," Becky called out, "we just got an IM sent by the Emir from the Kuwait Investment Authority. He wants to know what the hell is going on with Singapore? He can't trade out of his positions."

"Tell him to suck ice—he's making a killing on his oil."

"What happened to the December oil contracts in Taipei?" Raymond asked.

It spiked up 20% off market, but the imbalance of orders points to at least another few days of up-limit halts in Chicago.

"Becky, I need you to get in touch with either Dave or Bill at Carlyle and ask what they're gonna do with the ten December $2,500 gold contracts—we're giving them one hell of a discount. Either shit or get off the pot—do they want 'em or not?"

"I'm on it, Andy." Becky turned her attention back to the terminal in front of her. The muti-colored screen to her left illuminated her face and the numbers reflected off of her glasses as she typed in the digits. Her voice could barely be heard as she spoke into the mic, "Hi. Sorry to wake you, this is Becky again from MYB, I need to speak with Mr. Rubenstein . . ."

Andrew Stevens turned his attention back to the terminal the furthest back from the entry of the top-floor loft. Displayed on the screen in front of him was a spreadsheet of all of the oil and gold futures contracts he had purchased before the stampede started. The percentage gain he had made on each trade was displayed in a bright green. Crawling across the bottom of the screen were news feeds from around the world. On another screen were the options positions. Many were closed out at a huge profit. There was no question, they were sitting pretty in oil. Their other positions were being managed by the team in Cape Cod—who had been quietly taking on more and more risk all throughout the day.

The last computer screen, mounted on a bracket to his left, displayed the details of the purchases and sales of derivatives to different traders in other markets around the world. Metals, grains, currency, interest rates—it was all in play. The spike in oil prices threatening to throw the world into an extended depression.

Andrew was frantically manipulating the mouse and punching in digits from the numeric keypad. At the same time, he was talking into a bead microphone attached to a Bluetooth headset that covered his left ear. His voice was no more than a whisper as he issued commands in foreign languages to trading houses, resolved details with affiliates, and dodged the harried, panicked calls of other partners or counterparties. He was fully aware he had kicked off a world crisis, but the sooner the others sank, the better. The only ones who would survive what he had done were the ones who could quickly adapt to the changing circumstances. Of course, it was much more difficult for the others to swim since Andrew had thrown them all an anchor instead of a life preserver. And, for those agile enough to survive, he had one more trick up his sleeve. The trap was sprung.

*****

In Cape Cod, the den where Maxwell York usually sat was seeing a previously unthinkable stream of traffic. The men and woman coursing through the estate—all wearing their newly issued RFID identification tags—had to pass through the stately old room to get to where the computers were. Inside of the computer room, the talking was reduced to stifled whispers. No one wanted to disturb anyone else because they all had very important jobs to do.

Although he was only hired to manage security matters, it turned out Carl Simmons was also proficient with technology. Andrew had directed him to monitor the MIN-OPS network for any chatter about their activities in the world's futures and options markets. Up until that point, they had successfully utilized their many subsidiaries and hedge fund mangers under their control to shield them from detection. The world's exchanges were jumping all over the place, but no one recognized that MYB was the firm creating the havoc. It was a high stakes game and the longer they stayed invisible, the better.

Looking up and seeing the numbers on other screens, Carl saw the closing numbers of Dow and S&P 500 from the previous day's trading. The charts didn't slope down but dropped like they had fallen off a cliff. He saw gold and oil prices spike up in the spot market, despite the halt of trading on the exchanges.   To the man sitting beside him, Carl commented, "This is unbelievable!"

"Yeah," the man replied, "Our boss always liked George Bush. I guess you could call this Andy's version of shock and awe."

Through the headpiece attached to his jaw, Carl heard Andrew's voice, "Carl? Are you there?"

"Yeah, I'm right here Mr. Stevens."

"Any news on Sampson?"

"No, Sir. Major Sampson hasn't made a move yet. I'm waiting for an update from my team." As a former Marine himself, Simmons referred to Sampson respectfully, by rank. Even though the Major was retired—and they were going to cut him down like a dog—the man was still a legend. As the saying went, once a Marine, always a Marine.

Stevens blew out a cheek full of air in disgust. "I guess you don't want to tell me how Sampson spotted your men?"

"Major Sampson is the consummate professional, sir. He could sniff out a frog at a toad convention."

"Yeah, yeah, yeah . . . I read all about this creep. Why didn't you just go in and get him before he spotted you?"

It was Carl's turn to exhale in exasperation. "Because he'd probably wipe his ass with us and not even break a sweat in the process. Please, Mr. Stevens, don't worry about him—the situation is under control."

"Okay," Andrew relented. "Let's talk about that other project. Is your team ready to go in D.C.?"

"Yeah. I've got twenty of the nastiest, most pissed off veterans I could find geared up and in place."

"Please, don't tell me these are a bunch of drunken bums."

"No, sir, these are heroes who came back to the country they fought for and were shit on. They've all got PTSD or traumatic brain injuries, they've all got criminal records and none of 'em can get a job. The best part though, is that they can fight like badgers and shoot like marksmen. Trust me, they'll get the job done."

Andrew paused. The pause was so long Carl wondered if he was still on the phone. Finally, he spoke. "I like you, Carl, so I'm going to make you a deal. If your men in Washington can pull this off, not only will I buy out your firm for $100 million, I'll take you on as my head of security when the dust settles."

Simmons whistled in disbelief. "That's it? All I we have to do is hog-tie a few politicos and I'm in?"

"Well, yeah, that and take out Sampson."

*****

250

As a unit, the squad burst into the room. In a matter of seconds, every possible space, angle, and hiding place had been observed and checked for hostiles. The area ten paces forward and to the right of the front door turned out to be a large walk-in closet. There, the pointman, assigned to initiate contact with and take out any and all targets, could not believe what he saw.

Within nine-tenths of a second, the assault team had double-tapped two mannequins. Hanging by strings tied across the closet rails were mock-ups of two bodies. The dummies were made of strategically tied, puffed-out pillows, sheets, and towels wrapped in foil. On the floor was a fan, blowing the two dummies gently back and forth to create the illusion of movement. The foil also had a series of wire leads hooked up to a lithium-ion battery from dismantled electronic equipment.

Touching the foil on the human-shaped stand-ins, the men of the squad could sense heat. Sampson had rigged up two warm "bodies" to fool the sensors he knew they would use—and he used the battery of the device they were using to track him to do it.

Carl Simmon's voice crackled in the earpiece of the lead man. "Spider-One, Spider-Two, report."

"Spider-Two, here. Chicken Little has flown the coop, Webmaster. Over."

"Mike, look over here!" one of the men called from the door of the bathroom.

"Stand fast, Webmaster." John spoke into the mic. He walked straight to where several of his men stood, looking up at the bathroom ceiling. The missing square of plaster was just big enough for a grown man to squeeze through. "Webmaster, our man made an escape hatch—he's probably long gone by now, over."

Carl wiped the beads of sweat that were starting to drip down his slick forehead. If his men only knew what was at stake, they wouldn't have been so loose and would've seen anyone leaving that house, no matter how they got out.

"Shit!" Simmons pounded his fist on the desk. Everyone in the computer room in the Cape Cod mansion turned to look at him. He ignored them. "Go on, go ahead up there and check it out. See if he left any clues or if you can get a handle on where he might be going. After that, hightail it back over here, we've got to get ready to help our boys out down in D.C. Copy?"

"Copy that, Webmaster. Over and out."

Simmons was so angry that they lost Sampson that he was not paying attention to his surrounding, nor were his senses engaged to detect danger—as he had been trained to do. If Carl had not been upset to the point of distraction, he probably would have smelled the distinct aroma of fuel. Everyone else in the house smelled it as soon the heating oil delivery truck pulled up. Others on his security team did notice the smell—but they were the ones who let the truck onto the estate for what the driver said was supposed to be an emergency delivery someone at the estate had ordered.

In the time it took for the man who was watching the gate to verify if someone had, in fact, placed the order, the driver was gone and the residential oil tanker truck was left sitting right in front of the mansion. The sun had started its ascent and the morning breeze swirled the fumes all around the compound.

Carl looked up, wiping the sweat of frustration from his brow. He saw his number two man walk purposefully through the door of the computer room staring hard in Simmon's direction.

"Carl, we've got a problem."

"What is it now?"

*****

There were two very interesting details about Cape Cod that made Sampson's job easy. The first was that a lot of the older homes still used home heating oil. The second was that in order to restore the rocky, burned out soil where they grew grapes, the local farmers used a lot of fertilizer. The ability to do recon on a prior trip so he knew where to get what he needed surely paid dividends. Escaping from the bed and breakfast turned out to be the hardest part, and that was only because he was not alone. But, once off the roof, with Susan safely waiting for him, the rest of his plan went off without a hitch.

The fuse was strategically placed inside of the delivery truck full of heating oil, ammonium nitrate, and sugar. From a safe distance, Sampson used a disposable cell phone to do what he had seen done a hundred times in Iraq. He dialed the number to the cell phone attached to the fuse. Instead of sending electric pulses to the phone to make it vibrate announcing an incoming call, the electricity created a spark that ignited the fuse that set off the massive bomb.

The house on the estate on Cape Cod—along with everyone inside—was vaporized and a small mushroom cloud could be seen for miles. When the dust settled, all that was left was Maxwell York's debris-covered garden and a large crater where the mansion used to be.

Chapter Twenty Five

The copious traffic east of Boston toward the coast had brought the wide lanes to a standstill. Heading west, there shouldn't have been any congestion; no one in their right mind would be going anywhere near the big cities on the eastern seaboard. But, desperate drivers pouring out of the cities had co-opted the lanes heading toward the city to make their escape. Also, with so many driving at the same time, there wasn't any gasoline available anywhere. Those who ran out of fuel had their vehicles unceremonious rammed off the highways and were left to fend for themselves. The riots in Boston, New York, and Philadelphia had spread across the country and the mass exodus rendered most of the highways impassable. If it had been the middle of summer with the usual heat and humidity, the roads, which had turned into nothing more than occasionally pivoting parking lots, would have been torture.

Flying high overhead, the Piper Cub Sampson had stolen from the tiny airport outside of Hyannis was not burdened at all by the traffic. The cars were effectively providing him with a map. Instead of flying the scenic route over Nantucket and Block Island, and getting an amazing view of the East Coast, he decided to follow Interstate 95 until they were out of Massachusetts. After a quick stop in Cranston, Rhode Island to refuel, they took off again following the Connecticut Turnpike south. With no maps or flight plans, he figured the best way to get where they were going was to follow the long lines of cars.

Sampson's attention was focused on piloting the plane, trying to make sure they would not get off track. Still, he couldn't help but notice how Susan had been unusually quiet ever since their escape. The fact they had to jump from roof to roof had unsettled her to no end. Then, when he grabbed her, covered her mouth with his hand, and jumped off of the last house's roof onto the bushes below with her wrapped in his arms, he thought she might scratch his eyes out when he let go. How was he supposed to know her only fear was the fear of heights? It was just an old jump-school instructor's trick to get scared little eaglets out of the nest. It was cruel, but after it was employed few men ever hesitated to jump. He hoped she would get over her hurt feelings and warm up to him soon. They had a lot to discuss—and, strangely, he was starting to miss the sound of her voice.

They followed the Hudson River south to the Tappan Zee Bridge. From there, they flew over I-287 until they could see the spurs of the routes breaking off to the many alternates of Route 17. Because Sampson had flown into Teeterboro before, he knew which flight paths and approach lanes to use. At such a busy commercial airport, the lack of radio and air traffic was a surprise—and the fact that he could not pick up anyone in the tower was not what he expected.

After they snuck out of the bed and breakfast, bombed York's estate, and stole the plane, they had no way of finding out what was going on and had no idea how serious everything had become in a very short span of time. If they had been able to find one of the few radio stations still broadcasting, both Susan and Daniel would have known about the complete political upheaval.

Sampson remembered from what he had read in the files supplied to him by Andrew Stevens that civil disorder was a distinct possibility, but they were supposed to have plans to quickly restore the public's confidence and faith in a government—their government. There were certain things Maxwell York, Roland Troth, and the other elitist needed to achieve their goal of establishing a neofeudalism. At the top of the list was the rule of law. Without law or a power to enforce the law, the deeds, titles and liens controlled by the super rich would be unenforceable. They had to somehow lock the lower castes into a system of laws and some justice so the contractual obligations the rich relied on—and the laws they wrote to enforce them—retained the power of persuasion. Even the most elite realized that they could only rule by consent of the masses.

The entire plan of installing a neofeudalistic system depended on the ability to offer the people a seemingly better social contract than they had in the past. And, there were supposed to be people in high places who would lead the masses by the nose right down the path the new masters wanted them to follow.

Obviously, that hadn't happened. Sampson felt pretty confident that because Maxwell York was, literally, toast, everything had gone to hell. Instead of a semi-peaceful transition, what they were witnessing was pure havoc. All he needed to know was that no one was manning the air traffic control towers to understand the state of the nation.

Landing at Teeterboro did not present any problems. Although the runways were not completely clear, there was enough room from the dearth of traffic for him to make a safe landing. He brought the Piper Cub to a stop outside one of the many warehouses where shipped goods were unloaded from cargo planes to be held by customs. Again, he noticed there were no customs officers around, and the lack of activity at the usually busy hub made his hyper-sensitive perception and intuition especially acute.

Unloading just one Army Surplusduffel bag from the hold, Sampson hoisted it over his arm and behind him. He expertly caught the strap, counterbalancing the bulk across his shoulder.

"Okay, Susan. Where do we go from here?"

"I think we better get to Michelle in New York." Her voice was flat, lacking emotion from both exhaustion and too much drama.

"Did you see the roads leading to the George Washington Bridge? There's probably no way to drive across it and I'm willing to bet the tunnels are even worse." Sampson stared at her for a second to gauge her reaction. There was none. "How do you feel about driving as far as we can and then hiking the rest of the way?"

"Yeah, We could do that or we could steal one of those helicopters over there. It's not like anyone cares."

Sampson turned and looked over to where her eyes were leading. There were two helicopters sitting unattended near the fence of a maintenance company.

"You can steal a helicopter, right? I mean, you did steal the plane and you do have guns on you," saying this as she pointed to the duffel bag strapped across his shoulder with her chin. Although her voice was a little accusatory, it still lacked any true emotion. "Who's going to stop us?"

Sampson tried to read her state of mind but couldn't. She was either resigned to the fact that the world had gone to hell and that nothing they did really mattered. Or, she had gone completely off the deep end and was living in some sort of fugue state making up her own reality as she went along. The look in Susan's eyes was something he had seen before—it was the look of someone who had turned their mind off and was acting on instinct. If her instinct was to steal a chopper to get them into Manhattan, something he had failed to think of, then deep down inside, this woman was a warrior.

"Yeah, if one of 'em is in working order, I guess we could fly into the city. Do you know where Michelle is?"

"She'd be in a building owned by the trust off of Central Park West . . . I think the Upper West Side."

"You think?" His question was harsh and loudly expressed, as if in derision. "That's the best you can do?"

His sharp reply had the effect of focusing Susan's mind a little better. With the return of awareness came a bit of her attitude. "I have the address in my phone—if you just give it back to me and let me put the stupid battery in, I'll tell you exactly where the hell she is."

"I told you, keeping the phone active isn't a smart idea."

"I know, I know what you said . . . they can track us and can figure out where we are . . . .blah, blah, blah, but what you're not thinking about is this Mr. Military Man, who the hell is going to track us? Look around, do you see any police, any of your military buddies? Hmmm? There's no one left to care about where we are, don't you get it?"

Susan started to shake and Sampson thought she was ready to lose it—but not because the country had fallen apart. There was more to the story that she wasn't saying.

"You don't know that, Susan. You don't know who is in control right now or what agencies are still active—and let me tell you, I am not gonna be trapped off by some hit team because of something as stupid as a cell phone. Now, you're probably right—we probably can use your phone for a few minutes, but not here—not in the open like this with no cover and no way to escape. When we left the inn on the Cape, you saw them for yourself—the people watching us, the snipers on the roof across the street from where we were staying. Do you want to take the chance of them finding us?"

A touch of sadness was in her voice when she answered, "No . . . I don't want them to know where we are—but do you think I can use my phone just long enough to find out how my kids are?" The question sounded like a desperate plea.

Sampson handed her the disposable phone and the battery he had pulled out. She deftly reassembled and activated it and held it to her ear.

"Nothing. Everything is down."

*****

Carlos was lucky. Because he was in a rush, he had driven directly to the small airport outside of Limon, on the Costa Rican coast. There, he found a fully restored French made Dessault two-banger that was fueled up, and a man willing to sell it to him. The plane was a relic and the four-seater was big enough to carry a lot of fuel. If he stopped in San Jose, then he'd only have to make one more stop to refuel once he made it to the United States. From there, he'd be able to fly all the way to New York or New Jersey, wherever he could land. That was something he'd figure out once he got closer to the city.

Leaving the villa had been hard on Carlos. After explaining things to his wife, Helena, and to Susan's kids, he literally had to tear himself away. He knew one day he would return to the United States, but he never thought it would be under such perilous circumstances, or that he would be leaving his wife behind. From what Michelle had explained to him about Tommy getting killed and how the situation had deteriorated so quickly, he knew he had to go back and could not leave her alone to deal with everything. That would have been too much for anyone. Add in the fact that Susan was missing, and he had to get Darla home to take care of Tommy's funeral, there was little choice in the matter.

Taking the kids back with him was out of the question. In the villa with Don Jorge and Helena, Chris and Lisa would be safe and sound, no matter how crazy things got in the USA. As far as Costa Rica went, it was stabile—most of the people were already poor and the turmoil with the world's major currencies and oil meant little to them. The people of Costa Rica, Ticos, were not only used to taking care of themselves, they were also very good at it. Surrounded by farmers, the kids and Helena would have access to ample supplies of food and water. It was a no-brainer; they would all be much safer in the villa than anywhere in the states.

Darla Jones was sitting next to Carlos in the loud, twin-prop airplane. Although saddened by the loss of Tommy, her husband, it had not changed the person she was. At first, the news had been devastating. But, little by little, she taught herself to cope and feel better. As an independent woman who took each day as it came, she did her best to simply go with the flow and after several days of intense mourning, she started to heal. She did her best to not think of the man or men who murdered her husband.

In order to pass the time on the plane, Darla disassembled, cleaned, and reassembled the two 9 millimeter Berettas. It was hard work to overcome the pain and sadness of her loss.

Carlos watched Darla cautiously as she fiddled with one weapon and then the other. Part of him hoped she would put them away and start acting normal again—her single-mindedness was starting to give him the creeps. However, there was another side of him that was glad she was armed and deep down, mad as hell.

"Hey, Darla, put those things away. The airport's dead ahead and I'm going into a landing pattern."

"Go ahead and land, Baby doll. It'll be good to be on the ground so I can lay my Tommy to rest an give him some peace."

*****

Dan and Susan made quick work of unstrapping the helicopter that appeared functional. Always a creature of habit, Sampson took the time to do a preflight check of the engines and hydraulic systems. As anxious as she was to get started, she did not harass him about being careful. Helicopters terrified her and the last thing she wanted was for that bird to fall out of the sky with her in its belly.

260

Finally, after Dan was convinced the helicopter was safe he broke the lock on the fuel pump and started the process of topping off the tanks.

The uneasy silence between them continued, but Sampson sort of understood why Susan was upset. The fact she could not get to her kids, or talk to them, was bothering her to no end. With the world exploding, he imagined it must be difficult for her to be away from her offspring—although that was not an emotion he had the ability to empathize with.

Not even taking the time to consider the possibility what he was going to ask might make things worse, he threw the topic out like it was an afterthought.

"Listen, Susan—do you know any scientists or anyone who knows anything about genetics?"

"No, why?"

"There's a few things I need help figuring out."

"Why? Is there more going on that you haven't told me about?"

"Well, yeah, I mean what York and his people were doing wasn't just about money and property. There's a biological side as well."

The words made Susan turn towards him and walk closer. "Go on, I'm listening."

"There's a company called Hamilton Genomics and they made a virus that's somehow supposed to weed out the population, you know, thin it out until there's a lot less people."

"You mean something that's gonna make us all get sick and die?" Susan wanted to puke. What else was he going to tell her?

"No. I'm guessing the virus somehow stops humans from reproducing."

She was just a foot away from the helicopter and Dan holding the hose. The smell of the fuel made her eyes water. "How do you know this and why didn't you tell me about this before?"

"Because I didn't understand it myself. York gave me the files and I tried to make sense of them, but the science is way over my head. That's why I asked you if you knew someone. I need help figuring it out."

"Well, I'm not some dummy—why don't you show me the files or tell me what you remember, maybe we can figure it out together.

"I guess it's worth a shot." Sampson closed the hose's nozzle and brushed past Susan to allow the length of the hose to retract back into a coil. As he passed, he couldn't help but smell her hair. Even after more than a day on the run her aroma smelled sweet. He hung up the nozzle, turned to her, and continued, "Okay, beyond what I already told you, this is all I really know for sure. They designed a virus to somehow go after one of the sex chromosomes. When someone's infected, it changes people's DNA somehow—and don't even bother asking me how. I also remember reading about how some small genetic groups won't be affected at all, and for a very tiny percentage the virus will kill them right away. Something like 98.5% of everyone else will either have only one or no kids—at least that's what I think it does."

That struck a nerve with Susan. She remembered how hard it had been to get pregnant with Chris and Lisa— and how it had taken intervention by specialist or she would have been childless. It also dawned on her that she wasn't the only one. A lot of women from her generation had fertility issues. She didn't know all that many women or couples her age, but of those she did know, most were childless—and that included her sister, several of her cousins and Michelle. Thinking harder, a few others popped into her head, Donny's first wife and his sister-in-law, both were her age and both had died tragic deaths before having kids. It made her wonder if it was a coincidence—or if the lower birth rates had more to do with the changing times.

"What else do you know, like, how are they going to infect people?" She asked.

"Susan, it's not how are they going to—they've already done it. The virus is out there and it's already a part of us."

Thinking of her own children, she was stunned and saddened and only managed to breathlessly push out one word, "How?"

"That's one part of the files I did sort of get. They had a whole bunch of charts and graphs labeled with different kinds of bugs and success rates. At first, it didn't make any sense but then I realized those were the success rates of infection using fleas, mosquitoes all kinds of bugs as vectors. One report I read was actually in English and it explained how they got the virus into the human population. What they did was they grew a common bacteria as a carrier for the virus and sprayed that into wooded areas saying it was pesticide. Later, they went back and capture bugs to see if the bacteria lived, if the virus survived, and if it spread. Sure enough, the bacterial made it onto all kinds of bugs and the virus was alive inside the bugs. Before long, cases were turning up in those areas where people were getting sick from mosquito bites or Lyme disease . . ."

"Stop! Did you just say, Lyme? You mean from ticks?"

"Yeah, from ticks, and from those blood samples they proved humans were starting to infect each other with the virus through sexual contact."

"Oh, my God! Donny's first wife died from Lyme disease. Do you think this is connected? When did they start the spraying?"

"I don't remember, but——-"

263

"Dan!" She interrupted him. I can't believe I forgot about this. Donny has a brother, Richard—and his wife died from Lyme disease, too. Richard Clearmont is a scientist of some kind and all he's done since his wife died is try to prove the Lyme disease killed his wife and the medical community covered it up. You asked if I know a scientist, you're damn right I know a scientist."

"Well, where does he live?" Dan asked this with the most excitement he had all day. "Let's go talk to him and bring him the files I have."

"He lives somewhere here in Bergen County . . . I'm not sure where though."

"So, let's go find him."

"We can't! We have to get to Michelle. She might be in trouble."

The sound of two propellers cutting through the air cut off their discussion. Sampson signaled for Susan to take cover as they watched the Dessault bank to the left and slowly lose altitude for a soft landing. When she looked back over at Dan, he had already assembled a long rifle with a big sniper scope attached to the top. She looked back and forth between him aiming and the plane taxiing down the runway. Before long, it came to a stop near the Piper Cub already sitting awkwardly next to the warehouse.

When the door of the plane opened a smallish man stepped out, he was too far away for Susan to recognize any features. On the other side of the plane, a tall, thin woman stepped out. In her hands were two black objects that, even from a distance, looked like guns.

"Stay down behind that barrel, the woman's armed," Sampson ordered.

Susan turned to Dan and noticed his finger go from the trigger guard to a central spot on the trigger itself.

"Is that fucking necessary, Dan? We don't even know who they are."

"Yeah, but what I do know is the pretty black chick has two guns and she looks pretty serious."

Tall, thin, black chick carrying guns. That description fit an image in Susan's head. "What does the small dude look like?" she asked.

"Hispanic, pencil mustache, thin . . . as far as the woman goes, she was real pretty but you're gonna have to add a new distinguishing mark to the middle of her fore—-"

Samson heard the sound of boots on the pavement. Susan had jumped out of hiding and was sprinting faster than he could believe possible toward the two people who had just stepped out of the plane.

At the same time as she ran, she was yelling at the top of her lungs, "Carlos! Darla! Over here! Carlos, over here! It's me, Susan!!"

Daniel Sampson immediately removed his finger from the trigger and activated the safety. Susan DiGiovanni's two friends would stay alive, at least for the time being, he thought. He did not like the idea of sharing her with anyone.

Chapter Twenty Six

A line of riot police advanced down Fifth Avenue. They would soon be face to face with marauders who were breaking windows and looting stores. Further down the street, several blocks away, people were running in and out of the shops, their arms full of luxury merchandise once on display in the upscale boutiques. The police had on masked helmets and held their blackjacks and batons threateningly as they marched shoulder to shoulder down the avenue. Brave reporters and cameramen tried to capture the scene of what was gearing up to be the biggest confrontation of the day between the police and rioters.

As the fronts neared, the din of shattering glass, yelling, and stomping feet grew louder and louder. The street was starting to look more and more like a war zone with every passing minute as fumes from firebombs and acrid smoke from burning tires choked the air. Trash can fires belched out even more clouds of thick, black smoke, and the initial fingers of flames flickered out of the broken windows of several cars. Arcing projectiles rose from the hands of protesters and fell, smashing back down to earth. The rising tension in the air mixed with the smells and sounds of conflict made the entire block seem like it was convulsing.

The gap between the line of cops and the crowd of rabid protesters narrowed. The cops suddenly stopped surging forward, a substantial shift in demeanor, and there was nothing subtle at all about the transformation. They lowered their batons, turned to one another, and started to consult back and forth between themselves. The change in their posture and attitude was much less threatening and the level of tension between the two ever-nearing groups started to evaporate. Several riot police turned and walked back, shouting the others behind them or yelling to officers mounted on horses. It was only seconds worth of deliberation but then it was over. The decision was made.

The lines of hardened cops broke ranks and simultaneously lowered their weapons even more. Officers removed their riot helmets and some even tossed them to the ground and walked toward the protesters with their hands raised to show they were not attacking. Other cops ripped the badges right off of their uniforms and walked away from the discarded tin while even more stripped their shirts right off of their backs as a sign of open rebellion.

Witnessing the odd display caused an eerie silence to fall over the gathered crowd. The cowering reporters watched in amazement as the cops made gestures of peace and signaled for the protesters to come forward and join them. In bunches or groups, cops leaned forward to tell their former adversaries what was going on and upon hearing the news, murmurs turned to shouts which sent waves of jubilation through the crowd of protesters. In one big surge that exploded out in all directions like a kaleidoscope, the antagonistic groups, the officers of the NYPD along with the looters and rioters, bound through the broken windows and doors of the most exclusive Boutiques on earth.

The riotous mob felt no guilt at all grabbing the obscenely expensive Hermes handbags and Rolex watches. The Bulgari, Dolce & Gabana, and Piaget merchandise disappeared in a flash. Many less affluent of the city's residents were enraptured to haul away the Cartier and Swarauski wares they always admired but could never afford. With no civil authority and no threat of arrest, the streets came alive with people emptying the stores of their swank goods.

A reporter, Jamie Kerr, from the local FOX affiliate, was the first to get the attention of a pillaging cop. Her cameraman, dutifully keeping pace with her plunge into the madness, was right behind her. Jamie's dark brown hair was a mess and her suit was covered with soot from burning tires. The skin under her perfect nose was stained black from inhaling smoke. None of the hardships deterred her in the least. She knew filming the scene of the police breaking ranks and turning away from their duties was huge, and if she was the first to find out why, and get it on the air, it would be a catapult for her career. A Mexican woman as a news anchor in New York City, her parents would be so proud . . . that was if there was a station left when she went back . . . and if they had been able to start broadcasting again . . .

The anonymous cop Jamie grabbed was dressed in a bullet-proof vest with a plain white t-shirt underneath. His NYPD-issue weapon hung loosely in its holster, the safety snap undone. In his left hand was a stack of gold bangle bracelets that knelled in the low metallic clang of solid metal. His other hand was near the gun.

"Officer, officer, can you tell me why the NYPD has joined the looters?"

The man replied in a thick Brooklyn accent, yelling into the microphone she held in front of his face, "The mothahfuckahs took our money! We ain't got nottin'!"

Jamie had to coax more out of the indignant cop, "Who took it? How do you know—what did you hear?"

Slightly more composed, he answered, "The PBA sent word out. The bankers, those fuckahs got us too. They robbed us and took our retirement money."

As soon the cops heard the news from their union leaders and word spread, most of them simply decided to quit. The men and woman who had given their lives to the city, who had served valiantly for decades, no longer had anything to lose.

One investment bank went under, and then another, and another; causing the collapse of an insurance company, and then another, and another. Collectively, they took the

268

Police Benevolent Association's pension funds with them. Not only that, the salary the cops were supposed to collect would be paid in dollars—which were all but worthless. Risking their lives for nothing was not a bet the officers were willing to make. When the banks and insurance companies failed and the value of the dollar plunged, the mayor of New York lost his private army.

The cops did the only thing they could do, the only thing that made any sense—they joined in the looting to snatch up the only things that retained value. It was the only way they could get what was coming to them.

*****

Failing to connect with the SEC-DEF, he tried to reach out to others. Everywhere he turned to get concrete directives about the mission, he was thwarted with shrugs of indifference. Not one of his superiors wanted to take responsibility for making a decision and Major General Smythe found himself thinking the three and four-star generals above him were a bunch of spineless worms.

On the civilian side, the situation was even worse. Right down the line, an assistant-this or deputy-that gave him the same, "Gee, I don't know," and the not-so-subtle suggestion to keep his mouth shut and to do what he was told. Yes, the Executive Order itself was clear and he knew what he had to do. The problem was, no one had laid out specific rules of engagement for the mission.

The parameters of the operation and lack of limitations on his command authority unsettled Smythe. The Nation Defense Authorization Act had not only made it out of committee, it also passed the House and Senate and was signed into law as written. The critical provision, with the pertinent amendments neatly tucked away somewhere after the first thousand pages, was probably unread by most legislators. That it passed so easily proved the system of checks and balances was pure hogwash. If the politicians knew what they had enacted, they would have been appalled.

Being in charge of the task force's Rapid Response Team gave General Smythe access to massive resources and the ability to strike anywhere in the continental United States. At the same time, the charter for his commanded gave him an unbelievable amount of latitude. Someone with fewer scruples could easily use the special division for nefarious purposes. Still, he had no problem accepting the command he had been given—it was a tremendous opportunity and an honor—what bothered him was the idiotic strategy pushed by the politicians that could only lead to disaster.

Yes, the world had changed and many threats had materialized, but to authorize a commander to use special forces to contravene internal national security threat seemed like overkill, at least at first. The President's order to regain control of every major city—using any means necessary—was unambiguous in scope, and although he was authorized to do so, he didn't think the use of such force would ever be necessary. However, with the conflagration spreading rapidly across the nation, and reports coming in about police forces disbanding, those events rapidly altered his way of thinking. With city blocks burning all over the country, establishing a rapid response team under the auspices of the National Guard suddenly made perfect sense. A national crisis was already well under way.

The first steps the Joint Commission commander had to take were predetermined. Once the President's Executive Order came down, General Smythe activated a series of protocols to conduct threat assessments, select targets, and initiate counter-measures. The men and woman at the very top of the Task Force had seen the storm brewing and were prepared to deal with whatever may come. Isolated from the general population, and conditioned to follow orders, no one questioned their objective: **to stop the biggest threat the nation had seen since the Civil War using any means necessary.**

The protest organizers' moves and plans had been tracked from the start of the movement and continuously monitored for months. When all hell broke loose, the communications between insurrectionists grew exponentially. Despite the volume, everything intercepted by the Task Force's computers was cataloged and stored for analysis. The analysis of what people were saying to each other provided the leads the investigative teams needed.

The main participants, designated as primary agitators, hadn't even bothered to hide what they were up to when using the internet or cell phones. They built websites, hosted blogs, and were actively engaged in Twitter. They even posted pictures of what they had done and wrote about the crimes they planned to commit. In the internet age, notoriety was the death knell for an activist. The more followers someone had, the higher the threat assessment, and the bigger the target on their back.

As soon as the Task Force investigative team had all of the information they could handle, they did what the protocols directed them to do—stop the insurgents from communicating. Even though the move had been counter-productive in Egypt and Libya, the Task Force followed the exact same failed strategy by shutting down the internet and electronically hijacking every cell tower in the nation. The agents knew neither measure would last long. Eventually, hackers would crack the system and program in work-arounds. Then, they would then have to alter the blocking software and try to shut the whole thing down again. Both sides knew the game of digital cat and mouse would continue until the crisis ended.

It had been many, many years since the Alien and Sedition Act had been repealed, but the Commission's agents were able to use similar laws that were passed in the panic and paranoia that ensued after the attacks on the World Trade Center. The Patriot Act I and II provided many ways to press charges against those they felt posed a risk to national security. The recorded internet traffic and reports from other agencies across the country enabled the Task Force to track and identify the protesters. Then, the same data formed the bases for criminal charges. With so many targets to go after, the orders went down the line to focus all resources on the primary agitators in major cities and to prepare for action. The interment camps built and staffed by private prison corporations were finally ready to be utilized to their full capacity.

Chapter Twenty Seven

Hellbender, the one-time Coast Guard cutter, had set anchor right outside of Pleasant Bay. From its location, it was possible to see the coast on a clear day. Using powerful binoculars, it was even possible to see the details of some of the old forts and mansions along the shore.

Wearing a dark blue windbreaker with a flotation vest strapped over it, an elderly gentleman stood just outside of the bridge's hatch. A cold breeze lifted large locks of stiff gray hair up and set them gently back down in place. Using both hands, he held the foot-long binoculars up to his eyes and pointed them in the direction of where his home used to be.

Maxwell York was not a happy man. There was nothing left to look at—his Cape Cod mansion was nothing but a fond memory. "The son of a bitch!"

A man came up behind York from inside the bridge. "Mr. York, it's time to go below for another treatment. The doctor is waiting for you . . . Oh, and will Mr. Papas and Mr. Hensch be joining you for dinner?"

York lowered the binoculars and looked at the man with his ice blue eyes. "Yes, of course, but first I have some calls I have to make on a secure line. And, kindly inform the captain I need him to chart a course for the Port of Newark."

"Aye, aye, sir."

*****

A few hours after the sun set, nineteen men, all armed with modified COLT M-4's, a .233 caliber carbine-sized assault rifle, Glock 9's strapped to their thighs, and several flash-bang grenades secured across their chests, rode in under the cover of darkness. Clad in black with grease-blackened faces, they seemed to have crawled right up out of the mud of the Potomac. Three black, quick and silent inflatable rafts they came in on were tied to a branch hanging over the river. When they landed they came ashore silently. Without speaking a word or even signaling, the men split up into three squads of six and set out for three different destinations. One man was tasked with protecting the rafts—their only possible escape route was back down the river to safety.

The fact they had not received the "All-Go" from their boss, Carl the Webmaster, did not matter. They had already been paid $25,000 each and promised a lot more if they successfully completed the mission. A deal was a deal and they all needed the money.

Block by block, the squads used every skill they had been taught to maintain cover in urban combat. If they happened across people they couldn't go around or evade, they killed them quietly, usually with a dagger across the throat. If there were any unexpected barriers or crowds they could not dispose of silently, they found alternate routes. The squads were seeking out three different manhole covers so they could enter the sewer system at different locations. With all the disquiet in the streets of Washington D.C., finding and entering the sewer system turned out to be easily accomplished without alerting the authorities.

Once in the sewers, the first squad headed for the Capitol, the second the Old Executive Office Building, and the third the Supreme Court. Getting in or under the White House was impossible due to the security measures already in place. But, recent construction and renovations at or near the other sites made access a distinct possibility.

Their assignments were all the same, approach the target destinations and, as stealthily as possible, gain access to either the sub-basements, parking garages, or subway systems under each building. If they met resistance, they were to return back to the rallying point because they did not want to alert anyone of their presence and it wasn't supposed to be a suicide mission.

All three squads did come across barriers but were well equipped to bypass them with only slight difficulty. Once they found a means of entry at the right coordinates, they successfully placed modified satchel charges, activated the receivers, and set timers. As quickly as they could, they returned to the rallying point with no less than one hour before daybreak. The rafts were untied and hustled back down the river.

The mission went off without a hitch. In the sub-basements of the Capitol and the Old Executive Office Building, and in a new parking garage of the Supreme Court, a total of nine bombs were in place, armed, and ready to be remotely detonated by the hand of a man named Andrew Stevens or explode at a predetermined hour.

Since all nineteen men made it out successfully, and the bombs were properly placed and activated, each man was due an ice cold six pack of Coors and a cool $100,000 bonus. They couldn't wait to get back to the safe house and get in touch with Carl Simmons so they could collect their cash and their beer. The men had no idea they would never again hear from or see Carl. The group of nineteen who went on the mission, and the team leader who had stayed at the safe house, had enabled the coup of the greatest nation on earth at the cost of about a half-million dollars.

*****

The view from Major General Smythe's office was a data center one floor below his loft—what he liked to call the "Falcon's Nest." His suite overlooked hundreds of computer terminals and monitors with swarms of uniformed and civilian personnel moving from place to place in some indecipherable semblance of activity. The office was accessible by two secure elevators and the suite itself was protected on the sides by two-foot thick concrete walls. Bulletproof Plexiglas panels provided the view to the activity below.

Sitting behind his mahogany desk, Smythe could not hide the disturbed look on his face as he scanned over the latest reports. His advisors had sent their conclusions up to him and had put together a conservative estimate of the number of people who may be involved—not just materially offering support, but physically active in protests or riots. Based on the internet traffic and the number of connections to activists already on the street, they concluded the action could lead to a full-blown revolution.

There was no other way to look at it except as a legitimate threat to the current government and a threat to national security. Smythe never thought his own analysts and advisors would contravene the President, but he had to give it a shot and hope they came up with a different plan. They didn't.

It was stark news, he thought, and the situation would be made even worse if he ordered the wrong response. If no one else recognized it, Smythe instinctively felt the government's reaction up to that point had been all wrong. Back in the 1960's and 1970's, the prior periods of civil discord, there was no such thing as a phone with mobile, high-resolution camera. Now, they were everywhere. Americans seeing other Americans having their heads bashed in by the police and chemical warfare taking place on their streets had only increased the number of rioters. If everything continued on its current trajectory, events were going to spiral out of control and they wouldn't be able to end it. He knew that before he even read the next section and what the most senior and most secret of advisors had recommended about possible responses and containment strategies.

The politicians expected him to send the warriors in with guns blazing, but there was no way they'd be able to stop the rest of the country—and the world—from witnessing it, eventually. That was what scared the analysts and General Smythe the most. But the bureaucrats in D.C. wanted the best soldiers in the world protecting them and if that meant SEALs, Rangers, and Delta Force units taking out rioters, so be it. To Smythe, it was a confirmation that the politicians were no longer beholden to the people. Instead, they were now serving other masters. The Rapid Response Team would be both their sword and their shield. He knew what he was supposed to do but once again started to doubt his ability to follow through.

The final plan the analysts recommended to him was to round up the primary agitators, detain them in internment camps, and charge them with sedition. The news of mass detentions, they believed, would be a deterrent to the other protesters and snuff out mass rallies and marches before they even started. It would also buy them time to get the brigades under his command in place for quick-strike suppression. Following that strategy, at least, they could hopefully quiet things down enough so he wouldn't have to release his war dogs on the masses. If that didn't work and his real bosses upped that ante, the next part of the plan was something he did not even want to consider.

General Adam Smythe did not make a big deal out of his decision. Acting under the direct authority of the CIC who had given him leave to conduct the operation as he saw fit, he picked up the phone and pushed a speed-dial button.

His words came out emotionless, "This is Major General Adam Smythe, authorization code ALPHA-ALPHA-TANGO-SIX-SIX-NINER. Get a platoon of the RRT to the Capitol Building ASAP. Operation Black Hills is a go Colonel. Round 'em up and move 'em onto the reservation."

Chapter Twenty Eight

Interstates 80, 87 and 287, along with Routes 3, 4, and 17, the New Jersey Turnpike, and the Garden State Parkway could only be described with one word, pandemonium. The major roadways were not only choked with abandoned cars and trucks but the towns of Fort Lee and Teaneck had been overrun with fleeing New Yorkers, and resembled refugee camps. Some New Jersey homeowners even had their homes broken into for food and water. Parks and lawns along the Jersey side of the Hudson were turned into make-shift campgrounds. Gun shots could be heard in the distance, and the smoke from dozens of fires was visible across the entire horizon.

For those who managed to get away from Manhattan or the Bronx, it felt safer to pitch tents and sleep outside in the cold autumn air than to stay in the city. The northeast corner of the Garden State had been swarmed over by people fleeing the unrest and confusion of the Big Apple. Unable to handle or provide for the massive influx, the communities were quickly drained of available food and fuel. The people of Bergen, Essex, and Union County were afraid they would be run out of their own homes and their belongings ransacked. Looters could be seen crisscrossing from house to house, looking for easy entry. Because of the fear, almost everyone hunkered down with their doors locked tight as they kept watch over their food and other valuables.

Sampson was in his element. From Teeterboro, he protectively guided Susan, who was still abnormally quiet, through one residential neighborhood after another. With the main roads all but impassable, he skillfully enabled them to move north by northwest at a respectable clip without being noticed by anyone who could potentially pose a threat. Picking their way from backyard to backyard and from park to park, they made good time toward

Susan's sister's place and where Richard Clearmont once lived.

All the gear they had was packed securely in an Army surplus bag draped over Sampson's shoulder, while both he and Susan carried SA 9's tucked under their shirts in the back. His commando dagger, usually hidden unless he was on an operation, was strapped openly to his thigh. They had not seen any state or county police vehicles roving around or any of the many municipal police forces of the towns they traversed. Because of the unique circumstances, they had no uneasiness about being armed. They were much more afraid of being accosted, searched for food, and robbed.

Some of the establishments they passed hinted at the insanity that had taken place before society started to collapse. Signs in store windows had prices for bare necessities crossed off and increased several times with new, higher prices. One minimarket, with its doors open and shelves all but bare, had last priced a half-gallon of milk at $15 and a loaf of bread at $20. The fuel prices had forced rampant inflation and then the rush to safety had made the price of everything skyrocket. Gasoline, selling for $8 a gallon, must have ran dry days before. All around that shopping center and store, it eerily resembled a ghost town. Even though it, like the owners of the store, ran out of stock ages before Dan and Susan passed, it had only been a matter of hours.

Walking along Kindercomack road past the Oradell Reservoir, the area not only looked more peaceful, but gave off a completely different vibe than towns they navigated a little further south. The more serene atmosphere gave them confidence to leave the cover of private property, walk out in the open, and travel directly.

"So, where do you want to go first? You mentioned your sister, Lisa and her shop, and your house—so which one is it, Wyckoff or Hohokus?"

Susan put her head down and did not respond immediately. "How about we go to Costa Rica so I can be with my kids? I should be with them."

Sampson didn't really know how to respond. Never before had he been in such a close relationship with a woman—with anyone for that matter—and he certainly had no idea how to make her feel better about her kids. "Didn't you say that woman—"

"Michelle?"

"Right. Didn't she tell you your kids were okay and they'd be taken care of no matter what?"

"Yeah, but—"

"But what? You don't trust your friends or you don't think they'll take care of your kids? I think that's pretty messed up."

He paused and let that sink in. If he couldn't ease her mind, maybe a little guilt trip and a dose of reality would get her to snap out of her funk.

"I didn't say that, Dan . . ."

"You may as well have. Listen, you're here and they're there, and that's not gonna change anytime soon. Now, you've got to make a choice, Susan. Either you get your head out of your ass so we can find Richard and figure out what this virus is, or you can go on moping and let whatever Maxwell York and Hamilton Genomics infected us with kill your kids. I don't know about you, but doing something about this shit and finding a way to fix it makes a hell of a lot more sense than whining about what we can't do!"

Susan was taken aback at his harsh words, but he had hit a nerve. Her main objective was to protect her kids at any cost and if it was true about York and the virus, doing nothing about it was as good as giving up on her children. The mamma bear instinct came roaring out of her and immediately took control.

"Okay, Dan, you're right. Let's go to Wyckoff and find Richard, if he's still around. The trusts send a check to him every month for his expenses."

"So, it's settled, right?" Sampson asked this with almost genuine sincerity. "Your kids are going to be fine and you and I are going to make sure they stay that way, right?"

"Right."

A sense of peace came over her and for the first time in as long as she could remember, the ache of separation and the anxiety of potential loss receded from her consciousness. She was going to do whatever she had to so her babies would be safe—if that meant staying with Dan and finding Richard, so be it.

They turned and started walking with even more purpose towards Wyckoff. Reaching out with her left hand, she took Dan's hand into her own and felt comforted by the warmth and the roughness of his skin. He looked at her curiously and raised a eyebrow. She shrugged and cuddled her body up against his strong arm. Susan was happy they were going to do it together. He was strong, determined, and had ingenuity. She was starting to feel safe around him and he had given her good reason to trust him and his instincts. The man seemed to have his head screwed on straight and was not about any bullshit, at least he hadn't been. Sure, she knew he was involved with bad people, and she hardly knew anything about him, but she was determined for that to change.

"Ya know, Dan, after spending all of this time together, I don't even know your last name or anything about you."

"So, what do you want to know?"

"You can start with your name."

"My birth name is Daniel York, but you can just call me Sampson—no one calls me Dan. Actually, I hate that name."

Susan stopped in her tracks and turned toward him, pulling her arm as if trying to take her hand away from his. He did not let go.

"Susan, don't get upset. I just found out myself. For the first five years of my life, I was in an orphanage—"

His words were cut off by the sound of helicopters. They were flying very low and drowned out the words. On instinct, he grabbed her by the arm and tugged her into a hedge row, pushing her underneath the branches and making sure they were under cover. Seconds later, several Blackhawks passed directly overhead. They were painted black and at least one gunner at the hatch looked like he was actively seeking targets.

Sampson leaned close and put his mouth right next to her ear. "Change of plans! We're gonna get the hell out of here and stay out of sight until things calm down."

"Why? What's going on?"

"They just imposed Marshall Law and we have no idea who the hell is in charge. It's best if we wait it out where no one can find us."

"Okay, but where are we gonna go."

"Ramapo Mountains. It won't take us too long to get to the reservoir."

"Are you sure?" Susan pulled her head back so she could look into his eyes when he responded.

"Yeah, I'm sure. Come on, let's get out of here."

He looked up to make sure the choppers could not pick up a visual on them or their heat signatures. The big airships were moving away slowly, hovering low, either looking for a place to land or driving some unseen prey south. Recognizing they were safe, Sampson helped Susan up and together they ran north at a pace they could try to hold until they were in the clear.

As he promised, they reached the edge of the Ramapo mountains that straddled the borders of New Jersey and upstate New York a lot sooner than Susan believed possible. Despite the cool weather, her hair was wet with sweat and her body felt clammy under the heavy pull-over. Because there hadn't been time to break in her new boots, she could also feel sores starting to form on her heels. Despite the pain and the soreness in her legs, she did her best to keep up with the silent, furtive Daniel York Sampson.

She looked at the sign announcing they were entering protected land and ducked under the steel bar blocking the dirt road onto the state park. Sampson stepped over the blockade and stopped to wait for her to catch up."

"Well, we made it. What do we do now?" she asked, reaching out to take his hand.

Taking her tiny hand into his, he looked at Susan DiGiovanni, a woman he believed broke every preconception he had about females, and felt something he never felt before—an emotional tug at his heart.

"How about we get a little deeper into the woods and build a fire. I'll go hunting while you get out of these wet clothes. I bet your feet are killing you."

"How did you know? Was I limping?"

"No, you weren't limping, but those are new boots and you're gonna have some nasty blisters."

She was touched by his sensitivity and impressed by his insight. She closed the distance between them as they walked and lifted his arm to guide it around and behind her. They disappeared into the forest walking in lock step with her arm around his waist and his arm draped across her shoulders. At any other time, in any other place, they would have looked like the perfect couple.

Epilogue

The first television station to come back on the air and retain a steady signal was FOX out of New York. They were only able to display their logo, but it was a start. Shortly thereafter, other major broadcast networks lit up and every radio station in the city came back on the air. It took a little longer, but soon the cable channels returned and the internet started to show signs of life. Minutes later, all of the cell phone towers started the process of rebooting their systems and clearing the buffers of disconnected calls. Although unable to place calls immediately, the mobile devices and smart phone across the city started to be pinged with signals.

It would be the first time in days anyone had access to news, the ability to find out about the welfare of family, or to reach out for help. They weren't all that disappointed about the delay because everyone realized getting things up and running would take some time. They found hope in their screens that displayed the same singular line of text: PLEASE STAND BYE FOR A SPECIAL REPORT.

Word spread fast among the various groups of protesters, rioters, and looters. Night was falling, and the ability to once again hear what was going on in the world or maybe communicate with family did what the police could not do. The return of radio waves, satellite signals, and streams of digital broadcasts cleared the streets of Manhattan and eventually every other city in the nation. The only ones left behind were the drunks, the injured, the mad, and the dead.

As soon as people got off of the streets and went home, most of them turned on the television sets or sat down to log onto Facebook or Twitter. It seemed like ages had passed since the world went mad, and the people were tired, exhausted to the point of passivity. The restoration of media and return home was a much needed respite from the stress and anxiety of what had become a free-for-all. Settling in and waiting for the news, it gave families much needed time to come together to take measure of what had happened and what they had lost. Then, the Emergency Broadcasting System started to sound its beeping alarm.

Gathered around television screens all around the country, families and neighbors as well as strangers and travelers listened to the uncanny beeps and watched the text start to scroll across the screen: "THIS IS NOT A TEST. PLEASE STAND BYE FOR AN EMERGENCY ANNOUNCEMENT . . . THIS IS NOT A TEST . . . ."

On every station and on every computer able to process streaming video, Andrew Stevens appeared on screen. There was only one camera and it was zoomed in to focus on his handsome face and perfectly combed dark hair. He was standing at a plain wooden podium lacking insignia of any kind. As the camera panned back, the audience could see a line of men and women seated in chairs several feet behind the dais. They were sullen and still, not talking to each other, and they all wore morose expressions. The camera zoomed back in, moving from one face to another so everyone watching could see who was in attendance.

In the center was the President of the United States. To his right was the Vice President and to his left was Secretary of State. Also on the stage was the Secretary of Defense, the Speaker of the House, the President of the Senate; and both the majority and minority leaders of both houses. Standing along the stage were other members of the Cabinet and the nine Supreme Court Justices.

No one outside of D.C. knew about the explosions that rocked the Capitol, the Supreme Court and the Old Executive Office building. Very few beyond the President's inner circle knew about the secret meetings at Camp David or the rapid dispatch of messages delivered by heavily armed Secret Service agents. No one but a very select few heard the offers, counter offers, or rejections. And, only the President himself heard the threats that resulted in the explosions that caused three federal buildings enough damage as to be near collapse.

The President had been threatened, he had not given in—and then he had to be shown the truth. He was no longer in control. No one but Andrew Stevens saw the President break under pressure and agree to all of his terms for fear of many more explosions and a violent coup he did not have the power to stop.

It was impossible to determine the venue, but the caption on the screen read, "Washington, D.C." The cameraman panned back over to the tall man standing at the podium and held it steady. He looked directly at the camera and spoke in a deep, clear voice:

"My name is Andrew Stevens and I am speaking to you tonight at the direction of the President of the United States and with unanimous consent of Congress. As of twelve noon today, the United States of America was placed under Marshall Law. Until further notice, no one, I repeat, no one is to be on the streets or out of their homes after sundown. Teams from the National Guard have been dispatched with orders to kill on sight. This order will stay in effect until law and order is restored.

Furthermore, I am calling upon all civil authorities and public employees to go back to work tomorrow morning. Police, fire fighters, anyone involved and contracted under law to protect, serve, or administer to the needs of the people must return to work or face removal and detention. Believe me, I do understand the complex reasons why many of you felt the need to walk away, to go home and protect your families, and leave the streets at a critical juncture in this great nation's history. I understand your lack of faith and trust in the system. But, to all the police men and women, to all the fire fighters and other public employees—I promise you this, you will all be made whole, you will all be given amnesty, and you will be able to live the American dream once again—but we need your help to do it. The National Guard and federal authorities need your help to restore order.

And, that brings me to the reason why I am speaking to you and not the President. I, along with many other concerned Americans, have the means to offer you a new social contract, one where you will no longer be burdened by debt, where you can save for your retirement and earn a decent living. All I . . . we . . . are asking is for you to give us a chance to correct the wrongs that have been done to you.

To all of the public union members, return to work and return law order and justice to our streets and you will be the first ones rewarded. Through your unions, the twelve Federal Reserve Banks will renegotiate the terms of your mortgages, reduce the amount owed, reduce the interest rate, and extended the time to repay. Once order has returned, all of the banks connected to the Federal Reserve System will be working with us to do the same thing for all Americans. Imagine a future with manageable student loans, mortgages based on the actual value of your home, and more years to pay off your car loan or credit cards at much lower interest rates. In time, this future can be yours if you just give us a chance.

Now, in order to do this, we have to take steps to stabilize the monetary system and we will do so by requiring a fractional reserve, in gold, on all currency. We will also have to guarantee the principle and interest on all government debt, foreign and domestic. In short, a consortium of bankers and industrialist will have to bail out the United States of America. And the reason we are doing it is because this country, the greatest nation on earth, deserves to be saved.

In order to make all of this possible, we must take several critical steps. To enable us to make the changes we must make, I am asking you, the American people, to temporarily suspend the Constitution of the United States. This will only last until order is restored and a vote cast to reinstate it. The second thing I asks of you is to grant me, Andrew Stevens, temporary authority to administer the legal and financial affairs of this nation. Acting as a Special Master, with the advice and consent of the President of the United States, we can restore this country to stability.

To make these changes and get on the path of peace and order, in return for a secure financial future, I am asking every American of voting age to register online with the newly created Federal Election Registry and vote. What we shall see as a successful experiment in direct democracy.

Directly after this broadcast, more details and information will be provided to you. The voting begins immediately and ends at noon tomorrow. Unless you show your support through the democratic process by temporarily suspending the Constitution and granting me the authority I seek, I will have no choice but to step aside and retract the generous offer the consortium I represent has made.

I thank you for your time and goodnight."

He had gotten the attention of some Americas and inspired them. In a few towns cops started to return to their stations and organize patrols. With the permission and assistance of the National Guard, fire fighters returned to their fire houses and immediately started pulling out the engines to look for and extinguish fires that were still burning. A lot of Americans felt a sense of relief and hope that things would not just return to normal but be better than it was.

At the same time, a sizable percentage of the population was vehemently against both propositions. Some vowed to fight tooth and nail if the Constitution fell while others did not know who Andrew Stevens was and did not trust him. A small group of patriots were sure that the President had been hoodwinked and swore to find out the truth behind the conspiracy. As upset and vocal as the dissidents were, very few of them bothered to read the lengthy, arcane language of the bills that authorized the vote. All they needed to turn the tide was in plain sight and available to all whom took the time to digest the legislation. Very few did.

By six a.m., the next day, both question had been answered by majorities that could not be overcome. A slim majority voted to suspend the Constitution of the United States of America. By an even narrower margin, Andrew Stevens was democratically appointed to the position of Special Master of the United States.

Special Master was a position created by him with all but dictatorial authority over the banking system, the military, as well as every department in the executive branch. The bloodless coup was over. Andrew was in charge and would stay in charge. The only people who did not realize it were the citizens of the United States of America who voted to support him.

COMING SOON:

MONEY GAMES III

Contending for Gold

Chapter One

The peaceful view overlooking Central Park belied what was going on all around it. Although there wasn't a cloud for miles, the air was thick, hazy, dark even, fouled by the fumes from burning tires and other debris that had been set on fire in the streets.

Michelle looked out of the double-paned, leaden glass windows on the park side of the penthouse suite. She was leaning on one of two matching high-backed Victorian chairs situated to get the best view of the great lawn below. A faint, musky smell of age and disuse was all around her. No one ever bothered to use the place, she mused, let alone air it out or restore the ancient furniture. Still, the exquisitely decorated apartment retained the elegance and charm of the Gilded Age. But, none of that mattered now. That was an age that had long passed and would never return.

She took a long sip of wine, knowing it was not a good idea to bury her sorrows in alcohol. But, she had been trying everything in her power to suppress the hurt she felt from the loss of Tommy. Even though he had been married to Darla, Michelle loved him. His murder, to her, felt like a dull knife slowly slicing through her tender heart—the deeper it went, the more it hurt. As much as she wanted go on a mental vacation, she couldn't. Too many things were happening and she'd have to make time for it later.

Days before, the investment bankers from Goldman and the lawyers from Weintraub, Rothstein, and Warburg had left the penthouse in a rush. It was ironic. On any other day, if she had disclosed the discovery of a massive amount of gold to the underwriters, every snake at that table would have found a way to excuse themselves so they could pass off the inside information and then come back too try and woo her out of more shares. The initial public offering of a company possessing $80 to $100 billion dollars in recoverable gold ore was big enough to have made international headlines and would definitely have unsettled the markets. The fact the city had starting to burn must have curbed the vultures' capitalistic appetites.

Because of the conditions in the city, and the rapidly deteriorating circumstances around the world, the men didn't just call for their cars when they left, they also called for heavily armed, private security details. Manhattan was not a safe place for anyone at that moment, and it was an especially brutal city for one carrying a leather briefcase or wearing an expensive suit. She really didn't know how long ago that had been, when the news first broke.

Since then, the insanity had redoubled. Looking out the window, Michelle was alone with her own thoughts. She was shocked at how quickly the city had fallen apart. The mayor of New York City retained what could be considered his own private army 40,000 strong. They were armed with weapons and technology developed for and passed down by the military, yet the NYPD had no answer for what was happening in the streets.

No one was sure exactly what triggered the initial chaos. but, clearly the people had enough. After the Mining of the Straight of Hormuz, in short order, the stock market crashed and the price of gasoline doubled. Not long after, stores who had merchandise delivered into the city tacked new delivery expenses onto their prices. That combination caused a run on the banks and everything spiraled downward from there. The glass, concrete, and steel cathedrals of the world's biggest financial institutions were almost immediately under siege.

The situation had quickly devolved from marches and protests, to demands for the banks to return money, to window smashing and looting. Thousands of cops dressed in riot gear and armed to the teeth were no match for the hundreds of thousands of the city's denizens who, over the course of a few days, increasingly took to the streets demanding remuneration, justice, and a whole host of other unattainable concession. With no singular voice, the collective wants, needs, and demands of the people were drowned out by the melee and impossible to answer.

When the rioting first started, the NYPD was able to scatter the crowds around the cluster of Midtown bank headquarters and the multitudes besieging Wall Street. The marauding groups quickly reassembled and either went after another target or attacked again from another direction. The mayor then ordered the NYPD to use the untested, military-grade, crowd-control equipment to stop the rioting. That experiment was recorded on hundreds of cameras all over the city and the disastrous results broadcast all around the world. The police killed several protesters using microwave blasts that made their skin bubble and fried their internal organs. The airing of the gruesome footage was a major turning point—not just in New York, but around the world.

Almost immediately after the killings, the Mayor's mansion and many police stations were attacked by large crowds. The disturbances spilled over into residential neighborhoods and other commercial districts. The further the civil uproar spread, the more force the police used, the harder the crowds struck back. The amount of property damage cause by the rioting citizens increased with the level of force used against them. The vicious cycle of attack, counterattack, and escalation on both sides of the struggle rapidly turned into a free-for-all.

Seeing how quickly the city was deteriorating, Michelle had to try and plan what she was going to do. She had been watching the ever-expanding riots on television as the engagement spread from city to city, state to state, and nation to nation. She also watched and monitored the trusts' investments as the markets tumbled, froze up, and then went into free fall. Thanks to a panicked, rushed call from Susan—and some quick hedging—all of the two trust's liquid, dollar denominated assets were safely parked in tangible commodities in warehouses around the world. She was optimistic. After things calmed down, if things returned to normal, they would be okay, maybe even in a position of strength.

Michelle was glad she listened to Susan and was given the green light to go forward with whatever she thought was right. She was also lucky she was able to move as quickly as she did. During the hurried call from Susan—who was caught in the middle of yet another crazy odyssey and was, yet again, on the run—had only one concern—and that was the welfare of her children in Costa Rica. After Michelle gave her multiple assurances that the kids would be cared for under any circumstances, the line had gone dead.

Eventually, there was no way to watch or listen to the news. The radio and television stations went off the air. Every once in a while a few local stations would reappear—but the broadcasts were inconsistent and spotty. It looked like someone somewhere was trying to get things up and running again but just falling short. Then, internet went down and seconds later so did the cell phone networks. Only the basic utilities continued to function. Michelle hoped the electricity and water would hold out or else she'd soon have to find another place to hide. Being so many floors above street level made her feel safe, but without water, it wouldn't matter. As a precaution, she filled the tub and every container she could find.

Trapped in the penthouse, with nothing to do and no way to get any news, there was a lot of time for her to think. Prior to the internet and TV going down, there was a lot of news to digest on many fronts. Standing by the window, looking down at the eerily calm park, Michelle used her substantial brain power to try and piece everything together.

Before the incident in Iran and the Straight of Hormuz, yes, she had listed to Susan's warnings based on her gut instinct. But when she heard trading in U.S. Treasuries froze up, she figured it had to be the world's central bankers who caused the financial crisis. Only a few nations in the world had the power to choke the bond market by selling debt. When the bond market froze up, that was when she knew the game was over. Her familiarity with unstable South American currencies and the consequences of an impotent bond market on a fiat currency informed her what to expect next. Even if others were in denial or didn't believe it could happen in America, she knew for sure it was already happening.

Then, as if to confirm her suspicions, that fool Andrew Stevens pulled that stunt, somehow getting the people to agree to suspend the Constitution and getting himself named Special Master—and all hell broke loose all over again.

Michelle Alvarez-Rivera, a woman who had struggled all of her life to attain credibility in a world dominated by stuffy old white men with old ideas, felt it was up to her to figure out how to take advantage of the critical failures of the old-boy network. She wasn't in a position to change the world—but she sure as hell controlled enough gold to make sure the people she loved were safe and secure. She had the means and she had a plan. If she could pull it off was another question all together.

A loud knock on the door startled her out of her thoughts. Not expecting anyone, she had no idea who it could be. The elevator only came to the top floor if a special key was used, but with the world gone mad, Michelle couldn't be sure who had found their way up. Thinking her friends could not possibly make it through the traffic jams or treacherous streets, she had no idea who could be pounding on her door.

She walked quickly to the kitchen counter and picked up a snub-nose .38. As she slowly made her way down the hall and toward the front door, the bell rang and startled her into a complete stop. Without realizing it, she had raised the barrel of the weapon and was pointing it at the door.

"Whoever it is, I'm armed—just go away!"

"Michelle, don't shoot! It's me, Carlos."

"And it's me Darla. Hurry up and open the door, Carlos is hurt."

Michelle pushed the cabinet she had moved behind the inside opening door out of the way and fumbled with the locks and chains. As quickly as she could, she pulled the door open. Standing with an arm around Darla, Carlos leaned against her and held a blood-covered rag to his head with his other hand. Darla's shirt was ripped and where the skin showed, the grips of two large handguns poked out of the waistline of her pants.

"Oh, my God, Carlos! What happened to you? How did you get here?"

"It's nothing, Dona Michelle," Carlos answered weakly. "I got hit in the head with a bottle."

Michelle reached out and took his arm, leading him and Darla down the hallway. After she secured the door and helped Carlos to the kitchen table, she went to the freezer and got out a tray of ice.

Darla explained, "We flew from Teeterboro to the heliport but there was nowhere to land, so Carlos flew over the city until he spotted a place to land on the top floor of a parking garage. It wasn't far from here, just a few blocks, but as soon as we landed, a whole bunch of people stormed the building looking for us. Luckily, they ran up the ramps while we rode down the elevator."

Carlos added, "We would have gotten away clean but someone saw us and they threw bottles at us."

Although Carlos was awake and alert, it was clear he was in a lot of pain. He kept the rag pressed against his head to stop the bleeding, but stopped talking.

"It was a lucky shot it bounced off of a sign and straight down into his forehead. After that, it was easy. Child, we ran here like two baby gazelles on the Sahara bein' chased by a hungry pride of lions."

"Oh, God!"

As Michelle wrapped cubes into a towel, she asked, "So, how did you get a helicopter, I mean . . . ."

Michelle handed the ice pack to Carlos and pulled his hand away from the wound to check it. "Yeah, you're going to need stitches. That's a nice gash." She turned back to Darla for the answer.

Darla answered, "It was easy. When we flew into Teeterboro, Dan and Susan had already picked—"

"Susan? You saw Susan?"

"Oh, my goodness. Yes. Yes! Oh, Michelle, I'm sorry, Susan's doing just fine and she's in good hands."

"Where is she, Darla? Why isn't she with you?"

"Her and that guy she's with have to go find Donny's brother, Richard."

"What guy, and what do they want with Crazy Richard?"

"Michelle, Sweetie, you better sit down for this one—have I got one heck of a story to tell, and you're gonna have a hard time swallowin' it . . . But first, let's talk about Tommy. Where's my husband's body?"

Chapter Two

The Remington 700 sniper rifle was sitting straight and level on its bipod. The mound at the top of the hill not only provided a flat, solid surface but also kept her downwind from the target. Seven hundred yards away, the mark lowered his head and tore at a small patch of dry brown grass. His lips and long tongue extended out from the end of a long, narrow, brown snout. The buck's majestic 12-point rack tilted down and then up as the white tail deer, a big old stud, chewed on the snack with his grinding teeth. Usually, he wouldn't be out at that time of the day and should have been bedded down in his hide until nightfall. But, the sky was overcast and threatening snow. The smell in the air meant a hard snow was coming and in a matter of hours would make such a simple meal a lot more difficult to obtain. Besides, the plentiful tan and brownish grass did provide him with some camouflage and the meal was still easy pickings.

Lying prone, looking through the scope, Susan saw it all and watched the graceful beast pause and sniff around, trying to detect the scent of any predators in the area. When he looked up, she put the crosshairs directly on the white patch between the protruding muscles of his forelegs. Slowly, steadily, she exhaled and pulled the trigger. The sound of the report echoed through the valley at the exact same time as the buck dropped. Susan DiGiovanni had scored her first kill.

"Woo-Wee! I got him!"

"You sure did. Nice shot," Sampson's voice was filled with pride. "Now, let's get down there and carve us up some steak."

"You're not gonna make me eat the heart, are you?"

"Only if you want to."

Susan let go of the rifle and shifted her body so she could grab onto him. Sampson had been lying beside her

299

with a small spotting scope trained on the target. He turned defensively onto his back when she lunged in his direction but was unable to stop her from landing right on top of him.

"Whoa, whoa, what are you doing?"

"Well, I figure since today I'm the hunter and you're the gatherer, I was going to club you in the head, drag you into my cave and have my way with you."

"Feeling a bit aggressive, huh?"

He dropped the scope and grabbed her by the wrists. With an upward lift of his hips and a quick spin, he had her on her back and was hovering directly over her. The move shocked her but when she realized he had taken away her advantage, she squealed in delight and started to squirm. A second later, with his knees pressed up against her butt and her legs spread, Sampson buried his head into the nape of her neck and bit her gently.

"Oh! You bastard, you're going to pay for that!"

"Am I? You promise?"

Having no choice because he immobilized her body by pressing his body weight against her, and had her arms pinned above her head, she surrendered to him completely.

"Yeah, I promise . . . but now that you got me to submit, what are you gonna do with me?"

"Eat."

"Mmmm. Sounds delicious."

Sampson stood up and helped Susan off of her feet. He brushed the dead, dry leaves off her back and reached down to pick up the rifle. "As much as I'd love to have a taste of you right now, we've got a body down there that's getting cold and stiff and we better get down there, bleed him and clean him before the meat spoils."

"Party pooper!"

Sampson smiled at her childish response. Even though Susan was close to forty, her youthful demeanor and playfulness made him think of everything he missed as a kid and he was amused experiencing at least some of what he had missed. It was a complete surprise to him how much he was enjoying her company and their time together.

Several weeks had passed since they had hiked into the Ramapo Mountains. He knew the terrain and knew exactly where to go to keep them away from civilization. His initial plan was to camp out for a few days and then return to find out if the situation had settled down. But, as it turned out, there had been no need to return.

From several of his vantage points along the higher ridges, he could see warplanes flying overhead. Also, when on recon closer to the highway, occasionally he would see Army trucks heading south towards New York. An active military on American soil meant only one thing—Marshall Law was still in effect. As long as they were imposing Marshall Law, it made no sense to try and find Richard Clearmont. Just moving around could subject them to detention, or worse, and that would not be a good thing.

Staying with Susan in the mountains turned out to be a new kind of adventure for him. He taught her how to set up camp, to fish, and how to build a fire. He also showed her how to track game and how to properly clean and cook the kill to preserve as much meat as possible. She turned out to be a quick study, anxious to learn and to try new things. At the same time, he found himself thinking she was funny and charming and somehow brought out feelings in him he had never experienced before.

Susan had been more capable and more entertaining than any recruit he had ever trained. She was also the only recruit he ever had who he wanted to screw.

For her part, Susan taught him the most valuable lessons he ever learned. At first, she did not allow him any closer than to hold her and keep her warm at night. But, by being kind and tender, open and honest she showed him how to care, and eventually how to feel. For the first time in his life, he actually cared about someone more than he cared about himself. Oddly, he found himself wanting to protect her and keep her happy. When those feelings started to take root and grow in him, and she noticed, Susan, on her own accord, took things to the next level.

It was more than a week after they made camp that he started to teach her how to shoot and how to hunt. After the first time he cleaned and reassembled the Remington 700 he took her down into a ravine and let her shoot. That night everything changed between them. At the center of their camp, Susan taught him how to love and fucked his brains out.

Together, they cleaned and dressed the venison, returning to camp with more meat than they could eat in a week, but plenty to last them for a long time after they cured it. The sun was down but both of them continued to work and clean, making sure the strips of flesh over the fire were properly salted and cooked. The heat of the fire and the activity kept them warm even as the temperature dropped and it started to snow.

"So, what do you think about heading back?"

"What, now? What about all of this?" Susan stretched her arms, indicating all of the work they had done.

"No, not now. I mean when we're done. We can take some meat with us and see if we can find your sister. If we can't find her, we'll either try to locate Richard or come back here, depending on the circumstances."

"I don't know. It sounds dangerous, but Lisa might be in trouble and, who knows, she may even need food."

"Exactly. Once we're in town, we can find out what's going on and then go from there."

"Sounds like a plan to me."

Inside, deep down to her heart, Susan was touched. The fact Sampson thought of her sister and taking her food meant the world to her and showed what kind of a man he was. As distant and cold as he seemed when they first met, she believed she had read him all wrong. He was really kind and sensitive and thoughtful—and all of those attributes were wrapped up in a package that was to die for. As much as she hated herself for thinking it and feeling it, especially so soon after falling in love with and then losing Donny, she was really starting to fall for the former Marine, hit man, and abandoned son of Maxwell York.

Thinking they were done with the conversation, Sampson had turned his back to her and the fire, hanging strips of meat to cool off of the branch of a nearby tree. Susan walked up behind him and wrapped her arms around his waist.

She leaned up on her tip toes to whisper in his ear, "Hey, caveman, before we leave, why don't you drag me into your cave and do whatever you want to me?"

"I thought you were the hunter now and you were gonna do that to me?"

He turned to face her put his hands on her hips as she draped her arms over his shoulders.

"Yeah, but since you won our wrestling match and pinned me . . . I thought it'd be fun to submit to you . . . ."

Susan was unable to finish her sentence. Sampson picked her up in his arms and carried her to a warm, dry spot next to the raging fire. That night, they made love for hours and fell asleep in each other's arms.

*****

The news was first broadcast in Tokyo, Hong Kong, Singapore, and Sydney. Seconds later Al-Jezera and the BBC interrupted their regularly scheduled broadcasts and exposed the shocking episode to the entire world. On every American station, the regularly scheduled broadcasts were interrupted for breaking news. First Vice President of Iran, Reza Rahammami, had released a statement concerning the large devices sunk into the Straight of Hormuz. Included in the statement were the six locations of the devices and the exact nature of the large, metallic orbs. Rahammami then resigned his office in the only way that made sense to him. He put an ancient, souvenir German Lugar to his temple and blew his brains out.

As soon as it was suspected that the Straight of Hormuz had been mined the U.S. Navy sent out every available MH-60S Seahawk that was equipped with OAMCM—the latest Organic Airborne Mine Counter Measures hardware. The mine detecting helicopters had been continuously sweeping the narrow channel in the Straight, but the Navy had not been able to locate the mines. Once they had the exact coordinates, though, the seaborne minesweepers moved in and found what they were looking for. To everyone's surprise, Reza Rahammami had not been lying—the devices were not mines at all, but large listening devices that were built to monitor the channel for submarines.

Just like Rahammami had said, the devices were purely defensive and everyone, especially the United States military and the oil traders in the futures pits, had simply jumped to the conclusion that the objects lowered into the heavily trafficked Straight were, in fact, mines.

The prior day, all of the markets around the world had reopened under the heaviest security possible and with massive amounts of volume. Almost immediately after the news about the bogus mines broke, the markets started to go crazy—even the trading desks at markets that were in after-hours sessions saw order volume increase five-fold in a matter of minutes. The traders on the New York Stock Exchange, which had halted trading for the day because it had already dropped the limit and tripped the circuit breaker, were helpless. The NASDAQ was also paralyzed by the halt in trading, forcing everyone to flee to secondary markets and individual market makers. It was a lot less efficient and with the tremendous volume, the usually relaxed atmosphere of the boutique trading floors became the center of the world. Their less-robust trading systems were quickly overwhelmed with volume and one computer after another came crashing down to a screeching halt.

The markets in oil, gold, and silver had tripped the daily breakers on the upside for the day and they were closed as well. The Mercantile Exchange did have the unusual power to resume trading futures contracts under special circumstances, but that had never been implemented. It would not be implemented on that day either since most of the traders in the open-auction system had already gone home. The computers were not designed to handle the hard-headed negotiations that went on between the screaming, gesticulating pit traders. The options market, however, had no such barriers and the options on futures contracts were setting all kinds of records for volume and volatility. The news about the Straight of Hormuz being reopened within the hour was going to sink the prices of oil, gold and silver and most expected the recently crashing equities to spiking back up and go through the roof.

Some saw overcompensation and believed that the up correction would be overdone and that resulted in a massive amount of hedging, retreats, back-filling and upswings. Trying to gauge where the futures and stock markets would settle had become the most impossible puzzle in the world that every living traders was trying to solve.

Money Games Part 1

Review: Money Games 1 was a gripping, intense page turner that kept me guessing. Money Games 2 is even more intense and wouldn't allow me to put it down until I finished the book. Kimberly Barnes has really out done herself with this novel. I can't wait to read part 3! R. Jacobs,-Author.

Money Games II

Cross Artist

Prime Time

URBAN HOUSE PUBLISHINGs #1 Bestselling Author

R. JACOBS

MY LIFE AS A CERTIFIED CLAPPER

R. JACOBS NOVELS

Urban House Publishing Order Form

Money Games I, By Kimberly Barnes -
$15.00/ $3.50 shipping_____copies

Money Games II, By Kimberly Barnes -
$15.00/ $3.50 shipping_____copies

Cross Artist, By R. Jacobs

$15.00/ $3.50 shipping___copies

Prime Time, By R. Jacobs

$15.00/ $3.50 shipping___copies

My Life as a Certified Clapper, Br R.Jacobs

$15.00/ $3.50 shipping___copies

Send checks or Money Orders to:
Urban House Publishing
P.O. Box 1826
Montclair, N.J. 07042

*Books available at Amazon.com,
     CreateSpace.com, and
UrbanHousePublishing.com. Also available as
an E-Book".

Urban House Publishing Order Form

Money Games I, By Kimberly Barnes -
   $15.00/ $3.50 shipping_____copies
Money Games II, By Kimberly Barnes -
   $15.00/ $3.50 shipping_____copies
 Cross Artist, By R. Jacobs
_$15.00/ $3.50 shipping___copies
 Prime Time, By R. Jacobs
 $15.00/ $3.50 shipping___copies
 My Life as a Certified Clapper, Br R.Jacobs
 $15.00/ $3.50 shipping___copies

Send checks or Money Orders to:
Urban House Publishing
P.O. Box 1826
Montclair, N.J. 07042

*Books available at Amazon.com,
    CreateSpace.com, and
UrbanHousePublishing.com. Also available as
an E- Book".